TO SERVE, PROTECT, AND WRITE

COPS WRITING CRIME FICTION

Volume 1

SHORT STORIES

Edited and with an introduction by
A.B. PATTERSON

TO SERVE, PROTECT, AND WRITE

COPS WRITING CRIME FICTION

Volume 1

Published by A.B. Patterson   2022
Andrew Bruce Patterson
PO Box 1008
Broadway
NSW   2007
Australia

First Printing 2022

Cover design by J.T. Lindroos | www.oivas.com
Logo design by Stephen Hill | www.dylunio.com.au
Typesetting by Publicious Book Publishing | www.publicious.com.au

A catalogue record for this
book is available from the
National Library of Australia

ISBN: 978-0-6452661-0-8

Also available as an ebook:
ISBN: 978-0-6452661-1-5

Published with the assistance of Publicious P/L (Australia)
www.publicious.com.au

To all the law enforcement officers who serve
and protect their communities with selflessness,
bravery, and integrity

CONTENTS

EDITOR'S INTRODUCTION

I'm a crime fiction writer and a proud ex-police officer, both uniformed and detective. I've always been an avid reader and I still retain vivid memories of reading Joseph Wambaugh's books as a young uniformed constable back in the 1980s in Perth, Western Australia. Whilst Wambaugh wrote based on his experiences as a cop in wild Los Angeles, the stories resonated so deeply for their realism and relevance to being a cop on the streets, even if it was in Perth, somewhat more sleepy than L.A.

Shortly after I started my writing career in earnest, I set up a project on my website called Cops Writing Crime. My intent, inspired by my memories of reading Wambaugh, was to collate all the ex-cops (or still serving cops) around the world who had turned to writing crime fiction. I believe that the very best realism in crime fiction comes from those writers who have worked the streets as cops (and occasionally on the other side of the law). I thought my project would result in a small number of authors, but it has grown to more than 300 over the last few years, as I have done more research. The authors included in the project I refer to as "The Squad".

This anthology arose from the Cops Writing Crime project. Having collected so many authors, and read the work of a number of them, I was more convinced than ever of the delicious realism they bring to crime fiction. I had, over the same period of time, also become enamoured with the anthology format, having read many of these across genres, and had my own stories published in them. So, I reached out on my social media networks and tried to entice authors from The Squad to participate in the nascent concept.

The anthology project kicked off and has now come to fruition a couple of years later. The sluggish crawl to completion can be attributed to a number of factors, including the pandemic that has disrupted all our lives for nearly the last two years. I must also plead guilty to my own fumbling efforts as I navigated my first such project: the next anthology will be a lot more smoothly produced! But the biggest factor was ensuring a gender mix amongst the authors. Whilst I had received a great range of stories from male authors earlier on in the project, I was adamant that an all-male volume was neither desirable nor reflective of the range of talent and voices in the Cops Writing Crime community. So I spent several months cajoling female authors from The Squad to come on board. And we now have four wonderful stories adding strong female voices to the collection. It is so much the richer and deeper for their inclusion.

The stories you are about to read are incredibly varied in their perspectives and their takes on crime. As the back cover blurb announces, there is a great range of crime involved here, as well as perspectives of different protagonists, including uniformed cops, detectives, and criminals. You are about to embark on a reading journey that will be often dark and gritty, sometimes humorous, but always so, so realistic. Don't expect a comfortable ride: the emotions expressed in these stories are brutally honest. And that is precisely what you get when cops write crime fiction.

When I sent out the project brief to the authors, there were no story constraints. The only requirement was a crime story that was imbued with police realism. Hell, these authors have delivered in spades. The collection is as eclectic as it is heartfelt and authentic, and you can be assured that all the authors are writing from a very personal space. You are getting the ultimate in verisimilitude when it comes to crime fiction.

A big challenge I faced as the stories came in was how to order them in the final line-up. As it happened, of the fifteen stories two were set in the past and one in the future, with the rest being contemporary. That handed me a natural start and end point: the first two stories are about historical policing and the last is a rather dystopian view of policing in the future. For the remaining twelve in between, I tried to mix them up according to crime type, country of origin, and author gender. There was no obviously perfect solution, but I think the arrangement works.

I should also make some observations on the editing process for this anthology. The original project brief given to interested authors was that no content editing would be done, and therefore the stories they submitted had to be, in their views, totally polished and ready for consumption by readers. I have to say, I wasn't disappointed and I have personally enjoyed reading every story in the collection. I really hope you do as well.

As my first editing project of this kind, the most interesting challenge of all was the English language and its presentation in this volume. I am an unashamed addict to the English language (I did an Masters in English for pleasure!) and its variations and quirks are an endless source of joy. The authors in this collection, myself included, represent four different English-speaking countries with the four variants that represents. I decided early on that I would not touch any of the spelling variations that exist, rather I think they add to the rich variety of the language. So, as you read, you will probably note the spelling differences as you alternate between authors from the US, the UK, Canada, and Australia. The differences are there intentionally.

Where I did try to ensure consistency was in the use of punctuation. Whilst some of this is subject to generally accepted rules, some is also entirely a question of style and usage. I did not consider these differences to add to the richness of English, and so I strove for consistency across all the stories. And all the stories, including my own, had to compromise to a degree. I do feel strongly that the end result is a much smoother read, for you the reader. And, hey, you're the important one here!

My own story is included in the collection, and I make no apology for that. The writing world is full of those self-appointed judges of everything, and that includes those who dictate that an editor should not have their own work in the collection they are editing. Yes, they are entitled to their views, and I am happy to ignore arbitrary opinions. My desire in publishing this anthology is to showcase the great crime writing from authors in The Squad of Cops Writing Crime. And given it's my effort and funding that are enabling the collection, I am more than happy to throw in my own work. At the end of the day, I become one of the fifteen, and a very proud one of the group. This anthology promotes all their work, as well as crime fiction generally.

By way of final comment, and reflecting on the dedication in this volume, I would like to pay tribute to all the law enforcement officers in our liberal democracies who work hard and make huge personal sacrifices, sometimes the ultimate sacrifice, in order to serve and protect their communities. Every author in this collection would agree with me when I state that policing, in a free society, is a damned difficult profession. And like any profession, it is not perfect and there are individuals within it who are unworthy of our respect as they besmirch the decent majority. I remain proud of my years of service and of the many great colleagues I worked alongside. Failings and imperfections notwithstanding, the police institution is one I respect, and it is central to our rule of law.

So, here is Volume 1 of Cops Writing Crime: *To Serve, Protect, and Write*. I'm very proud of this collection and am looking forward to it being the start of a great series to come. If you want realism in your crime fiction reading, then there is no better source than Cops Writing Crime. As I said in the back cover blurb, it is all about those brushstrokes of daily police life, and the special and unique flavour they bring to crime fiction.

Please enjoy!

Cheers,
Andrew

A.B. Patterson
Sydney, December 2021

THE STORIES

THE STORIES

ALL GOOD THINGS MUST BEGIN
(The First Frank DeGrae Case)

Christopher Allen

- 1 -

Calvin and I turned the corner and as we approached the address I turned off the headlights. I rigged for silent running and parked about a block away quietly and under the cover of darkness. Easing down Central Avenue I coasted off the street into a school parking lot as we passed under the last street lamp. Slowing to a crawl I applied the parking brake with one final hard pull and the car came to a complete stop. I shifted back into Reverse and turned the ignition key back to the left. The purring idle of the engine fell silent.

We walked from the patrol car the final half-block to the office building. When we got there we could see the smashed first floor window and debris scattered on the ground below. As Calvin and I stood assessing the situation, two more officers walked up to us from wherever they quietly parked their patrol unit. The four of us were discussing our plans when the shade was pulled back from inside and a young man started back out with some piece of office equipment. Before anyone could do anything he looked up and saw us. The adding machine was dropped and he fled back inside.

Calvin and I entered through the broken window almost immediately with Roberts right behind us. His partner remained as a lookout at the corner of the building near their parked patrol car. In a desperate attempt to get away the burglar made a dash to a set of steps leading down into a cellar with an adjacent coal room. Calvin was hot on his heels and Officer Roberts had managed to get between Calvin and me and followed also. I paused at the top of the stairs just in case we missed an accomplice and to cover the rear.

After a moment I could hear the sound of breaking glass and a mass confusion of several voices yelling over top of one another. Then a shot rang out. Then I could hear the iron coal chute door slam open directly below where I stood. I quickly exited the shattered window we had made entry through in order to head off the suspect's escape from the outside. There came more commands from the basement area for the suspect to stop and then a number of more shots rang out from a police issued Smith & Wesson .38 Special revolver. The suspect, a young man of about twenty years and wearing clothes appearing to be inherited and a bit too large for him, now lay lifelessly at the iron coal chute door, half in and half out. His newsboy cap was lying nearby and coal dust covered much of his face and hands. What wasn't darkened from crawling through the coal bin was richly colored of blood.

***

Sometime later while standing in the alley I asked Calvin, "Are you sure? You must remember something."

"I remember running down the stairs, across the room, and grabbing the guy's shirt. Then picking myself up off the floor with a huge headache. That's it," answered Calvin for the second time.

"You gotta remember something bud," interjected Officer Roberts. "The guy reached a window but it was too high to get out so he turned for the coal chute. I ran across the room to cut him off when you shot him. I know you thought he had a gun. It's an honest mistake."

"At least everyone is alright. The sergeant is on his way so let's just try to settle down and collect our thoughts on this for the investigation," I told the others.

Apparently my partner saved the day down there but he hit his head on something and was having trouble remembering everything. While we waited for everyone else to get there I was helping Calvin with a bump to his head that was still bleeding a bit.

In a short while the scene was covered up by all kind of cops. Other on-duty uniforms as well as the plain-clothes guys. Everybody gave it their all to come help but it was long over before anyone could get to us. The only thing left to do was for the detectives to conduct their investigation. And for me and Calvin to make our report to the sergeant.

I was still trying to get my partner to get his head looked at when through the maze of parked patrol cars and buzz of other officers everywhere I made out the figure of Sergeant Malcolm heading straight for us.

"You guys alright?" Malcolm asked as he stepped up.

"Yeah, Sarge. Except I think Calvin here bumped his head," I replied. "What's up with the head Akers?"

"I'm fine, Sarge, just a little bump."

"DeGrae, take your partner to get that head checked out and I'll talk to you guys later."

"Alright, Sarge. But ... "

"Now, Frank."

"Yes sir. Come on Calvin," I said taking my partner by the arm.

***

A few days had passed since the shooting and I started picking up on some rumors that were floating around. The scuttlebutt had it that my partner was mixed up in some rum running gang stuff and shooting that kid was somehow part of it. I naturally became very concerned mainly because if he was to be implicated everyone would assume I was in on it too. Or at least knew about it. Now I had to figure a way to bring this up in conversation with Calvin without making him clam up on me. Or worse yet, have him turn on me. We spent so much time together I couldn't possibly believe any of it. He didn't have enough time off to himself to get into anything like that. But I had to bring it up.

It was on a Monday, and our first day back to start a new work cycle, when I was approached by the Lieutenant in the hallway. He asked me to come back to his office after roll-call. This didn't sound good.

Entering Lieutenant Hunley's office he looked up from behind his desk and said, "Close the door Frank." This already looked bad. I said nothing and turned to pull the door closed. "Have a seat." I walked to a chair across the desk from the lieutenant and sat down.

"Frank, how long have you and Calvin been partners?"

"Oh ... about four years, I guess," I answered while still moving about in the chair searching for that position of stature. "That's right. We were assigned together in March of twenty-eight."

"March twenty third, nineteen twenty-eight to be specific", the lieutenant interjected. "We have a little problem here I need your help with."

3

"Alright lieutenant. I'll be glad to help if I can", I replied while still wondering why he had pulled our personnel files.

"Good. I know how close partners are out on the street but I also know you're an upright guy. Look Frank, I know what I'm about to tell you will be hard to take but I'm getting this from the IA guys and the Chief's office so I need your strictest confidence."

Still oblivious as to what he was talking about I simply leaned in as if I did know and answered, "Sure lieutenant. Anything to help."

"Thanks Frank. It seems your partner has been watched for some time now. "Oh?"

"Yes. And we're beginning to see a connection with a couple of rum runners."

"What?! Calvin? No way!"

"Frank, I know it's hard to believe. I mean, your partner and all. I get it. But I need your help. The department needs your help."

"I just can't see it lieutenant. We're together all the time."

"Alright Frank. Here's the deal. You help us on this and we don't go after you along with him."

Now I was angry. I knew some of the guys took a drink and there were even a few I heard rumors about being paid off but this was beyond the pale. Calvin and I worked together every day and even spent most off-days together. Neither of us liked anyone else. I stood up and while staring the lieutenant down I quietly answered, "Let me sleep on it. I'll get back to you tomorrow."

"Alright Frank. That sounds fair," Hunley said as I stepped around the chair and headed for the door.

- 2 -

"Okay Roberts. I know you have. But just once more. Just for my own curiosity. It's not official or anything. Look, I sat down with Hunley the other day and he told me everything already. I'm in this now too," I said as I raised my beer bottle and he threw his third dart. Roberts just closed his triple twenty and was feeling pretty good about himself. My praise of his unmatched skill elevated his pride even more.

"Okay wise guy. I have a proposition for you. If you bite, you're in," Roberts said as he turned to pick up his frosted beer mug.

"Sounds fair. So give."

After downing a long swallow of the ale Roberts replied with, "Meet me here Monday night. Say around eleven. I'll have you meet a guy or two and we can seal this deal."

"Monday? Eleven? So, what's up with that?"

"It'll be alright. We'll meet right here. At this table and board. There'll be people everywhere. Nothin'll happen."

***

"It's going to be alright Calvin. Just trust me on this thing," I said as I checked my watch. "It's ten o'clock," I continued as I pulled the patrol car to the corner and stopped. "Hang on while I check in."

"Alright Frank," Akers answered with a dejected tone.

As I got to the callbox a shot rang out. I dropped my ring of keys and hit the deck. More shots came and Calvin rolled out of the passenger side of the car. The shots stopped. I rolled onto my other side where I could look back toward the parked car and saw Calvin on one knee with his duty weapon drawn and he was aiming it in a Weaver stance.

Not moving and keeping his sight picture along the top of the revolver Akers called out, "You alright Frank?!"

"I'm good Calvin. Thanks."

"Let's go Frank. We'll use another box."

"I'm right behind you Calvin."

Calvin covered me as I moved back to the street and got back under the wheel. When I was ready he turned around and jumped in as I eased off the clutch. Before his door was closed I gunned it and let the clutch pedal pop on up. We were out of there like a shot.

"What the … ," Calvin said as he was slammed back against the seat and the door closed on its own.

"Thanks Calvin. I'm not sure that was just a normal sniping."

"What?"

"Right Cal. That's what I've been meaning to get to. Now's as good a time as any to lay this out. Pay attention." I went on to explain to him about my little meeting with Hunley and the upcoming meeting with Roberts again at the Three-Oh-Eight Bar. He went from being mad about us getting shot at to utterly incensed. He was much nicer with simply being shot at.

"You mean to say, I'm being investigated and they want you to spy on me?"

"Correct. And I just heard someone wants to hang that shooting on you as a murder."

"Now they're really going too far. I don't even know who that kid was."

As I cruised along the avenue our continued conversation was so intense we almost forgot about being shot at. I finally spotted another callbox and reported in.

***

As I tossed the dart and reached for my beer, Roberts stepped up saying, "Hey Frank. Ready?"

"As ready as I'll ever be."

"Come on," he said and turned back toward the bar. I followed. At the end of the bar we turned into a dark narrow passageway and then a quick right to a locked oak door. Roberts gave a series of four short raps and it mysteriously opened. When I closed the door and turned back to face the room Roberts began to introduce me to everyone.

There were three people I immediately recognized. They were fellow officers of the 16th, better known to the locals as The Tenderloin. These boys played for keeps.

Picking up a stack of banded bills from the edge of the desk Roberts turned to hand it to me while saying, "Everybody, I think you already know DeGrae here." I reached and took the cash and Roberts continued. "Here Frank. This is your sign-on bonus." Looking back to his confederates he said, "El Tee told me Frank here was coming on-board and he's gonna shore up pinning the Curley Hunter murder on his partner, Akers."

Still looking down and flipping through the bills I responded with, "Thanks Roberts. Glad to be aboard. This is starting to look like it's going to be quite mutually beneficial."

"There's a couple of other fellas I want to introduce you to tomorrow but right now we need to seal the deal with drinks and another game of cricket."

Tucking the money into an inside pocket I said, "Right behind you

Roberts. Let's go." Turning back to the fellas I raised my left index finger and with a tip of the brim, "Later boys."

A couple of days later I caught up to an old academy buddy who had moved up pretty quick. He worked in the Deputy Chief's office as a liaison between the Command Staff and the Operations Division. I'm sure the law degree didn't hurt either. I, more or less, chummed it up with him fishing for anything he may have run across regarding Akers or myself. Surprisingly he seemed to know nothing. Absolutely no word about either of us. It took a while. I didn't want to seem too anxious so I went the long way around the block bringing up several other guys that had been caught dirty. However the name Curley Hunter came up a few times connected to a couple of New York's finest who were no more. My first piece of the puzzle had materialized.

My next shift with Akers was Friday. In the early afternoon, a little before roll-call, I asked Calvin how the bump on his head was coming along when he slammed his locker door and turned abruptly toward me. "Frank. I think they're really after me. I was called a couple of days ago and went in yesterday. I was grilled like a prisoner. They finally told me they knew I killed Curley Hunter because he knew too much about what I was into. What has happened?"

"It's going to be alright. What about your head?"

"My head!? I'm serious Frank ... "

"Me too Calvin. I need to know specifics about your head. Where exactly is the bump and what did the doctor say about it?"

I realized it was time to get serious about what was happening and I was probably in the crosshairs as well. I was being used as a pawn to get at Akers and then I would be disposable too. The only thing about all this was that I was aware of the game so I started doing a little homework in addition to a few little insurance policies I had already secured.

After we got out of roll-call we headed over to the crime lab. I was beginning to get the idea that no one could be trusted but I needed to get a little info. The trick would be to do so and keep on the low down about it.

"You want to do what?" asked Akers.

I eased the clutch out and the engine caught. We eased into the intersection and I made the right turn onto 63rd. While pulling hard, hand over hand, on the wheel and pushing the gear shift up into second I started explaining again, "I heard about this thing they have where they can test someone to see if they shot a gun or not." I pushed in the clutch pedal and yanked the shifter down to third. Easing up on the pedal and hitting the accelerator I continued. "And there's a thing for checking for blood on stuff too. That's why all the questions about your head. We need to go back and see what you hit your head on."

"I've been curious about that too. I can't remember much about down there and I certainly can't think of a thing I hit unless something just jumped out and hit me from behind," Akers said.

"That's exactly my point Calvin. I'm thinking maybe something else happened down there."

"Wait a minute. Are you suggesting Roberts did something?"

"Look Calvin, we've got to start looking at any possibility right now. But we need to keep all this to ourselves. You know what'll happen if it gets around we're free-lancing an investigation into other cops. Worst case is we disappear and best case we wind up hated by everybody."

"You're right Frank. And you're right that we have to do something. Anything."

"So keep cool and let's walk this thing through by the numbers and keep our mouths shut while we do this. And you need to know I've already got my neck so stretched out my head's about to pop off. I paid a visit to the Feds when this whole mess fell in my lap and started looking real ugly."

"You what?!"

"Who do you trust around here?" I asked him. There was a deafening silence.

- 3 -

A couple of weeks went by business as usual. Everyone knew what was brewing but the smoke seemed to have settled quite a bit. Me and Calvin, along with Roberts and the others, kept showing up for roll-call and patrolling our beats. Then one day after roll-call Calvin and I started out the back door and down the steps when Roberts was walking back inside and we had a minor traffic jam. "Hey, Roberts, let's take lunch together. I've got something to show you later", I said while trying to stay balanced carrying our case and clipboard. Calvin came from behind me and pirouetted around Roberts and myself as he held his kit bag in one hand and the Winchester pump in the other.

"Sure Frank. Later," was heard as he hurried back inside without even slowing down. I descended the four steps to the pavement and followed Calvin out to our patrol car.

Around nine o'clock or so, Akers and I met up with Roberts at Callahan's. We were met at the *maître d*'s dais, just inside the front door near the cloakroom, by the proprietor. He noticed us as we entered and came to meet us, as he always does.

"Good evening gentlemen. How are we tonight?" he asked the group.

"We are capital my friend. Just wonderful," I replied. "Could we possibly be seated in more remote ... say ... private area where we won't be disturbed?"

"Why of course Mister DeGrae. Not a problem. Come this way."

Me and the boys bypassed the usual checking of hats and coats and left the *maître d'* at his station to greet the commoners. Since it was the middle of the week there was no music but the hum of conversations and clinking of glasses and silverware seemed loud enough.

We ended up in a much smaller dining room with only four tables and no other patrons. We were assured no one else would be brought back while we were here.

"Alright. This is more like it," I said as I walked around to the back of the table and pulled my chair out. Akers and Roberts were already seated when I started to sit down.

"Will you gentlemen be needing a menu?"

"I'll just have coffee," I said. The others looked at me with raised eyebrows and expressions of query. "Go ahead and order guys. If you want to. I'm just not that hungry tonight." Since I called the meeting the others decided to follow suit and ordered the same. It was quickly understood we may not be here long.

As soon as we found ourselves sequestered Roberts wasted no time in asking, "So what gives Frank? Why are we here? It certainly isn't to eat, now is it?"

I slowly leaned into the table toward Roberts. His aggressive posture melted a bit as he sat straighter from his forward leaning position. "Alright tough guy. Here it is. I'm going to cover this one time, and one time only, so you better listen good and have your smart cap on. Capeesh?"

"Now just who the hell do you think you are bud?"

"Officer Roberts. There are three Federal agents seated at table number seven out front waiting to hear from me. Do I have your attention now?" I answered. He went flush and suddenly had no color in his face.

"So, uh Frank, uh, what's this about?" Roberts continued with a much more yielding manner.

"Remember friend, this is a one shot deal here tonight. Screw with me and we're done."

"Got it. Go ahead."

"I know what happened in the basement. What you did down there with my partner here. And that boy. Curley Hunter I believe was his name?"

"I didn't do anything. Akers here shot Curley," Roberts replied.

"No. Calvin didn't shoot anyone. It was you. Here's what happened. After looking into a few things involving some small time hoods moving money around it came up that Curley was working for Lieutenant Hunley. But poor Curley was about to spill it to the Feds because he didn't think he was getting enough scratch for his trouble. So Hunley needed Curley dead. That's where you come in."

"You're crazy Frank. And you can't prove a word of it."

"Ah, but I can. Hold on a minute. You showed up as LT's golden boy even though you're just a mere rank and file officer. You work for him too. Not only at the precinct, but on his extracurricular activities too. So you were recruited for the hit."

"Prove it Frank. You're blowing smoke."

"I'm getting there. You spilled it to Curley, via his girl Val, the stripper at the Gray Fox, about an easy job at Melman's. You even guaranteed an easy in and out telling her you would cover it for him keeping the rest of us away from the place."

"You're boring me now Frank. I'm outta here," Roberts said as he pushed back from the table.

"Hear me out or you head straight on up to FBI Headquarters tonight."

Roberts stopped pushing. With an ice-cold stare he said, "Alright smart guy. Go ahead with your fairy tale."

"Having baited Curley into Melman's you made sure the alarm was sounded so you could respond with the rest of us and finish the job for Hunley. Curly played into the scenario perfectly when he ran to the basement. You also made sure to let Calvin go down the steps first and when at the bottom you clobbered him in the back of the head. You stunned him enough to take his revolver and shoot Curley with it and put it in Calvin's hand before he woke up."

"Alright Frank. That's a nice story but what do you have besides a wild fairy tale and speculation?"

"Jason, I have a swab from the butt of your Smith and Wesson. One of the FBI's lab boys gave me a couple of phenolphthalein wipes. A variation of a Kastle–Meyer test for the presence of hemoglobin."

"Hemo-what?"

"Blood you moron. The butt of your service revolver still had Calvin's blood on it from where you cold-cocked him with it. I also had a chance to try one of their new toys on your jacket."

"My jacket?"

"Right. Your jacket. Still hanging in your locker with your gun belt and gun. You see, you could go home and wash your hands and even your clothes to get rid of any gunshot residue that would have shown you as being the shooter but you forgot about your coat. People always forget about their coats and rarely wash them. As you failed to wash yours. I was offered to spray it with a new mist solution that detects nitro- compounds from the partially burnt and unburnt propellant particles. Your jacket still carried the gunshot residue from where you used Calvin's gun to kill Curly. It was murder Jason. A pre-meditated, well thought out murder. He wasn't even armed. You set a trap for him, lured him in, and murdered him."

"Alright Mister Honesty. What about the money you took at the 'Three-Oh-Eight'?"

"The thousand dollars you guys gave to me to guarantee Calvin takes the fall?"

"What!?" asked Akers.

"Yeah smart guy," said Roberts.

"You'll need to ask Special Agent Jim Ellison about that. I gave it to the Feds so I have no idea where it is."

This was the boys' cue. When the G-men walked in Roberts looked at me with pure contempt. "You son-of-a ... "

"Later my friend."

***

"You know when this gets out you're through, right?" asked Akers.

Turning the wheel and heading uptown I replied, "You're probably right Cal. I've been giving that some thought already. I know this new mayor is an upright guy and all but we still have a ways to go. It looks like we're still years away from cleaning out this Tammany snake pit so I've made a decision."

"Oh, you have, have you?"

"Look Calvin. You're still squeaky clean around here on either side of the fence. If you stay on the narrow path you have a future on this police department. I don't."

"What are you saying Frank?"

"Calvin ... we had a good run but I've got to move on now. I don't know who is still dirty or who will simply hate me for turning in a fellow cop. I know there are still a lot of good guys around here but I don't know who they are yet. I think I can do more good at helping end this corruption blight and stay safer for my own sake if I go it alone in the private sector."

"You mean ... "

"I'm turning in my resignation Calvin. I'm quitting and getting my P.I. license. I know I'll still need to watch my back for a while but I already have clients lined up through attorneys and outside agencies. I'll be okay."

"Frank ... I don't know what to say. I know you fell in this crack watching out for me. Stay in touch and let me know if there's ever anything I can do."

"Oh, don't worry Calvin. I'm not going anywhere and I'm sure the day'll come you'll regret having made the offer."

In the following days and weeks I managed to set up shop and leave the NYPD behind. Work was actually pretty good and the company coffer was looking healthy.

Having caught wind of what happened to me opened the door to the Mayor's office and even he was sending business my way. Calvin just made it on the list to be promoted to sergeant so I guess things were working out for him too. I knew he had a future there. A great guy.

My old friends Lieutenant Hunley, Jason Roberts, and the gang of good ol' boys from the 16th were already out of commission. It seems that about the time I was about to spring my surprise some other insiders were onto Curley's girlfriend Val. They got to the poor girl before she could make a deal with the DA too. She was found in the East River.

After the night the Feds were in Callahan's with me, Calvin, and Roberts, along with what happened to Val, it wasn't long before the hits on Curly and Val were directly linked to Lieutenant Hunley issuing the orders. Officer Roberts sang like a bird once down at FBI headquarters.

As for me ... I was afraid my career in New York was over. As it turned out, it just started. With our new mayor it was highly publicized that corruption among city officials and the police department was over. Our little burglary call had also snowballed into a major headline and sent the rats into hiding and jumping off of the boat. In the end I was quite happy with my connections in the police department, with the Feds, and at City Hall. The days of systemic corruption were coming to an end and my town would be taken care of by the most professional police department in the world. It was more than worth the risk.

* * * * *

JOHNNY WALKER

Thonie Hevron

June 1936, San Francisco

Jack pulled the black '32 Ford unmarked car to the curb in front of the Kearney Street Hall of Justice. Captain Ronald Bertrand lumbered over to the passenger side. He settled his bulk while holding on to the door-frame. Bertrand had added a few pounds since last time Jack had seen him. The sour expression hadn't improved, either. Jack's stomach was in knots. Picking up the brass for a homicide scene wasn't a normal occurrence. But he could always count on Bertrand to make his day tougher.

Nestling into the seat, Bertrand glanced at Jack. "You look like crap, Herlihy."

"I just have a sick headache." And the captain wasn't making it any better.

"Bad booze, huh? You should stick with the good stuff. Like Johnny Walker. Then you won't get sick."

"I can't afford your whiskey, Captain."

Bertrand patted his jacket pockets. "I have just the thing for you: Goody's Headache Powder. My sister in North Carolina sent me some last week. Just came out in the stores. Mix it in water, drink it down and the headache is history." He checked his pants pockets, then threw his hands in the air. "I guess I used the last one. Sorry."

"'S Okay."

"Been a while since we been on a call together, huh?" Bertrand lit a cigarette and blew a blast of smoke. He smiled, showing teeth but no sincerity. "Since that caper down on Jones Street, right?"

Jack remembered. The vivid images of a brutal gang hit still haunted him. Bertrand had been his patrol lieutenant at the time while Jack sported a shiny new detective badge. Despite hours of scrutinizing the scene, interviews, and every piece of evidence, they'd never turned a suspect. He also remembered Jack's partner throwing a chair across a desk as Bertrand stonewalled the investigation.

"I saved your butt on that one, Jackie Boy."

Herlihy winced at the nickname. "What do you mean, Captain? We never found out who did it."

"Exactly my point. The brass was getting lots of pressure from the DA to find the doer. For your first case, you were thorough, but …. well, it didn't matter if you couldn't find who done it. The DA wanted your badge, but I put him off. I knew you had lots of potential, even if you couldn't find one measly Eye-talian."

Herlihy knew he was supposed to say thank you, but his lips wouldn't form the words. He didn't like being indebted to Bertrand; didn't trust how Bertrand had kept the chit until it needed to be called in. But called in for what?

Bertrand drew on his cigarette. "How's Vivian?"

"You mean my wife, Verna? Fine." No requirement to answer with any depth since he couldn't even remember her name. "Too bad about yours."

"The bitch ran out on me." The Captain made a project out of extracting tobacco from his lip. "Took me to the cleaners, too."

It was Jack's cue to change the subject. "So, what brings you out, Captain?"

Bertrand's head whipped around to Jack. "Just worry about your driving," Bertrand snapped.

"Take it easy. I was just asking."

They took a yellow light at Van Ness just as it flipped red. Bertrand asked, "What's the call, homicide?"

Jack nodded. "Caucasian female in the Embarcadero. Landlady found her. Strangulation."

"Then let's get to it." Bertrand flicked his cigarette butt out the window, dropping into a sulk for the rest of the ride.

A lonesome foghorn moaned in the bay long before Herlihy saw the waterfront. Fog had stolen in and obliterated the sunset. Dampness blanketed the street, deserted after the teamsters left for home. The two-story boarding house sat on bare ground. It looked like it had been slapped up in a hurry after the earthquake thirty years before. The siding was chipped, prey to the marine air. The sagging front door now stood open.

Herlihy's nose wrinkled at the sour smell of cooked cabbage. The lace curtains were shredded and the Oriental carpet worn through. Bertrand's jaw set while he waited for Herlihy to walk the hallway. It was something Jack always did at the scene of a crime: look over the entire building. Bisecting four rooms on the first floor, a hall led to the kitchen and dining room in the back of the house. Many a mediocre meal had been cooked here, Jack thought as he scanned the messy room. He'd send the photographer in here to take pictures, even though nothing remarkable caught his attention.

The body was on the second floor, front room. Jack motioned the patrol officers to back out to the hallway so he would not be disturbed. The department photographer followed them. The only window faced the commercial shipping piers; no other doors. Jack's gaze moved to the pale, lifeless woman lying across the rumpled bed. The Medical Examiner bent over the body making his initial observations. Herlihy took his time. The woman could wait. First, he examined the room as he had done in the kitchen.

It was a single room with a bed, nightstand and a battered oak dresser. A pole suspended from the ceiling by kinked wire held two dresses and a coat. A green Bakelite radio on the dresser next to drugstore perfume bottle sat in mute testimony to an austere life. A dented hotplate on a small table in a corner, was surrounded by a bottle of expensive scotch, a pitcher and two dirty glasses. Trash from the can underneath overflowed onto the floor. The only picture was on the nightstand: a small framed photo of a woman holding and young girl. From the clothing, Herlihy estimated it had been taken in the late teens. Maybe it was the victim as a child with her mother. No signs of a struggle other than the bed and corpse.

Time to inspect the body: 34-year-old Connie Franco was a bottle-blond with a frown line fixed between her eyebrows, even in death. She wore a grayed nylon slip and bra, no panties.

As Jack listened to the Medical Examiner, Bertrand muscled through the officers in the hall. "What the hell's the idea, keeping me out?" He nudged Herlihy in a poorly contained show of aggression.

Herlihy paused to re-orient himself. Squinting at his captain, he chose his words carefully. "I'm getting a feel for the scene. Other people in the room pull my attention from something that might be important."

"Aw, bullshit," Bertrand grunted. He elbowed past Herlihy to the bed opposite the ME. Too loud, he said, "Looks like a two-bit hooker to me. C'mon, wrap this up."

The ME peered over his rimless spectacles and frowned at Bertrand.

Bertrand's eyes widened at the ME's disrespect, then he took a step back, stumbling into a table. After an awkward turn, his hands reached to steady the bottle of whiskey. Before he could catch them, the bottle and glasses slipped, shattering on the wood floor. Kneeling, he looked at the broken glass. "Aw, Jeez, what a mess."

Herlihy's Irish was up. He strode the four paces across to his captain and leaned into his ear. "I don't care if you're the boss or not. Get outta here."

Bertrand rested his hand on the floor between chunks of glass and wadded up papers and pushed his other hand heavily off his knee. He stood, out of breath, his chest heaving, and pissed. "All right, all right. I'll wait downstairs."

Two days later, Bertrand appeared at Herlihy's desk. As a lieutenant, the detective rated a small office of his own. Bertrand pulled the door shut, dropped into a chair and leaned on his knees. "So what's the word on the homicide on the Embarcadero?"

Herlihy sat back. "Funny you should ask, Captain." Jack reached across his desk and pulled a packet from a stack, a finger flipping the intercom open. He unsealed the envelope, placed it on the desk and said, "I'm glad you stopped by. I was just going to call you."

Herlihy could see alarm bells go off in Bertrand's head. "Oh, yeah?"

"Did you know the deceased?" Jack had just passed the point of no return. A personal relationship with the victim of a murder wasn't the end of the world for a cop. But, it *did* cast aspersions on his character when he didn't tell the investigating officer. If Jack was wrong, it could kill his career.

Bertrand rubbed his meaty hands together, started to his feet then sat back down. His face was blank. "If you're asking, you must know the answer."

"Go on." Jack's heart thumped in his ears.

"There's nothing to say. She was just a girl."

"How'd you meet her?"

"She's a waitress at a diner on Market Street. That's all." Bertrand's chin jutted out.

"How well did you know her?"

"Whaddya mean?" Bertrand blustered in his chair, like it would put off any further questions.

Jack leaned toward the Captain. "You know what I mean."

Bertrand backed down and appeared to relax. "Not well."

"Ever been to her room before?"

"Nah, why should I?" He picked at a hangnail.

"You know why someone killed her?"

Bertrand's skin reddened. "Now, look you. I had about enough of this." Bertrand splayed a hand on the desk to push himself to his feet. "You may be the star detective of this unit but ... you owe me, Herlihy ... " His chest puffed out.

Jack stood. "Sit down." In a quiet voice, he said, "I don't owe you anything. Sit down."

Bertrand fell back in the chair, his eyes protruding with panic. Jack leaned over him. "You're lying, see?" He shut down Bertrand's protest. "I talked to the landlady. She identified you as being there on many occasions."

"So what? Connie liked cops." He squinted.

"Then there are the fingerprints on the broken drink glasses and scotch bottle. We've found enough for an identifiable print. We'll be taking yours to compare."

Bertrand's face flushed a luminous red. "Maybe I touched the glass while we were there."

"No. You didn't." Jack left no loose ends. "The ME said he watched and that you didn't touch any of the glass at any time. You did, however, pick up a piece of paper and put it in your pocket."

"What are you talking about?" Bertrand's jaw set like a bulldog.

Jack pulled a stack of photos from the envelope. He pulled one out. Then another. Two black and white glossy 8x10s. So many times, life hinged on such small things. "See? These were taken at Connie Franco's room. This wadded up paper?" He dealt out another photo. "It's the Goody's Headache Powder you told me about. Remember? You couldn't find it in your jacket. Now you know where it was."

"You're out of your mind, Herlihy. You can't prove ... "

" ... that Goody's Brand is yours? How about this: you told me yourself. It isn't sold on the West Coast or anywhere else except for North Carolina. I talked to the company just to make sure. I checked your locker and found the box of headache powder, the same brand in the victim's trash can. And now, Captain, we're going to take your fingerprints to see if they match the ones we picked up on the glass and on the paper wrapper."

Bertrand stood, leaning in, his nose inches away from Jack. "No, you're not. I ain't saying another word. Not till I get a mouthpiece."

The door flung open hard enough the knob smacked the wall. The DA and the Chief filled threshold. "That's enough." The DA nodded. Over his shoulder, the Chief said to an officer, "Cuff him and book him for homicide."

Bertrand struggled against the handcuffs making it difficult for the uniform to steer him through the office.

Jack remembered something. "Oh, and the brand of whiskey was even yours: Johnny Walker."

The dark glance Bertrand threw over his shoulder told Jack that he'd heard.

* * * * *

19

I REMEMBER WHO I AM

Michael O'Keefe

My name is Robbie Meyer and I'm a cop. Most people would describe me as a big strapping guy: six foot nine, and a very solid two hundred and eighty pounds. I have a shock of red wiry hair on my head, and freckles that remind people of leprechauns. I'm forced to duck and turn my shoulders to fit through most doors. Everybody in this town calls me *Irish*. This is ironic because I don't have a drop of Irish blood coursing through my veins, not one.

The other name by which I am known, but only very rarely, is *Mad Robert*. I'm slow to anger, but when I do, my size and strength ensure that massive destruction usually ensues. My fury is brief and is more a product of frustration than any real impetus. Most often, I am able to catch myself before I hurt someone beyond their ability to heal.

Now that I've established that I am not Irish, and am not in fact mad, it bears asking what it is I *am*. I am Jewish, and proud of it. This is a rare phenomenon in a town like Dunson, Ohio. We have very few Jews, proud or otherwise. Even so, I'm not talking about some pedestrian, reformed, only-Jewish-on-the-High-Holy-Days kind of Jews. I was a rabbinical student with big plans. My father instilled in me a love of the law and an unquenchable desire to know and understand God's justice. I couldn't have been a rabbi in Dunson. There's not enough of us to constitute a real Jewish Community, so we have little need. Leaving wouldn't have worked for me either. I was hopelessly in love and Dunson is where she lived, and therefore where I needed to be.

I left town briefly to study at Yeshiva University, in New York. After immersing myself in the Torah and Talmud for four years, I was no closer to understanding God's purpose for us all and was utterly befuddled by his sense of justice: random as it seemed. The laws in Judaism are written, and they're clear enough, but nobody seems to obey them unless they feel like it, and God remains silent on the matter.

I yearned for the Old Testament God. He spoke up and made his opinion clear, and smote the wicked when he felt the urge. There was nothing vague or inscrutable about God's intent back then.

Of course, to us Jews, it's not called the Old Testament. We just call it the Bible. This New Testament thing is a Christian invention. That's okay by me. The ethos for both religions is largely the same. *Don't be a dick* seems to be the common thread. It's good that I can find a kindred spirit with Christians. My wife was Catholic and so are my children. For that matter, so are almost all of my friends and neighbors. There are a few other Jews here in Dunson, but they don't seem to think advertising the fact especially important, so for the most part we keep our religion to ourselves.

In fact, the only real devout Jews I ever knew in Dunson were my mother and father. My father arrived as a boy after World War II. Years later, my mother met him in New York at a support group for families of Holocaust survivors. My father was a speaker at the event, and for some incomprehensible reason, my mother fell madly in love with him. Following him back to Dunson, she soon married him.

I loved my father deeply, but I could never see the attraction. My mother was gorgeous; a dead ringer for a young Ingrid Bergman. He, on the other hand, was slight of stature and had poor posture, as if he were trying to invert his body to disappear into himself. He spoke quietly and slowly and seemed the saddest man I ever knew. But my mother brought out the best in him. She gave him a light he never had on his own. Even more glaring than the discrepancy in appearance between them, was the seeming impossibility that someone as large as me could have been produced from someone so slight. Other than the little remaining red tinge to his hair, and his sad, thoughtful, blue-grey eyes, we shared no physical traits in common.

I asked my mother about it when I was old enough to understand.

"Your father spent years in the camps," she reminded me. "They were his most important growing years. All of the internees suffered horrible malnutrition, but it was worse for children. By the time he was liberated, his growth had been stunted. He weighed only forty-five pounds. He filled out some and grew a little, but there is no telling how big he might have been if the Nazis' cruelty hadn't dwarfed him."

"Was his father big?" I asked.

"He remembers very little of his father. The trauma from watching his murder left him nothing but a picture of his face, and that as a nightmare."

"I don't understand," I admitted.

"When he remembers his father, all he sees is the sad, surrender in his eyes when poor Weiskopf cut off his head at Birkenau. He has no other family to ask. They all perished in the camps."

I never broached the subject with him. I don't think he and I ever had a meaningful conversation until I was ten. He was much older, even than my mother. So, it wasn't like we had a lot in common to talk about. Other than the Torah and the Talmud, and of course, Hebrew, which he was teaching me in preparation for my Bar Mitzvah, there was very little conversation between us.

Another thing that confused me growing up was how an emaciated, seven-year-old, Polish Jew ended up in Dunson, Ohio. My mother, the keeper of our family record, explained.

When Birkenau was finally liberated in April of 1945 by the US Army, Private Robbie Hardcastle, of Dunson, Ohio, found my father sitting among the dead bodies of his mother and sister. They had succumbed to malnutrition a day apart. When the other prisoners removed the bodies from the barracks to the burn-pit, my father followed. He was sitting with them awaiting his turn to die when Private Hardcastle found him.

Hardcastle was a schoolteacher, and already a father of three. The liberation of Birkenau broke his heart. The level of inhumanity he observed there very nearly broke his mind. He needed to do something decent and human to counterbalance the evil he witnessed. If he could save just one innocent, he thought, perhaps he could hold his shattered psyche together. Finding my father among the dead like that felt like a mission sent from God.

First he saw to my father's health and wellbeing. Then he made arrangements to have him declared his ward. After the war, he brought my father home to be raised as one of his family. Hardcastle would have adopted him but felt there was a greater duty to ensure my father knew and understood what was done to him, done to his people.

"Noah," Hardcastle told him. "You are as much my son as my other three. I love you with equal vigor. But you have a responsibility to be Noah Meyerowitz. Noah Hardcastle can't do what needs to be done. You must remember who you are, and you must tell the story of what they did to you. No one must be allowed to forget that this kind of evil exists, that it is among us. If we forget who we are, and the wickedness men are capable of, we are doomed to repeat it."

Toward this end, Hardcastle arranged for a rabbi to come to the house to instruct my father in Judaism and Hebrew. He found the small Jewish community in Dunson and got my father over to them every sabbath, so he could practice his religion and stay in touch with his ancestral self.

Because Robbie Hardcastle was a schoolteacher, my father became one as well. He finally shortened his last name in sympathy for his neighbors, who couldn't get their minds or mouths around Meyerowitz. He knew who he was, he assured Hardcastle. The last syllable was unimportant. When I was born, he named me after his mentor and savior. I wish Hardcastle had lived long enough for me to meet him.

I was ten-years-old the first time I saw my father's tattoo and asked about it. A blistering heat wave gave him cause to bare his arms, which he never did. Six indigo numbers crudely etched into his left forearm. He said he was just seven when he was interred with his father, mother, and younger sister at Birkenau. Taken from their home in the Polish Ghetto after the uprising, they were told it was a work camp. It wasn't. The only work being done was their systematic starvation and exposure to disease, and of course, removing and burning their fellow prisoners who had already perished. Most of the extermination work had already been completed before the Nazis opened their first can of Zyklon B.

He finally told me in excruciating detail how he lost his family, beginning with his father. Most of it he witnessed firsthand. Some of it he gleaned from the testimony from the Nuremberg Trials. He remembered my grandfather as a proud man who made the mistake of ignoring a guard at the camp who gave him a senseless order. For the snub, he was butt-stroked to the ground. But, this was evidently a great offense, far too severe to be satisfied by merely being beaten with the butt of a rifle. The guard was the worst one to possibly offend. SS-Obersharfuhrer (the equivalent of a Staff Sergeant in the

U.S. Army) Klaus Wunschman was better known by his sobriquet of *The Beast of Birkenau*. After offending *him*, my grandfather's survivability had dropped to zero.

Wunschman was diabolically cruel. While he had no problem just shooting a *Juden* in the head, he much preferred to use the prisoners against each other, thus dehumanizing them further. So he waited for a better opportunity to address my grandfather's transgression.

When Wunschman caught my grandfather's best friend, Jacob Weiskopf, hoarding food for his starving children, he had the leverage he was seeking. He told Jacob he had a choice: kill Benjamin Meyerowitz or watch his own children die. Weiskopf begged to be released from this odious task.

"Fine," Wunschman said, pulling his SS dagger from its holster on his belt. "It is the children then."

"No!" Jacob shouted. "Give me the knife. I will kill Meyerowitz."

Wunschman handed him the knife and told him, "Don't stop cutting until the head is clean off."

Jacob came upon my grandfather as he was walking with his family about the muddy yard. The prisoners had come to understand that a moving target was less likely to incur the guards' random cruelty. It was also a good way to stave off the communicable diseases rife among the prisoners. A static and airless environment was a breeding ground for the infectious diseases the prisoners knew were being inflicted upon them as experiments by the camp doctors.

Jacob plunged the dagger into my grandfather's neck without warning while he was holding my father's hand. My grandfather's only defensive move was to kick his son out of harm's way. After that, he had no strength to defend himself. He was already weak from malnutrition, having been hoarding his own food to feed his children.

My father watched in stunned silence as Weiskopf began furiously sawing at his throat with the dull dagger. He remembered my grandfather's only response was to bleed, gurgle and twitch. Finally, Weiskopf held the severed head up in front of him. He dropped it and the dagger at his feet before storming off toward the barracks, leaving my grandmother and her daughter to shriek and wail, while my father looked on in stunned confusion. He said the guards later used his father's head as a soccer ball. Even though he never engaged in hyperbole, I refused to believe such casual cruelty could exist in the world. He identified that as the moment his spirit broke. He admitted he was never the same.

"Weiskopf was an evil man, Papa, as evil as the Nazis," I said.

"No," my father corrected. "Weiskopf was a good man who loved his family. He only sought their protection. When he was confronted with an impossible situation, he forgot who he was. When he remembered, he was so horrified with what he had done, he took his own life, hanging himself from the center beam in the barracks."

"What became of his children?" I wondered.

"They were poisoned during medical experiments a few weeks later."

"So, Weiskopf killed your father for nothing?"

"When the Lord turned his back on my father, he turned it on Weiskopf as well."

"Doesn't that make you angry?" I asked. "Don't you want vengeance?"

"My father foresaw his end," he said. "He told me that the Lord is just and will even the scales in his own time. Vengeance is not *ours*. If we seek it, we forget who we are, just like poor Weiskopf."

"But, that makes no sense," I argued. "Wunschman has to pay."

"And one day, the Lord will see that he does," my father said, ending the argument.

It was this quandary of injustice that sent me into the study of the scriptures. I needed to make sense of this type of random brutality. It took me many years, but I finally surrendered. *God is inscrutable, and his justice may be beyond our reckoning,* I realized. After achieving a degree in Talmudic studies at Yeshiva, I was no closer to understanding the Lord. I was also in love, and missed her terribly. So, I came home.

I met my Irish wife in high school. Her family had moved from Donegal when her father, who worked in textiles in Ireland, was attracted to the opportunity for advancement available in Dunson's booming textile mills. Our relationship was almost foreordained. We were the two greatest athletes ever to attend Dunson Regional High School. Both brilliant students, we took all the same honors classes throughout our time there. Our love began in the ninth grade and burned hotter as time passed. We were perfectly suited for each other. She was a beautiful and talented soccer star, *the* Irish girl, and I was the big, handsome donkey and captain of the football team. Except that I wasn't Irish. Maura didn't seem to mind.

Amazingly, our religious differences never posed an impediment to us. Neither of our parents objected. They understood love and devotion. They appreciated that it was a rare and precious thing, not to be constrained by anything so unimportant as what house of worship one attended, or what name you called your God. Maura took a scholarship to Ohio State and turned it into a master's degree in education. She returned home to Dunson to become a math teacher and soccer coach.

I shrugged off numerous football scholarship offers and went off to Yeshiva to chase the cat's tail that is the will of God. After four years and getting no closer to his purpose, I returned home to take this job and marry the love of my life to build a home and family: eternal bliss. Or so the dream went. Just because it's what should have happened didn't necessarily mean God would let it. His random, capricious justice fell on our happiness like a building collapse.

Five wonderful, happy years and two children later, my Maura developed an inoperable brain tumor. Ripped from my life, she was gone in a month. I would have rent my clothing, smeared ash on my face, and cursed the cruelty of my God, but I had two children to raise.

I sold our home and used the proceeds and life insurance settlement to buy a five-bedroom fixer-upper in town. It turned out I had a knack for construction and home improvement. My parents moved in with us, and my mom took care of the kids while I switched to mid-nights. Late tours satisfied a lot of our needs. I was able to be at every important moment of my children's lives. I slept in the mornings and was awake to greet them as they came off the bus after school. It might not have been a typical existence, but it was good.

As the kids got older, they developed athletically, as their parentage would have suggested. I made every practice and game of their high school sports careers, sometimes shuttling from field to field to catch half of one game and half of another. With my parent's help, I was able to raise two healthy, well-adjusted, happy children, who are conscientious contributing members of society.

They've moved away to pursue their careers. My son is a young prosecutor in New York and my daughter has begun her first year of residency at University Medical Center in Cleveland. I miss them, but they call frequently. I'm not much of a conversationalist, but they know how happy I am to hear about their lives. It works.

Despite putting my personal ambition as a cop aside to raise my family, I've still managed to have an eventful career. Dunson is a suburb, situated halfway between Cleveland and Cincinnati. While we don't have a crime problem of the magnitude of the big cities, we still have one. Gangs, drugs, guns, theft, murder, and greed are part of the human condition. They don't look at a zip code and go somewhere else. So, even in uniform, I've done my share of hard police work. In twenty-five years, I've been awarded Dunson's Police Officer of the Year a half dozen times. The plaques are on the wall behind my desk at my daughter's insistence. She's proud of my service and far more impressed with it than I am. So, they're up there for her. I've turned down promotions to detective and supervisor dozens of times. I'm content with the solitude of late-tours. They let me examine my thoughts in a way only the darkness will allow. I need that kind of introspection. So, there I remain.

My reputation as a cop has grown. Given my history and outlandish size, most people are wise enough not to challenge my authority. But, stupidity is also part of the human condition. There are a handful of criminals who would tell you if they still could, when I order you to drop your weapon, you should comply. I don't know if their deaths were God's judgement or mine, but one of us had a final say in the matter.

Two years ago was a bad year. I lost my mom to cancer. But, my loss was pale compared to my father's. I watched what little life he had left drain right out of him. His eyes – never beacons of light – became wan, hollow, and somehow even sadder than they always had been.

A week after my mother succumbed, my father crawled into a hot bath and opened the veins on his left arm, next to that hideous concentration camp tattoo. I found him. Curiously, my sadness at his death was muted by my relief at the end of his suffering. He left a note. It wasn't an apology.

Dear Robbie,
This world is a cruel and harsh place. I bore it as best I could. But after the death of your mother, continuing seemed pointless. I was always weak. The Lord gave me people like Robbie Hardcastle and your Mom to shore up my weakness. But, Birkenau killed my spirit over seventy years ago. The gifts God bestowed on me kept me going. You kept me going. But, I can go on no longer. I have told my story again and again in the hope it wouldn't be forgotten.

In the end it was—by everyone but us. I'm tired now, and don't want to tell it anymore. I'm content that I have kept my promises—to you and the Lord. I've never forgotten who I was. If you do the same, you should be alright. You're a good man. You help people. As long as you remember who you are, you will continue to be one.

I'm confident I will see you and your mother again. I think with all I have endured; God will forgive me for taking a life that was not mine to take. I made good use of the years since Birkenau. I have not seen the Lord's justice yet. Perhaps it was never meant for me to witness. I still believe in it though, as should you. Just continue to remember who you are. God will show you the way.

I love you,

Papa.

After burying my father, I didn't believe in the Lord's justice anymore. I would never see it, because it didn't exist. I believed God had forsaken us all a long time ago. Things that happened were merely pointless, random occurrences. God had disappointed me for the last time. I wasn't expecting anything more from him.

A month later, I was on patrol in the old north-east section of town. I got a radio call for a man down in his home. I discovered the front door unlocked and could hear moaning from inside the house. When I entered I saw an elderly man lying on the carpet. He was clutching his chest as if in pain and rasping as he struggled to breathe. I could see, from the way his left leg was bent, he had broken his hip. Something about the room seemed peculiar. The man seemed to be lying between the living room and a hidden chamber behind the false wall which was hinged open. I was about to announce my presence when I looked past him into that small secret room. On the wall were two flags in four-foot shadow boxes. One was the banner for the Waffen SS, the other the classic swastika flag of the Third Reich. These were bracketing an old framed official military photo of Klaus Wunschman.

Festooned about the walls were framed pictures I recognized as being from Birkenau. These were many of the same photos I had seen at the various Holocaust museums I had visited over the years to get a better understanding of my father's suffering, and how a merciful God could permit it.

I realized these pictures were not grim reminders of the depths of depravity of which man is capable. These were part of a shrine. They were a celebration. I looked closer and was astonished to see a photo of my father as a boy, looking frightened and forlorn. Then I saw a photo of Nazi guards kicking a human head around like a soccer ball. I could see a seven-year-old Noah Meyerowitz staring on mutely in the background.

I could feel the fury begin to radiate through my limbs, a wash of crimson from my surging blood coloring my skin, which prickled hot like goose flesh. My jaw ached from clenching it so tightly. I squatted down to get a better look at the old man. Though in his nineties, I stared into the unmistakable face of evil. This was the monster who haunted my nightmares since I was ten-years-old: Klaus Wunschman.

"Oh, thank God," he said through a thick German accent when he saw me.

"God isn't here, Klaus," I assured him. "You need to focus on who *I* am."

He looked back in pain and confusion.

"I am the son of Noah Meyerowitz, and the grandson of Benjamin Meyerowitz," I said. "And you are *The Beast of Birkenau*, murderer of them both."

His eyes went wide at recognition of the names.

"It was not me!" he wailed. "It was Jacob Weiskopf. He killed him!"

"Yes, I know," I said. "With that SS dagger you have displayed over there under glass on your desk. You gave it to poor Weiskopf and ordered him to kill my grandfather, or you would put his children under the knife. Don't you remember? Your adjutant testified to this at the war crimes trials. You're proud of that knife and it's bloody history, aren't you?"

"No!" he pleaded. "I was only following orders!"

"They tried that argument at Nuremberg," I said. "They hung you Nazi scumbags anyway."

"I've changed! I swear. Forgive me!" he begged.

"Forgiveness?" I scoffed. "That's between you and the Lord. I'm just here to arrange the meeting. But you can rest assured, you *will* be in excruciating agony when it occurs."

I loomed over him, allowing all of my mass to shadow him in my darkness. I raised my enormous patrol boot and stepped down hard on his broken pelvis. His screams were horrible, even muted as they were by his chest pains. I kept exerting more pressure, grinding his brittle, old, hip to dust, when I heard the voice of my father in my head.

"Vengeance is not ours, Robbie. It belongs to the Lord. Remember who you are."

Wunschman gasped as I stepped off his shattered hip and slumped my shoulders in resignation. He looked confused as I keyed the radio microphone pinned to the epaulet of my uniform shirt.

"Central," I said in a dispassionate voice. "This is sector Alpha, Bravo. I've got an elderly male with an apparent broken hip, experiencing chest pains. Roll an ambulance and a paramedic forthwith."

Klaus began weeping. Through his tears, he sobbed, "Thank you."

"Do not dare thank me," I warned. "I will crush your skull with one ugly stomp. You only live out of respect for my father's mercy. But I have none. You will be exposed to the world as the miscreant you are. You will finally pay for your crimes at Birkenau."

For the first time, I saw real fear in Wunschman's eyes. He had been living in dread of this day for seventy-four years. Nothing – least of all an atrocity – can stay hidden forever. Now that he was discovered, alone, with no one to hide or protect him, he knew he would die for his sins.

As I had promised, Wunschman made it alive to Dunson Medical Center. He was placed under police guard while I made sure he was still wanted. Wikipedia verified the death warrant from Nuremberg, where he had been convicted *in absentia*. He was still listed as one of the top ten fugitives by the Wiesenthal Center for Justice. They had tracked him to Buenos Aires, where he remained until 1950. After that, he seemed to vanish into the ether. With no further sightings, Wunschman was presumed dead. So, no one had been looking for him any longer, until God put me in his living room.

In the morning, I contacted the FBI in Cleveland. An Agent Degrassi was thrilled to look into the case. It's not every day you get to arrest a Nazi war criminal. The US Attorney was beside herself with delight. This was the kind of high-profile case that could propel her into the governor's mansion.

The case played out with Wunschman getting the exposure and loathing from humanity he had always been due. He was convicted of his crimes again, this time in Cleveland. He was sentenced to die, at the time the most reviled man in the world. But, he succumbed to his shame and old age before the sentence could be carried out.

I was more confused than disappointed. Why did it have to happen only after my father's death? Why have it happen at all if Wunschman was going to snuff out a few months later? I finally realized I was never supposed to understand the will of the Lord. I certainly was never meant to be his avenging angel. If that were true, Klaus Wunschman would have ended with his head as a bloody footprint on his living room carpet. And as far as the Lord's justice was concerned, perhaps the *Beast of Birkenau* received it.

God allowed me to be an instrument of that justice. While in my opinion it was incommensurate with the evil that earned it, it was not *my* vengeance. So, I didn't get any say in its severity. I will have to content myself with the fact that the Lord is mighty and just, and I'm not. Ultimately, it is none of my business how he chooses to wield that particular sword.

So I get along with the knowledge that I do what a good man does, what he should, that to which I've sworn. It should be enough, but sometimes the injustice of life is so overwhelming, the fury and frustration build to a cataclysmic crescendo. Confusion tilts me until I feel myself slipping into the abyss. I want only to rip, and tear, and destroy every discordant thing in my wake. But then I hear the calming voice of my father: soothing, rational, patient. He reminds me that I am not the Lord. I am not his instrument of vengeance. I am but a man. He calms me. My fury begins to ebb. The frustration and ignorance seem to matter less. At my father's gentle prodding, I remember who I am. I am alright again … for a while.

* * * * *

DUBLIN TO LIVERPOOL

Barry Lees

Detective Constable Trevor Massingham was sitting in the departure lounge at Dublin International. He had spent four days in the airport, watching people, looking for a sign that they were committing crime.

The week before, he had been summoned to the office of his Head of Department, Detective Chief inspector Joan Long of Liverpool Police H.Q. Intelligence Division. The message had carried with it a warning of confidentiality. The wording suggested that the situation was serious. On arrival at Long's office, Trevor learned that there were three other intelligence officers seated around the table.

"Come in Trevor, phones switched off please," announced Joan Long.

Trevor complied and took his seat. He knew the others, but he tended to work alone. A nodded greeting was conducted before the D.C.I. commenced the briefing.

"We have had five young people admitted to hospital in the city over the weekend. They had all been out in the nightclubs before they were taken ill. Three were at the Moondance and another two at Dreamfields. They were found to have taken ecstasy. The forensic lab found that the strain they had imbibed was one they had not come across around here before and it was particularly dangerous. Two are in Intensive Care and another is on a life-support machine. We don't know how many other people are at risk."

"We are trying to trace the source of the batch and our colleagues in the Irish Republic have intelligence that has given us a lead. They believe that the pills are coming in from Dublin. The Garda are working on the origins of it, but we have to find who is carrying it and stop the supply at that point. Once it gets into the city centre, we will have no chance."

Trevor was both surprised and fascinated. In his experience, which was extensive, it tended to be the bigger cities that distributed drugs to the smaller ones. He expected them to go from Liverpool, but, logically, they had to get to Liverpool somehow. Joan Long was ready to deploy her team.

"Teresa, Kath, you are to take the ferry port. A search team will be at your disposal."

The two women nodded.

"Mark, you will be at the airport, and Trevor, I need you doing the same in Dublin."

The instruction was brief and clear. The task was laborious and vague. The hours he must put in would be demanding and the work repetitive. He understood the need for it and, if any further motivation were needed, he had two teenaged daughters who had shown their desire to dance the night away in the entertainment venues of the city centre. Five youngsters in hospital, risking death, he had to do what he could to stop that.

Trevor had been given a room in a hotel adjacent to the airport terminal. He did not see much of it. Flights to Liverpool did not take place during the night, but the daytime brought a constant flow of travellers through the terminal. Finding a needle in a haystack, that was his task.

The airport staff had to be briefed as to Trevor's intentions. Passengers come and go, but they never stayed there all day, and for several days. They were told that he was on the airport security team and they seemed to have accepted that. The days dragged on and Trevor's tolerance of airport cafeteria food diminished almost to the point of rejection. When it came to Friday, he was all but spent.

He entered the terminal with his small suitcase, which had contained nothing since his arrival, but was now full for his return home. He was booked on the 6.35 p.m. flight on the budget airline which carried most of the travellers in and out of the country. He checked in, for real this time, and took a seat in the departure lounge. He considered making one last visit to the duty-free shop, but he had examined the merchandise so many times, the thought made him shiver. Instead, he looked around him and watched the people one last time.

There was a group of twenty schoolchildren, aged between seven and nine. They wore matching jackets announcing the name of their choir. The conversations gave away that they were going to England to compete in a televised singing competition. They were excited and chatty. The adults fussed and counted their flock, who had appeared to Trevor to need no such attention. The matronly lady at the helm of the group, in her fifties and broad in build, corralled the children into the wide window bay from where the planes could be seen on the runway.

Several couples were holding hands and passports as they found seats in the rows. One pair, in their thirties and wearing gaudy Hawaiian shirts of different designs, appeared to be attired for a trip somewhere warmer than the north of England.

A noisy crowd could be heard approaching through the shops. It got louder. Male voices were nearly in song but far from in harmony. Their numbers and volume made them more intimidating than entertaining. When they came into view, it became clear that it was a sports team, all male, eighteen in number. One was carrying a pewter trophy bearing football insignia, whilst another carried an inflatable sheep, presumably for comedic purposes. When a recognisable song did form, it was a lewd version of a well-known nursery rhyme. Trevor hoped that the children of the choir were not tempted to join in.

A sobering sight followed. Struggling to pass through the bawdy crowd, a woman in a wheelchair came into view. She was being pushed by a man with a sombre expression. The football team made barely enough room for the chair and its acolyte to pass. There were some disapproving glances, but thankfully no confrontation. The footballers ceased their singing and a comparative lull ensued.

A fussy-looking, mature woman in a Burberry suit approached the gate, which was yet to open. A member of staff was preparing it when he was accosted by her. She was dragging a small case on wheels and carrying a pink and white plastic animal cage with a mesh across one end.

"I say, young man." Her manner was haughty and impatient. "I must insist that I be allowed onto the flight as a priority. My Henry is a pedigree and must not be jostled by anyone."

Through the mesh, a pointed nose appeared, accompanied by a pair of twinkling, wet eyes. Henry was lying on a fluffy, white cushion. Trevor silently hoped not to be seated next to the pet owner, or Henry. The staff appeared used to it and remained unperturbed by the request.

Trevor swivelled to look across the room and saw the departure seating fill up. There were people in business suits with purposeful expressions. Some spoke on their phones, whilst some flicked the screens of their tablets. One man in a raincoat, with a fake tan and blond streaks in his hair, appeared to be counting cash in full view of his fellow travellers. Trevor considered this to be unwise. He toyed with the idea of telling him so, but that was really a task for uniformed police officers. His role was not to be disclosed unless an emergency occurred.

The arrival of a huddle of eight young women ignited the flames of admiration amongst the football tourists. The girls were all in their late teens or early twenties and had Dublin accents. Several were finishing drinks bought at the duty-free shop that were meant to have been consumed after the journey. They were trailing luggage and seemed to be almost ready for the night out they were inevitably heading to. Trevor was surprised to see that most of the girls were travelling with curling rollers in their hair. In his youth, Trevor had often seen the old women of his neighbourhood with their hair in rollers, hanging out the washing in the back yards of the terraced houses. How times had changed, he thought.

The footballer boys flocked like moths to a flame in the presence of the young women, whose faces were already fully made-up. Trevor again thought of his daughters. He could not imagine them preparing for a night out in that way, but he was in another country. Perhaps it was considered normal here.

The gate staff removed the cord and invited the Burberry lady and her pampered pooch to board first. She disappeared along the sloping tunnel to the plane. At the gate, a queue had formed. Trevor took his place in it. A zigzag formation of ropes on short pillars made the line into a snake, the participants edging forward with tedious obedience. The children's choir formed up at the front and Trevor spotted the matriarch of the young singers dart off to the ladies' room with some haste. She pushed open the door and disappeared inside. Within ten seconds, the suntanned man with the blond streaks emerged, but from the ladies' toilet.

Trevor rubbed his eyes. It had been a demanding week. Had a man really been in the ladies' loo, or was it not a man after all? He could not imagine that the choirmistress would have failed to notice. Nevertheless, when she emerged after less than a minute, she gave nothing away. She rejoined the choir and encouraged the children to be ready to present their passports at the gate when they reached it.

Trevor was wondering where the pair had gone with the wheelchair. They were not in the queue. There was probably a simple explanation, but Trevor had grown to suspect everything, until an innocent explanation had come to light. The pet owner in Burberry had been given priority boarding, surely the family with a wheelchair user should be afforded something similar, thought Trevor.

He was distracted by the arrival of a police officer. He wore the dark-green uniform of the Irish Garda. He was handcuffed to a young man with oily black hair dipping over his brow. He wore faded jeans and a green parka coat. He was carrying a black bin-liner containing his belongings. His face showed the gloom of incarceration, but it also had an air of acceptance about it.

The football team, who had become interwoven with the nightclubbing girls whom they outnumbered two to one, brought up the rear of the line. Trevor could overhear the elevated conversations.

"We love it in Liverpool. It's just got so many great places to go," explained one young woman in a Dublin accent. "The clubs in Dublin are crap!"

A confident young fellow with an English accent sought to broaden her horizons as well as his own.

"Nah! Liverpool is nothing. You wanna get to Manchester. Much better. I'll show you around."

"Maybe next time, love. We are in a hotel for the weekend and it's all booked," answered a girl who was checking her face in a vanity mirror.

"How about I come to your hotel tonight and you show me around?" he suggested with clear intent.

Her friend interjected, "Nah. We've been saving for months for this trip. You lot should come out in Liverpool tonight," she proposed. "We will be in Dreamfields later. It goes on all night."

Trevor heard the name of the nightclub where the bad batch of ecstasy had been traced the weekend before. He hoped that the girls would steer clear of the drugs that were being distributed there. The accents and night-out preferences of the football boys showed that they were from further afield. At least until another of the football team spoke over the chatter.

"We were in Dreamfields last week. It was alright. I don't mind going back there if you girls will be there."

Perhaps, thought Trevor, there was a connection. He was exploring the possibility in his mind that the footballers had something to do with his current task. Frequenting that particular nightclub, as well as travelling between Dublin and Liverpool. It was a start.

Trevor recalled the couple in the loud Hawaiian shirts. Where were they? Had they boarded early? There was no evident reason for that, no disability, no sensitive, pedigree dog. Trevor scanned the line behind him. He spotted the couple, but they looked different. Gone were the gaudy colours, replaced by more sober and anonymous shades. Had they done this to make themselves less recognisable? If so, why? The man was transformed. He wore spectacles and his manner seemed apologetic. The woman, who had been holding his hand when Trevor had first spotted them, was sitting three seats from him. It was as though they were trying to appear unconnected. When the call came for them to join the queue, they remained apart. Had they fallen out? Was their liaison temporary and secretive? Or was the reason for the distance between them more sinister?

The queue shuffled on toward the final examination of passports and boarding passes. There were no pre-booked seats on the budget flight. It was first come, first served. Had it been a longer journey, Trevor may have made the effort to maximise his comfort. However, for a flight across the Irish Sea lasting less than an hour, he was prepared to put up with whatever was happening around him.

As there was no stowed luggage, some passengers had taken liberties with the volume of the items they had brought into the cabin. Some of the girls were also carrying clothes on hangers. Trevor's modest flight case went into the overhead locker without issue, whilst some of his fellow travellers tried to stow cases that were never meant for such spaces. After a few struggles, it fell to the cabin crew to officiate. Under-seat alternatives were suggested and all except one party seemed satisfied with that.

The tanned man with the blond streaks, whose emergence from the ladies' toilet at the departure gate continued to gnaw at Trevor's mind, found himself unable to stow his case. When the staff suggested that the owner of Henry, the prize-winning canine, agree to sharing Henry's seat with a stranger's case, the Burberry-clad woman objected strongly.

"The answer is no!" she announced.

"Lighten up love, its only a bloody dog," commented a voice from a seat behind where Trevor was sitting.

Trevor knew that the quip was going to be incendiary. The owner and defender of Henry rose to her feet and turned to glare at whoever had spoken. She locked eyes on Trevor first and he was about to express a gesture of denial when the offending voice added to their earlier viewpoint with another one.

"A dog shouldn't be on a flight, never mind having a seat to itself."

The lady was nearing boiling point.

"I'll have you know this seat is all above board and paid for. Why don't you share yours, hmm?"

She resumed her seat and tended to Henry's comfort with soft words through the mesh front of the travel cage. The stewardess found somewhere else for the oversized case. The man who had brought it had made himself scarce. Trevor had noticed a small number of empty seats on the right and just behind him. The man had probably gone to one of them. Confrontation over, the cabin crew got into position and wearily carried out the safety lesson to a largely disinterested planeload of people.

Finally, everyone was placed, and the seatbelt checks were complete. The Captain made a predictable introduction, in a light-hearted manner, through the public address speakers along with some reassuring observations on the acceptability of the weather and the timeliness of the flight. A short taxi to the runway, a pause for clearance from the control and the plane took to the air.

Once through the clouds and levelled out, the seatbelt light went out and an orchestra of clicks released those who wished to move. Trevor was in an aisle seat. By leaning to his right, he could see along to the door to the flight deck. The footballers were mainly at the front whilst the group of girls were behind him. It came as no surprise that several of the young men had headed to the back to speak to their new acquaintances. They took up positions in the centre aisle, from which to command the undivided attention of their targets. They were undoubtedly impeding the movement of the cabin crew, who did not seem concerned.

Trevor looked for the other people who had caught his eye earlier. The couple who had changed out of their colourful shirts were still sitting four rows apart. There was an empty seat between them, further raising Trevor's suspicion. It was possible that they had been unable to sit together because they had been among the last on the plane. However, the party of two that included the man in police custody, had been the last to board and they were sitting together.

As he watched them, a figure obstructed his view. It was the choirmistress, who had been fussing and herding her young choristers onto the flight. The choir were animatedly chatting between themselves, but their leader seemed tense and perplexed. She may have simply been a nervous traveller, but she had done and said nothing when she appeared to have found a man in the ladies' toilet. Trevor realised that some of her young charges were sitting apart from the main group. Rather her than me, thought Trevor. He had only ever had two kids to look after and that had been exhausting.

"Where is it? Where's the base? The base!"

The words were loud and urgent. Trevor saw who had shouted them. One of the football party was standing in the aisle, holding the trophy they had all been so joyful about. It somehow looked less impressive than it had at the departure gate at Dublin. The black base plinth, bearing the tiny, engraved plaques with the names of previous winners, had become detached and the current possessor was most anxious about it. He was moving his fellow players aside in their seats in a frantic and humourless attempt to find the black, cylindrical platform, on which the silverware was supposed to be displayed. There was some laughter at the expense of the panicking young man.

A hand shot up and in it was the missing trophy plinth. It was passed around whilst he was concentrating on the spaces under the seats. The joke was on him and he was the only one unable to see it. When the penny dropped and he stood upright, he saw the plinth and lunged for it. He landed on his own teammates and nearly on another man who was not in his party.

"Hey! Watch what you're doing," objected the traveller who had been forced to take evasive action.

By then, the plinth was back safely in the hands of the anxious trophy holder.

"I'm sorry, sorry," he pleaded, clutching the two parts of their prize closely to his chest.

He was pummelled by his teammates with the inflatable sheep to hoots of derision. He joylessly retook his seat and went out of Trevor's range of vision.

Trevor scanned to his right and saw the disabled woman in the wheelchair. She was occupying a space by the emergency exit halfway along the cabin. The man with her was seated behind her. Trevor felt some sympathy for their plight. Perhaps the choirmistress's task was not so difficult after all. The man who had been pushing the chair stood up to attend to the disabled woman. In doing so, he used the handle of the chair to pull himself up and the handle broke off, falling onto the floor and out of Trevor's sight. The man ducked down with some urgency to retrieve it.

Trevor saw that the top of the tubular metal frame of the chair was exposed. A hole, probably two centimetres wide, could be seen. Sticking out of it was something white. It was clearly visible against the black painted metal of the chair. The man came back upright and, with haste bordering on panic, he tried to replace the handle. He missed the hole and became flustered. The stewardess saw this and took over. After wrestling it from him, she calmly positioned the handle and pushed it down into the aperture, once again concealing whatever it was that had been in sight. Trevor was curious. What was it that he was so keen to cover up?

Trevor was distracted by some movement at the front. The Garda officer had, for the duration of the flight, removed the handcuffs from the surly young man in his care. The prisoner rose from his seat and headed for the toilets at the centre of the plane. There were four cubicles. Two on each side of the aisle. The guard was happy to allow him to perform his ablutions in private: after all, where could he go on a flight? The young man entered the cubicle, as the guard watched him from the front of the cabin.

The air pressure in the cabin had changed. Henry the dog was feeling it and he let out a series of pained yelps. His owner had decided that it was the fault of the irresponsible few who had been standing in the aisle and talking loudly.

"You rabble are upsetting my Henry!" she complained. A youth with a Manchester accent aired his rejection of her allegation.

"It's probably you it doesn't like. Have you thought about that?"

Laughter ensued and Henry yelped his discomfort. The Burberry lady finally realised that she was getting nowhere by complaining. She opened the cage and took Henry out to comfort him. As he came out, a small white package, no bigger than a letter-sized envelope, fell from the cage and onto the floor of the aisle. With surprising dexterity, she dipped down and snatched up the item before anyone could assess what it was.

"Oh, Henry. You have dropped your special pillow." She pushed it back into the cage and carried on cuddling the miniature dog.

The cabin crew came along the aisle, negotiating their way past those who had spent most of the flight standing whilst talking to their new acquaintances. Henry was replaced in his travel cage, but his plaintive whimpering continued.

"Return to your seats now please, we are coming into land. Thank you, thank you." The crew were beginning to sound like they had been having a long day.

Their entreaties were received with reciprocal lethargy. Slowly, the football boys peeled themselves from the magnetic attraction of the party of young women. As the aisle came alive with movement, Trevor spotted the man from the Garda peering over the seats. He must have been looking for his prisoner.

The lad had been a long time in the toilet, Trevor thought. He looked at the Irish policeman's face. There was clear worry expressed on it. He may have been regretting his decision to allow his charge to go to the toilet alone. What choice did he have? The cubicle was barely large enough for one person. It was not realistic to have accompanied him in there.

Before everyone had returned to their seats, the uniformed man squeezed past the first human obstacle only to be blocked by more. Only when the girl-chasing footballers had sat down could he make any progress, but he encountered another problem.

"Sir, you must return to your seat now please," urged the stewardess.

"But, my prisoner. He is in the loo. I have to get the 'cuffs back on him before we arrive."

"Please return to your seat, Sir. I will check the toilets." The cabin crew reassured him.

With some reluctance, and continually trying to look back at the toilets, the Garda man sat down and buckled up. The stewardess swept along the aisle, checking that seat belts were properly applied. At the halfway point, she examined the four toilet cubicles, paused, and checked them again. She continued down to the back of the cabin. A pensive look had come across her face. She dashed with unusual haste to the front to speak to the policeman.

"He's not there. The toilets are empty."

The cop was about to express his anger when the intercom sprang into life.

"Cabin crew prepare for landing."

The stewardess apologised for her inability to render any further assistance at that moment. She sat in her seat and clicked on her belt.

The plane descended toward the tarmac of Liverpool John Lennon Airport. The Garda man continued to make his protest, but there was nothing that anyone could have done at that precise moment. Trevor had seen a part of what had happened and was trying to work out the rest. He needed help. As the wheels touched down, Trevor deactivated "Aircraft Mode" on his phone and made a call. The stewardess was too far from him to be able to object.

"Mark, this is urgent. Make the call to stop all the passengers on the six thirty-five flight from Dublin. Try to delay them at passport control. I need you and a team to get down here ASAP."

He clicked off the call and undid his seat belt. The Garda officer was already up and searching the cabin for his missing detainee. Trevor was also looking for him. He had disappeared.

People were unclicking belts across the cabin. When they began to stand in the aisle, there was no chance of searching for anyone. Through the window, Trevor saw the stairs on wheels being shunted into place toward the front. Unfortunately, there was another set of stairs being manoeuvred into place at the back of the plane. Two exits meant that there could not be any effective screening of people as they alighted. Trevor hoped that the call he had made was acted upon without any delay.

"The time is almost seven-thirty," started the unseen Captain. "Have a safe onward journey and thank you for flying with us. We hope to see you again."

Trevor thought that his hapless Irish counterpart would not be keen to repeat his travel experience. Trevor wanted to help him, but as he was an experienced intelligence officer, he would only step in when there was a clear and serious risk if he didn't.

The doors came open and the passengers descended the steps into the warm but cloudy Liverpool evening. The procession of people snaked along the tarmac to the glass doors of the terminal. Trevor positioned himself toward the back in order to see more of them. As they entered the building, Trevor was sure that they had all gone through. Nobody had had any opportunity to leave in any other way.

At the passport control, the line stopped. The zigzag tape channelled everyone into one wide room. Trevor saw that the checking booths were not yet staffed. At the first appearance of a member of the Immigration staff, Trevor broke ranks and headed along the empty side aisle to the front. A uniformed checking officer saw him and came to see what he wanted. Trevor produced his warrant card and told him exactly what was required. The man heard it once and responded immediately. Trevor took a position at the side and awaited his colleagues.

***

"It appears that you have had the most interesting week, Trevor," began D.C.I. Joan Long at the conference table in her office. Teresa, Kath and Mark were also attending the debriefing session. Trevor took a sip of coffee and replaced the mug on the table.

"It wasn't so interesting during the week at Dublin." His colleagues had experienced a similar level of interest at their respective places of deployment. "But it got going on the way home. I had a few suspects, but I couldn't pin anyone down. There were so many places a passenger could conceal something small like a bag of pills. It made me suspicious of just about everybody. Then there was the Irish police officer who was escorting a lad in custody. He was wanted in the UK and was being extradited. We caught him at passport control, trying to pass himself off as another passenger. A fake passport has been recovered and two accomplices have also been arrested."

"Go on Trev. Don't keep us guessing," urged Teresa.

"There was a guy with a fake tan, a raincoat and bleached blond streaks in his hair. I saw him come out of the ladies' loo at the departure gate. A woman who was escorting a group of kids in a choir went into that loo just before he left, but she didn't say anything about it. She looked like the sort who would. She was fussing about in the cabin, getting in the way of me watching everyone. I was sure she was doing it deliberately. We know now that she is the mother of the lad in the handcuffs. She had volunteered to help with the choir only the day before. It was her husband in the costume with the fake tan and streaked blond wig. Near the end of the flight, he went into the loo and got changed, leaving the costume for their son to put on when he went in there after him."

Trevor sipped his coffee again.

"The dad, in his new appearance, found an empty seat near the back and blended in. He had his own passport, having left the fake one in the pocket of the raincoat in the toilet."

"So, you had to stop them leaving?" asked the D.C.I.

"I needed them to be held up at passport control. After that they could have disappeared. The Immigration staff were brilliant. They just made it look normal, until our search team arrived."

"Good job, Trevor," noted the boss. "But there were more arrests, I believe."

"I was listening to a lot of conversation before and during the flight," explained Trevor. "It was amazing how many of the passengers brought suspicion on themselves. The hard part was whittling it down, but someone did give themselves away with careless talk. It was one of a group of girls who were coming over to experience the nightclubs of Liverpool. I heard one say that they had been saving for ages for the trip and the same girl later let slip that they had been in Liverpool the previous weekend. That didn't add up."

"It's a bit thin to make arrests on that," declared Kath.

"I agree," added Trevor. "But the search team at the airport found eleven bags of pills, each containing about fifty."

"How did this not get picked up at Dublin?" enquired Joan Long.

"An easy mistake to make," said Trevor.

"What drew you to them, Trev?" enquired Teresa.

Trevor allowed himself a smile.

"It's going to sound daft, but I remembered the old ladies of my neighbourhood when I was a kid. I used to be able to see daylight through the things they had on their heads. On the flight, when I saw that theirs were not hollow, but solid, it made me suspicious. So, I asked the search team to look inside their hair rollers. That's where they found all the pills."

* * * * *

44

HIS FIRST

P.J. Bodnar

Helen Mathews sits in front of a fireplace in her Central Maine farmhouse flipping through packets of manuscripts, a bottle of expensive red wine on the early 1900s Gustav Stickley side-table next to her. Its twin sits on the other end of the couch, and a matching coffee table holds the stacks of manuscripts she hasn't yet read.

Antiques fill the house because they fit the period, not because she particularly cares about them. That is, except for the piece that came from her grandfather. It's on the mantle and chimes on the hour. The clock is the only thing she truly treasures in the house, and it only has value to her.

Although Helen isn't a particularly mean literary agent, she is brutally honest, and won't support something she isn't in love with herself. This fall evening, she opens one horribly boring disaster after another. The depths of one of the writer's inability to capture a scene make her laugh out loud. Her laugh is pleasant, but others have said it turns into a cackle when she really gets going.

Page after page gets tossed into the fire, increasing the warm glow of the small formal living room. There haven't been any good novels submitted to her in a long time, and she could really use a winner, so she tortures herself a bit longer.

Just when she's about to turn in because she can no longer take the agony, she comes across the manuscript for a crime novel. The author is a bit different: his writing seems to come from real life experiences. His descriptions need work, but the bones are there. She finds herself turning page after page.

As the fire starts to die down, she realizes how much the temperature has gone from chilly to outright cold outside. Getting up to stoke the fire, she observes that there is no more wood in the old bin that sits to the left of the fireplace, near the cast iron blacksmith-forged fire poker.

For the first time in a while, she feels like she might be heading down the right path, and her mind wanders to those who told her she was crazy for leaving a big literary agency and going out on her own.

The split-style farmhouse door that leads outside is the only original part of the kitchen, and includes the original early 1920s hardware. Although peaceful up here, she's still a city girl at heart, so the doors are always locked, top and bottom.

Helen walks onto the back porch and gets that uneasy feeling again, that somebody is watching from the tree line. She hurries with her work, collecting an armful of logs, grabbing as much wood as she can in one. She carries just one piece in the other in case she needs to swing it at something. She's mostly convinced herself the anxiety is just her nerves, but locks the door the moment it shuts as the cold chill runs down her spine.

With the wood box and her second glass of wine both full, Helen's nerves began to calm and her body settles into the oversized couch she bought from some online retailer. She pulls a quilt she won at the town's July Fourth Fair up over her legs and places the manuscript on top.

The wine caresses her tongue. It's from a winery on the Central Coast of California. She spent time there on vacation a few years ago and brought back a case. She only brings it out when she's feeling low.

Helen drifts back into the fictional world of the book. She's always preferred these made up realms to real life.

The chime of the mantel clock rings its Westminster tune and brings her back to reality. She hadn't realized how late it had gotten. She is expecting her nephew to arrive soon. He was due earlier in the afternoon, but called to say he was taking photographs of a sunset and would head her way when he was done. He told her that he could sleep in his fifth wheel if she turned in before he got there so not to wait up. With all the reading she has to do, she will probably be up long after he has arrived and gone to bed.

As she continues to read, Helen is transported to a small somewhat fictional beach town just south of San Francisco where things are going horribly wrong for one local rookie beat cop.

***

Helen's city street senses prove to be more accurate than she realizes.

He has been watching her from the tree line, as well as from inside the house. The 1920s hardware is nothing for his technically sophisticated mind.

Tonight, however, he isn't just peering through her windows or strolling unnoticed around the house, nor is he passing through the yard on to one of the other homes he's been watching. No, he's decided that it's time to let his urges free. He will have her at last.

He knew she would be his first the second he laid eyes on her at the local farmers' market. He'd followed her home at a distance, and had been visiting as often as she'd been in town. She wasn't young like some of the girls he liked to watch, but she was a city girl and he knew that meant she would be much more experienced. He needed someone with that spark. She had it in spades.

A warm smokey scent drifts on the wind across the field. The air has turned cold as fall fades into winter. He pulls the collar of his coat up and moves his hat down over his ears. His breath warms up his hands. He rubs them together, doing his best to keep them from going numb. He brought gloves but they're thin latex.

As he approaches the living room window, the sound of the dry leaves seems to echo across the yard. He worries that she'll hear him. But after listening to his heart pound for what seems likes fifteen minutes, he realizes that he's safe.

Then he smiles, because she's the one in trouble. Sitting there lost in her manuscripts …

She has no idea the horror that stands right outside her window.

Staring at her.

He starts getting aroused at the idea of what is about to happen, and begins to worry he won't be able to control himself. It's the one problem he doesn't have a contingency plan for. After a few breaths of the cold night air, he regains his composure.

The pack he carries hangs low on his back and he tugs on the straps to tighten it. In it is an assortment of tools he wants to try out on her. He's researched all kinds of predators to find a few techniques that intrigue him. He brought a large Bowie knife to keep her under control, but has ropes and smaller knives he'll use to decorate her flesh.

He overheard heard her talking to the clerk at the market. She said she's locking herself in the house for next several days so she can read that stack of manuscripts. Perfect. No one will be looking for her. He has all the time he needs to experiment. When he's done, the house will burn to the ground, and take any evidence he was there with it. Old farmhouses like this one are known in the area to be fire-traps if they haven't been updated. He checked the last time he was here, and knows exactly how to make it look like a horrible and tragic accident.

A cold breeze drives the chimney smoke down on him and his spine shudders. For a moment he wonders if he can go through with this. His mother always called him a quitter like his father. He never met the man, but no one ever had anything good to say about him, especially his mother.

No, he won't be like his father. Tonight he'll finally follow through with his plans.

Peering over the sill, he can see that she hasn't moved from the couch. The air is quiet and no noises come from inside the house except the quarter hour chime of the mantle clock. That is the first part of his plan. Use the chimes to cover his footsteps through the house. He has fifteen minutes to unlock the kitchen door. It won't take him more than two or three at the most, but he likes to know there isn't any pressure. He takes his time making his way around the outside of the house to the kitchen door. It takes him just under two minutes to unlock and open. He waits, counting down the minutes.

Off in the distance a dog barks, and he wonders if someone else has a visitor tonight. The thought of what is finally about to happen quickens his pulse. A knocking sound catches his attention. He looks down to see his hand tapping his leg.

A few more deep breaths and he calms down again.

The cold air makes his body shiver again. The last he was here, he oiled the door hinges to make sure they wouldn't squeak when he entered. A glance at his watch tells him the chime should begin soon. It tends to run a little quick. He wonders if she knows that or not.

The dog barking again in the distance brings his thoughts back to the present. His mother had always yelled at him when he would drift off into his own mind. Her words echo in his head. She's right. He needs to keep focused on the prize. His prize. He's been very patient, and now he gets to enjoy it.

The chime begins, and he opens the door. Making his way through the kitchen, the sound of the fire popping stops him in his tracks. From the doorway though, he can see her facing away from him, still engrossed in some silly book. A smile fills his face: he is about to give her more excitement than any writer could.

He wraps his finger around the handle of his knife. Adrenaline fills his body. The sweet taste coats his tongue. His heart begins to pound so loudly he can't imagine she can't hear it. He kneels down behind her, and breaths in her scent. Intoxicating.

The house creaks as if it can feel the tension of what is about to happen.

This is the closest he has ever been to her, and he soaks her in.

She turns the page of the book, and he pulls the knife from the sheath. He has practiced the next move thousands of times to make sure he gets it right.

With his left arm, he grabs her around the neck and puts the knife right in front of her face.

Her scream is deafening.

***

Darren Knox is lost.

He knows his destination, but his life is meandering like these back roads.

A year ago, after a hard break-up, he sold his house in Santa Barbara, CA, bought a truck and fifth wheel, and took off across the U.S. to find himself. So far he has a computer full of amazing images, but he's no closer to knowing where his life is going than he did when he left. The freelance and stock photography jobs he's been doing pay the bills, and the creative aspect of his life is rewarding, but he's searching for something more exciting, something more meaningful.

Eventually, Knox pulls into the driveway of his aunt's house. The property is large with several outbuildings. The one with the hook-ups for his trailer is close to the road but a bit of a walk to the main house. The sun has long since gone down as he backs the truck and trailer up to the old red barn.

Getting out of the cab, the cold air raises the gooseflesh on his arms, so he grabs his favorite sweatshirt from the backseat and pulls it over his head. He walks to the trailer and starts the task of disconnecting the two vehicles.

When he checks his watch, he thinks it's early enough to head up to the house and see if his aunt is still up. Plus he thought he'd make his grandmother's famous white bread rolls. He's one of only a couple family members who have the recipe, and they are his aunt's favorite.

After hooking up the trailer and grabbing the ingredients for the rolls, he walks down the long winding driveway up to the farmhouse. Before he approaches the house, he can smell the fire and knows that his aunt must be waiting up for him.

As he walks onto the porch that leads to the kitchen, gooseflesh covers his arms again, but this time he isn't cold. A dog barks in the distance, a sad long howl. Knox walks to the door to knock and sees that it's open. His aunt would never leave it ajar. All his senses start working on a different level. He can feel in the pit of his stomach that something is very wrong.

He backs off the porch and pulls out his cell phone. He exhales deeply. Somehow he has service. He dials 911, and it connects him with the dispatch of the Maine State Troopers. He tells them where he is and they connect him to the local police department. He explains the situation and they tell him there are officers on the way, but it may be a bit as his aunt lives a ways out.

The next thing Knox hears is a sound he will never forget. The scream carries out across the field and is met with an echo from the sad dog out somewhere in the countryside.

Knox puts the cell in his pocket and runs into the house. The kitchen and living room are empty. Papers are strewn all over the room, with a wine glass and the coffee table dumped over on the floor. He grabs the heavy fire poker from its place near the fire and moves with purpose. He keeps his breathing steady and his head turning to make sure there are no threats coming up behind him.

A loud thud comes through the floor. He ascends the stairs two at a time.

Knox walks into his aunt's bedroom and finds her on the bed underneath a man easily twenty years Knox's senior. The fear and pain in her eyes lights Knox up like a torch.

Something in her body language must have changed because the piece of shit on top of her looks over at the doorway, and steps off the bed with a hunting knife in his right hand. He is easily six inches shorter than Knox but probably weighs almost as much.

"Who the fuck are you?" the piece of shit says and turns towards Knox.

Knox glances at his aunt, who at that moment could have been his mother's twin. Years of anger and pain fill every ounce of his body. Everything he has been pushing down pulses through all 6'5" and 250 pounds of muscle.

The piece of shit yells again, "Get the fuck out of here or I'll kill both of you, you little fuck."

You can never really know whether you're capable of killing someone until the moment the act is presented to you. Knox has no doubt this piece of shit is about to die a very painful death.

Knox had raised German Shepherds as a boy. He loved the fact they didn't bark unless commanded, especially as they were about to attack. They would just explode like an overtightened spring.

As the piece of shit raises the knife towards him, that's what Knox does and he closes the distance between them in an instant. The attacker takes a sloppy arching blow at Knox with the knife. It's obvious he's never had to fight someone his own size or bigger. Knox ducks easily underneath it like his German Shepherds used to do during training. This move leaves the lower abdomen and ribs exposed: it's a painful place to be bitten.

Some people would swing a fire poker like a bat, but Knox uses it like a broad sword with a fish-hook on the end, and he is about to gut this guy when the attacker turns towards his aunt. Knox hooks the piece of shit on the collar-bone causing him to scream. Knox can feel the poker tear both flesh and bone. The piece of shit spins back towards him.

There is a moment in every fight when both participants are squared up staring face to face. One knows he is the hunted because the eyes of the other show no fear. They know they will win the fight before it even starts. They want it more. Knox knows this piece of shit needs to die.

The attacker attempts again to cut Knox with the Crocodile Dundee-style Bowie knife, but a blade that big is slow and heavy. Knox steps back like a fencer and lowers himself into a crouch like his dogs. He grabs the poker's handle with both hands and launches himself up at the attacker, aiming at a point about two feet behind his intended target. He drives the poker into him just above his belly button until it stops with the crunch of bone. When he pulls back on it as hard as he can, the hook on the end tears through the piece of shit's insides with a sort of slurping, popping sound. The handle becomes slippery as blood pours down it like an outdoor spigot.

The knife clangs to the floor. Knox pushes the poker back into him and lifts him off the ground until they are again eye to eye. The image of his mother fills his brain, the pain in her eyes even more intense than his aunt's. He slams the piece of shit's body to the ground with the force of a WWE wrestler doing a suplex. He pulls back on the poker again, but slips in the blood that is covering the hardwood of his aunt's bedroom floor. He lands on the attacker face to face and watches as his pupils dilate. The last breath he will ever take brushes against Knox's cheek.

Knox realizes his aunt is still screaming on the bed. He pushes himself off the piece of shit and sees his hands are covered in blood. He wipes them on the dead guy's clothes and stands. Walking over to his aunt, he grabs the quilt from the floor and covers her with it. He sits down on the bed next to her. "I'm sorry I was so late," he says to her. She buries her face into his chest and sobs.

"Thanks for saving me, Darren."

They sit there for what seems like hours but is no more than ten minutes before sirens can be heard blaring in the distance.

Knox gets up to lead them upstairs to the scene, but his aunt doesn't want to be in the room with the body of her assailant still on the floor. He helps her down the stairs. As they enter the living room, the cops are coming in the front door with guns drawn. Knox looks down at the blood covering him, and realizes what the cops are now thinking.

He looks up and sees two cops not much older than he is, both clad in tan uniforms with baseballs caps on. They start yelling orders at Knox at the same time, but the orders are not the same. Knox is unsure if he should put his hands up or lie down on the floor. He decides to turn away from them and raise his hands in the air. One of the cops takes charge of Knox while the other tries to calm Knox's aunt, who is screaming that he isn't the threat. Knox knows they have to get the scene under control before they can sort things out, and the fact is, he's covered in someone else's blood and did in fact just kill the man.

Knox is told to kneel down and cross his ankles. His hands are on top of his head. The cop steps on Knox's foot as he grabs his wrist and twists his arm behind his back. His other arm is handcuffed and brought down to meet its match and they are cuffed together. The cop gently leads Knox to the floor face down.

Knox's aunt continues to fight with the other cop, when a third officer walks in the door. Knox can tell he is their superior by the way he takes over the scene. He asks if the house is secure. They look at each other and draw their weapons and walk out of the room.

Knox watches as the Chief takes up a position with his back to a wall where he can see both entrances to the room. His sidearm is in his right hand but down behind his leg. Knox's aunt pleads with him to let Knox go. He tells her that he will get to that when he knows everyone is safe.

Knox tells her to let them do their job. He is fine, and everything will be okay. Knox can hear the other two clearing the bottom floor of the old farmhouse as the mantle clock begins its quarterly chime. He remembers when he was a kid. He would be on the floor of his grandparent's playing Matchbox cars on a rug just like this one. He thinks it's an odd memory to have at that moment.

The Chief's radio crackles to life. The words, "We've got a body up here, Chief," come over the mic loud and clear. Knox's aunt yells that he's the one who tried to kill her, that Knox saved her life.

The Chief walks over to Knox and lifts him off the carpet. "Son, I need you to sit in the backseat of my car while we get all this straightened out," the Chief says.

"I understand, Chief," Knox says looking him right in the eye, then starts walking out the door ahead of the older cop.

From the backseat of the Chief's car, Knox watches as the local fire department and ambulance corps show up and evaluate the scene. They bring his aunt out of the house on a stretcher. All three cops interview Knox, and he gives the same statement to each. His aunt had confirmed his story, and added details of what happened prior to Knox's arrival.

Sitting there for this long, Knox's legs start to cramp and the cuffs pressing against the seat pinch his wrists. He tries his best to find a comfortable position but gives up realizing there isn't supposed to one in the backseat of a police car.

The Chief walks over and opens the door. He helps Knox out of the cramped seat. "Sorry we had to keep you in there that long, son," the Chief says and Knox feels as though he means it.

"No worries, sir. I appreciate you guys helping us out tonight. I know you have a job to do," Knox says as he rubs the imprint of the cuffs on his wrists.

"The evidence in there corroborates your stories," the Chief says. "In fact, we've had a few run-ins with that piece of shit up there. Never thought he'd go this far though, but the world won't miss him. That's for sure."

Knox smiles hearing the Chief use the same term for the suspect as he had.

"What's the smile for, son?" the Chief says.

"Nothing, sir. Am I free to go? I'd like to check on my aunt unless you guys need something else from me?" Knox says looking slightly down at the department head.

"Yeah, son. We're going to need your clothes as evidence, but after that you are free to go," the chief says. He turns to walk away, but stops. "I must say that I'm pretty impressed. Not many people could have handled themselves the way you did tonight. We could use someone like you on the force. You ever think of becoming a cop?"

Knox looks down at the bloodstains on his favorite sweatshirt and wonders how he will feel in the morning when the adrenaline has worn off. "It crossed my mind a few years back. I don't know, sir. I'd have to give it some thought. Right now, I really just want to make sure my aunt is okay."

"When you're ready, you give me a call," the Chief says and hands Knox his business card. "Cell phone number is on there too, if you need anything."

Knox takes the card, and thinks, *maybe this is the direction I've been looking for all this time.*

* * * * * *

COLD COMFORT

Desmond P. Ryan

It was one of those nights where the rain was colder than the air, and the air felt pretty damned cold. Even so, Detective Mike O'Shea and his partner, Detective Ron Roberts, needed to get out of the office. Grab a coffee. Go for a spin. Something.

Although they were partners, the two men couldn't have been more different. Mike was a squad guy with a ways-and-means attitude, while Ron was a dyed-in-the-wool traffic cop who lived and died by rules and regulations. At least, that's how they were when they first partnered up. Over the years, much to each other's chagrin, they had begun to pick up each other's traits and the differences between them became less stark.

"Johnny's is closing," Mike said as he settled himself in the driver's seat, adjusting the mirrors.

"It's closing or being closed?" asked Ron.

"A little from column A and a little from column B, I suppose," Mike replied, looking over his shoulder as he put the unmarked silver Intrepid into reverse to back out of the crowded parking lot behind the station.

"Can't say I'm surprised," Ron said, adjusting his tie and pulling down the lapels of his suit jacket. "I always figured there was more going on there than just selling coffee. Is that where we're going, then?"

"Why do you have to be like that?" Mike said, waiting for a car to pass before backing onto the street.

"You mean honest?"

"I mean so fucking cynical," Mike said, clicking the windshield wipers up another notch before driving on.

"I'm a cop," Ron said as the rain lashed against the car.

***

"IV Two on the air?"

"Go ahead, dispatcher," Ron said, picking up the microphone attached to the radio beneath the middle console.

"I've got a call for you when you're ready. Possible sudden death."

"Go," said Ron, pulling out the steno pad he had brought with him.

The dispatcher read out the address and a few details of the call.

"Good thing we were already on our way," Mike said.

"Unless Johnny is the sudden death. I told you there was more than overpriced coffee going on there."

***

"Where's Johnny?" Mike asked the uniformed officer at the door, wiping the rain off his jacket as he entered the coffee shop.

"And I thought you guys were the investigators," Johnny called, sitting in the far corner of the shop, rubbing the stubble on his face, a cigarette dangling from the side of his mouth.

"You're not supposed to be smoking in here," Ron said, flicking the water from his fedora as he took it off.

"Watcha gonna do? Arrest me?" Johnny laughed. "What about the stiff in my freezer downstairs?"

"Have you been drinking?" Ron tilted his head sharply to one side, looking like a bird dog catching a scent.

"*Have* I? Don't you mean when *haven't* I been drinking. Real bright spark, this one," Johnny said, taking a drag, rising unsteadily to his feet, and then removing the cigarette from his mouth.

"Are you the one who called?" Ron continued, looking at this dishevelled little man who looked remarkably similar to the homeless people that wandered up and down the street outside of this shop at any given time.

Johnny looked exaggeratedly from one side of the empty coffee shop to the other. "See anyone else here, Sherlock?"

"Maybe I should handle this one," Mike muttered to Ron.

"Good idea, Watson," Johnny said, taking one last drag from his cigarette before dropping it to the floor and grinding it out with the toe of his shoe. "Or, I guess, you're Sherlock now, aren't you?"

"Yes. He seems like *your* kind of people," Ron huffed.

"What do you know?" Mike said, addressing Johnny while pointedly ignoring Ron.

"I know there's a stiff in my freezer downstairs. That's about it," Johnny said, making his way past the two detectives to get behind the counter. "Want a coffee?"

"No, thanks. We're good," Mike lied.

"Do you know how … *the stiff* … got there?" Ron asked, his eyes following Johnny.

"I thought *he* was asking the questions." Johnny said, looking over to Mike.

"Play nice," Mike said with a sharp nod to Johnny.

"Alright. The freezer in the basement. I was gonna leave it … "

"Leave it?" Ron asked.

"Yeah. Lease is up. I'm not renewing. Landlord is changing the locks tomorrow. I'm trying to do a midnight dash." Johnny poured some hot water into the machine to make himself an espresso. "Thanks for blowing my cover, boys!"

"So you're just grabbing all your stuff before you get locked out?" Mike clarified.

"Exactly. I was trying to get everything out I could. But look at the size of me, man! Do I look like I could carry half the shit out of this place on my own? No. So I hired some guys from the corner these past coupla nights to empty the place."

"Names?" Mike asked.

"Dunno," Johnny shrugged, taking a sip of his espresso. "In fact, I've never even seen them. When I said I was closing and wanted to gather up some shit, one of my regulars said he'd take care of it for me. Knew I was kinda feeling a little pressured, if you know what I mean. Losing my shop, my livelihood, my whole life … "

"Fair enough," Mike said. "Let's get the freezer printed. You don't mind if we take your prints, too, do you, Johnny?"

"Pfff. You guys already have my prints. Had to get 'em done for my firearms acquisition certificate. You guys should know that. Maybe after this shit is all over with, we can go to the range and fire off a few rounds together. I bet you've got some pretty good shit to use."

"Let's just get your prints, okay?" Mike said.

"I'm going to take a look at the freezer," Ron said, starting down the steep stairs to the basement. "Watch your head. Low ceiling."

"Be my guest." Johnny called after him. "Might as well add your prints to everyone else who's had a look inside."

***

Ron walked along the narrow hallway that led to the kitchen at the front of the shop. The freezer was just to the right of the door. Careful not to contaminate the lid any further, Ron snapped on a rubber glove that he had in his pocket and opened up the freezer.

Inside was a fully clothed man looking as if he had been intentionally posed seated with his head tilted back, dead eyes staring up at whomever opened the freezer. He looked peaceful, except for the slightly distended tongue that Ron knew meant he had been strangled to death. Ice had started to form by the corners of the man's mouth, suggesting that he hadn't been on ice for very long.

Ron let out a sigh and closed the lid.

***

"We can certainly call Homicide," Ron said as he reached the top of the stairs. He looked at Johnny. "You know him?"

"Nope, and I'm going home."

"Don't go too far away, okay?" Mike said.

"I live around the corner. Every cop in this division knows that."

"Because we've been to your place that often?" Ron asked.

"Yeah," Johnny said, raising his middle finger behind him as he walked away. "To par-tay."

***

"Well, boys, what have you got for me this time?" Detective Sergeant Amanda Black asked, her stiletto heels tapping as she made her way down the steep stairs to the basement, the rain still dripping off of her long coat. "Better be good. I was out for dinner with my husband when I got the call. Almost made it to the main this time."

Mike opened the freezer.

"Looks like a come-to-Jesus moment to me," Amanda said, peering down at the body. "No sign of a struggle. Was likely choked to death before he was put in the freezer. Was that a No Frills I saw around the corner? They're having a sale on frozen chicken. Sold out in my neighbourhood. I'll give my husband a call and have him pick some up."

Ron looked over at Mike and rolled his eyes.

"Hey, when you've got a daughter into competitive sports, you go through a lot of chicken. It gets expensive. Who else has touched this freezer? Is Ident on their way? And the coroner?"

"I've got a list of everyone ... ," Mike began.

"A list? Whatever happened to containing the scene?" Amanda said, looking at directly at Mike for the first time since she arrived.

"It s a short list."

"Better be."

"I called Ident. Amy's coming," said Ron.

"Great. I love that girl. Okay. And coroner? And where's the person who discovered the body?"

Mike and Ron looked at each other.

"Come on, boys! Tell me you know ... "

"It was Johnny," Mike spluttered.

"Great. Who the fuck is Johnny and where is he at now?" Amanda snapped.

"He's the owner of the place and he's at home," Ron said.

"Home?" Amanda repeated, her eyes focusing on Ron. "How the hell did that happen?"

"He just lives around the corner," Mike said.

"Well, either he comes to us, or you go to him. You decide."

***

"Want one?" Johnny offered, wobbling on his feet as he opened the door to the detectives, a can of beer in his hand.

"We need to talk to you," Ron said, looking down his nose at the open can.

"Great. Want a beer?" Johnny called over his shoulder as he turned around and walked back into the house.

"Maybe I should look after this," Mike said quietly to Ron.

"Maybe," Johnny called back as he opened the door to the fridge in the kitchen at the back of the house.

"What a disgrace," Ron mumbled.

"I bet you're good for a beer?" Johnny said.

"I'd love one," Mike said, walking into the kitchen.

"Wha … ?" Ron began.

Mike waved him off. "My people, remember?"

"Now we're talkin'. You're probably a good guy when you're not saddled with this asshole," Johnny said, pulling a can of beer from the fridge and passing it back to Mike. "Cheers!"

"Sláinte."

"Sláinte," Johnny repeated, closing the fridge door and turning around to face Mike. "That's an Irish thing, right?"

"Yeah." Mike said, tipping the can and taking a gulp.

"I like it," Johnny said, raising the can to Mike. "Sláinte."

"Now, about the body in the freezer," Mike said.

"Yeah. Fuck. I had these guys, not exactly from the corner, but … "

"From where, then?" Ron cut in.

"I'm talkin' to Irish," Johnny said. "Look, when you run a business like mine, you know everybody but nobody, you know?"

"I bet," Ron said, pulling out his steno pad.

"One of my regulars told me he knew some guys with a truck. They've been in and out of the place for the past two nights. Moving shit to my garage out back. Wanna see?"

"Not right now. But, yeah, eventually," Mike said. "So do you even know these guys?"

"Nope."

"You let people you don't even know move your things?" Ron said, looking up from his steno pad.

"Dude, nothing in there is mine. It's all chattel. Belongs to the landlord. I'm stealin' it. Oops! I guess I shouldn't be telling you that, eh?" Johnny said with a smirk.

"Don't care," Mike said.

"I knew I liked you. Want another?"

"No, I'm good."

"I'm havin' one."

"I think you've had enough," Ron said, disapprovingly.

"I think you should go fuck yourself," Johnny said, flipping the tab on the can.

"Any surveillance cameras in that back alley?" Mike asked.

"Which one? Behind the shop or here?"

"Either. Both."

"Nope. But I've got a camera inside my garage."

"We're going to want to grab the footage. Maybe there'll be a good enough still on there to ID someone."

"Be my guest."

"So how did you come to look in the freezer in the first place?"

"Sláinte." Johnny lifted the newly opened beer can to Mike before taking a big swig. "I thought," he added with a belch, "that I should go see what was going on down there."

"Why tonight?" asked Ron.

"Last day of the month. Locks will be changed at midnight."

"Fair enough," Mike said. "So what happened?"

"So I go downstairs to have a piss, the cans are down there. After I take a squirt, I wonder if there's anything left in the freezer worth taking."

"Like what?" Ron asked.

"Like a big stash of weed or something like that."

"Okay," Mike said. "So you open the freezer. And then what?"

"And then, after I fuckin' hold back my fuckin' cookies, I close the lid and call you boys."

"So *you* called the police?" Ron said.

"Has he been drinkin' tonight or have we?" Johnny smirked, taking another big swig of beer.

"He's just like that." Mike replied.

"Fuuuuuck … " Johnny said, rolling his eyes as he finished off the can.

***

"That third guy, there," Mike said, looking at the security tape they had pulled from Johnny's garage. "I know him. Third-rate B-and-E guy. Had him in court a few weeks ago. Judge gave him bail. And here he is. Sur-prise."

"Now who's being cynical?" Ron said with a slight smile.

"Guess I've been hanging around you too long," Mike said. Both men leaned closer to the computer screen on Mike's desk.

"B-and-E and homicide are a world apart," Ron said.

"Maybe, but he's worth talking to," Mike said, hammering at the keyboard, bringing up the man's record. "I've got an address. Let's go see if he's there."

"Unlikely."

"Says he's on conditions not to leave his place of residence between the hours of ten p.m. and eight a.m.," Mike read from the screen and then looked down at his watch. "He should be home now."

"Assuming the time on the video is correct, we've got him in the garage at two a.m. this morning."

"So we've got something to bring him in for and we'll go from there."

"*If* he's there."

"He'll be there."

***

"Officers, what a pleasure to see you."

"Save it, Kavitz," Mike said to the third-rate B&E guy from the video.

"Now who's being the bad cop?" Ron muttered.

"I suppose you'll want to come in? Check for alcohol? Drugs? Known criminals that I shouldn't be associating with? As you can see," Kavitz said, making a sweeping gesture around the filthy room behind him, "I'm alone here and have none of those horrible things in my humble abode."

"Step outside for a moment," Mike said.

"Why? Am I under arrest? For … ?"

"Breach of bail conditions. Got you on video outside of your … humble abode … this morning around two a.m. Hands behind your back."

Suddenly, a man scrambled out from under the bed and tried to push past the three men in the doorway.

Mike shoved Kavitz back inside the room towards Ron as he grabbed the loose-fitting shirt of the fleeing man. The man quickly turned, struggling to slip out of his shirt. Mike moved in towards him, forcing the man's head down as he wrapped his arm around the man's neck, his other hand pushing on the man's back. Within seconds, Mike's opponent was on the ground. Mike pivoted his body and put his knee in the man's back to hold him down. He slapped one handcuff on the man's left wrist and then pulled the arm sharply and painfully across the man's back before cuffing the man's right wrist.

"I don't know who you are or why you're running, so, at the very least, you're under arrest for assault police," Mike said, pulling the man up off of the ground as he got himself up.

***

"One or both of you killed the guy in the freezer. Which one is it?" Mike said to the two men sitting in the back seat, not taking his eyes off of the road ahead of him.

"These fucking cuffs are too tight," the second man said, squirming as he tried to raise his arms up behind him.

"Then stop moving," Ron said.

"I didn't kill nobody." Kavitz was almost crying. "You know me, boss. I'm not a killer."

"Then who did?" Mike said, taking his eyes off the road to look into the backseat through the rear-view mirror.

"I dunno," Kavitz said, looking down as he shook his head.

"Yeah, you do, Kavitz. And you want to know how I know?" Mike said, eyes now on the road ahead of him. "Because you aren't a killer. Hell, you aren't even a good B-and-E guy."

"You got that right, boss," Kavitz laughed.

"But your friend here. He's a killer, isn't he?"

Kavitz looked out the side window.

"Isn't he?" Mike repeated.

"Don't fucking say a word!" the second man hissed quietly.

"What's your name?" Mike asked.

"Fuck you," the second man spat back.

"Okay, Fuck You. You killed that stiff in the freezer, didn't you?" Mike said, watching the road in front of him. "Owed you money? Drugs? Fucked your girl? What was it?"

Kavitz began to whimper.

"Shut the fuck up!" the other man said, glaring at Kavitz.

"The guy pissed you off. You choked him. Maybe a little too hard. He fucking died. So you put him in the freezer, didn't you?" Mike said, stopping at a red light. "But that wasn't enough. He never said he was sorry. So you set him up like he was begging you to forgive you. That's what you wanted, wasn't it?"

Ron stared straight ahead, letting his partner do what he did best.

"Did he fuck your girlfriend? Is that what he did?" Mike said, turning his head to look back at the men in the backseat. "I'd be pretty pissed off if someone did that to my girlfriend. I'd lose my mind, actually. Wouldn't mean to kill him necessarily, but I'd certainly want to make him think I would. Is that it?"

The other man looked down while Kavitz's whimpering turned into sniffles.

"And then ... fuck, he's dead. Now what?" Mike turned his attention back to the road as the light ahead of him turned green. "Fucker never really got what was coming to him, did he? They say strangulation is pretty painless. You didn't want him to die without pain, did you? So all that was left was setting him up to look like he was praying for forgiveness. Am I right or am I right?"

"If you say so," the second man said.

"It's not what I say that counts, is it?" Mike replied. "You were man enough to choke a guy to death, and now you're not man enough to admit it. I find that kind of funny."

"Do you."

"Yeah. Because I never had you pegged as a wimp. I mean, any guy that would kill another guy for fucking his girl ... "

"Pfff. I couldn't care less if he fucked her or not. He owed me money. Lots of money. So yeah, asshole, I wrapped my hands around his neck and squeezed."

"Until he was dead."

No one spoke for a couple of moments.

"What's your name, buddy?"

"Manfred. Jerry Manfred."

"So you choked him until he was dead, didn't you, Jerry?"

"Yeah. Until he was dead."

"And then you put him in the freezer, sitting him up like that to make it look like he was sorry."

"Yeah. Me and Kavitz put him in the freezer."

Kavitz let out a wail as if he'd just been stabbed in the gut.

"How many times did you go back to that freezer, just to see the look on that fucker's face?"

"Few times."

"I bet. And he just looked up at you, those fucking eyes, unmoved. Let you almost convince yourself that he was sorry for what he did, right?"

"Yeah."

"How long did it take for you to strangle him?" Mike said, putting his turn signal on.

"Dunno. Couple of minutes, maybe?"

"But you don't really remember that part, do you? Because you just wanted that fucker to feel your hands squeezing the life out of him."

"I wanted to squeeze the fucking money out of him. Every last dime."

"Why?"

"Because he owed me. Big time."

"This is about more than money, isn't it, Jerry?"

"Yeah. I was going to get out. Get set up. Take that money and give myself a chance."

"For what?"

"What the fuck? A chance to have a life, asshole. To be somebody. To be The Man. To drive that car, live in that house, have that hot wife. Not fucking sleeping on mattresses that stink like piss because you got 'em out of the dumpster. Not fucking being with some chick who makes her money fucking the men who drive those fancy cars. Not sitting back here talking to you."

Mike waited a moment before going on.

"And then he fucking gave up," Mike said.

"Yeah, he fucking gave up. Not me. Him."

"He was dead, Jerry."

"Yeah."

"You fucking killed him, didn't you?"

The clicking of the turn signal almost echoed in the quiet car.

"Yeah," Jerry finally said. "I killed both of us."

"Jerry Manfred, I'm charging you with the murder of John Doe, also known as the man in the freezer, pending formal identification of the deceased."

Jerry looked out the side window for a moment.

"You can't use any of this in court," Jerry said, as Mike turned the car into the back parking lot at the station.

"No, I can't, but Mister Kavitz here is going to recount this whole conversation for me on video in exchange for the opportunity to possibly avoid prosecution as an accessory, aren't you, Mister Kavitz?"

Jerry glared over at Kavitz with the eyes of a man who had just seen his whole life slip away from him. Kavitz, who had been sitting with his head down, tears and snot running onto his lap, looked up, hopeful for a moment.

"Or," Mike continued, before Kavitz could answer, "you can spare us all a lot of shit, Jerry, and Mister Kavitz here will also go down for the murder, should you decide to give me a full confession once we get inside and I read you your rights. This is your chance to be The Man. You get to decide."

* * * * *

THE LADYSMITH

Pearson O'Meara

Deputy Rory Comeaux spotted the door marked with a skirted silhouette and gave it a shove. Inside the women's restroom, she bent at her waist and peered under the doors. All the stalls were empty. She tapped the bottom of each industrial-green metal door with the toe of her Danner boot, swinging them open to judge the cubicle's cleanliness. She lingered at the spacious handicapped stall, but the media ramifications played out in her head. "Fully-abled Lafayette Parish Sheriff's Deputy caught using bathroom stall reserved for handicapped. Will she be terminated? Tune in for our full report at six."

She stepped into the least disgusting stall and shuffled to her left in the tiny space, knocking the stained stainless-steel toilet paper holder with her holster. She tried forcing the broken door latch closed but couldn't line up the male and female parts. "No wonder dating is such a mystery," she mumbled.

Rory pulled the door towards her and squeezed out sideways, rattling past the toilet paper holder and pawing at the spider web of a cord that attached her portable radio to her shoulder mic. She released the mic from her left shoulder lapel then clipped it to her radio's antenna. The antenna swayed with the mic's additional weight.

She shouldered open the adjacent door like she was making a SWAT entry. Seeing no toilet paper, she pilfered a roll from the first stall by opening the dispenser with her handcuff key. Then, she backed into this now fully equipped space, her radio squawking.

Rory yanked on the coat hook to make sure it could withstand the weight of her belt and all its accoutrements – polished-by-hand brass buckle, holster, two pairs of Smith & Wesson handcuffs, two ammunition magazines, and a Motorola XTS 5000 portable radio valued at ten percent of her yearly salary. Finally, she slammed the latch closed and began her bathroom ballet.

In one smooth and practiced movement, Rory unholstered her weapon, then, using both hands, gingerly set it on top of the toilet lid. The lid was slick with humidity and not level, and when her Glock 17 with a chambered 9mm round slid off, she snatched it in mid-air like a chameleon's tongue catching a fly. She jerked her head away from the firearm and flinched. Hearing and feeling no accidental discharge, she exhaled. With zero regards for muzzle safety, she unzipped her uniform shirt and shoved her Glock, barrel first, between her 36Cs and her Second Chance ballistic vest.

Next, Rory unsnapped the three belt keepers on her leather Safariland duty belt and peeled the duty belt back to separate it from the under belt. The rip and tear of Velcro, the creak of leather, and the jingling of handcuffs were the music of police work.

Unless you were a woman.

If you were a woman in uniform, the sounds signaled countless hours in cramped bathroom stalls taking equipment off and putting it back on and praying everything was in the right place.

Rory turned to hang her duty belt on the back of the stall door. After double-checking the hook, she hung the belt as carefully as she would a Renoir landscape. She leaned back, admiring her work. With the most delicate touch, she hoisted it up, eyeballed it, then set it down again on the hook. *Balanced!* A pair of her handcuffs slipped from their case and clattered to the tile floor.

Rory pressed her hand against her chest to keep her gun from falling out and bent over to pick up her handcuffs. When she raised her head, she bumped into her radio. Her shoulder mic came unclipped from the flopping antenna, so she jerked hard on the cord. The cord contracted, and the mic popped Rory in the lower lip like a runaway yo-yo. She got her duty belt, radio, mic, and handcuffs in custody, but in the commotion, she pressed her radio's emergency button.

The Dispatcher bleated, "The net is Code Three. Ten-thirty-three. Dispatch, I-seventy-six. What is your emergency?"

"Accidental. I'm Code Four," Rory reported, trying to sound confident and controlled, not sweaty and flustered.

"Ten-four. The net is Code Two. I-seventy-six stand by for ten-twenty-one."

Rory's cell phone rang, and she fished it out of her back pocket.

"Are you okay?" the Dispatcher asked. "You sounded out of breath."

"Yes, I said I was Code Four."

"Yeah, but your emergency button went off."

"I know. I accidentally pressed it."

"How can you accidentally press your emergency button?"

"It's a long story."

"Where are you?"

"Generally? Or specifically?"

"Specifically."

"In a bathroom stall."

"Oh, okay, that explains everything. By the way, you're supposed to be using plain English on the radio now. Didn't you get that memo from Headquarters?"

Growing up in a law enforcement family with the chatter of a police scanner constantly in the background, Rory knew her ten-codes before she knew her alphabet. For her, ten-codes *were* plain English.

"Ten-four," Rory answered and hung up.

She dried her sweaty hands and forearms on her pant legs and took a deep breath. She cursed the department's wool-blend Class A uniforms, unsuitable for bathroom stalls in South Louisiana, or South Louisiana period.

Her cell phone rang again, and she saw "Bill" scrolling across the tiny screen. She accepted the call and waited.

"Are you about done?" Bill asked. Her partner's impatience was palpable.

"Yes, dear," she answered in plain English. She flushed the toilet to appease him, and he hung up on her.

Finished, she washed and dried her hands and re-applied her against-department-regulation tinted lip balm. Lipstick in plain English. She made sure her hair was still in place after the struggle and double- and triple-checked the stall to make sure she hadn't forgotten anything, especially her Glock.

Before leaving the restroom, Rory stopped and checked her uniform in the full-length mirror. Appearance was important in a paramilitary organization like the Sheriff's Office, and she took it seriously with hand-polished boots and pressed uniforms, all tucked in, zipped up, snapped, and aligned.

She was considered attractive, but the men she dated also considered her too independent, hard to handle, aloof, and generally a pain in the ass. Most recently, she had been informed that she was emotionally unavailable. Rory conceded the unflattering characterizations were all true, probably, because she rarely shared her innermost feelings, especially about *the job*. Part of her duty, she felt, was to protect those she cared for from the sheer ugliness she witnessed.

Rory snapped out of her maudlin thoughts and made a mental note to put in for a plain-clothes position so she could dress up like a high-priced prostitute and work a sting operation just like Angie Dickinson did in *Police Woman*.

Outwardly, to anyone old enough to remember and willing to listen, Rory lambasted Angie Dickinson, calling her a false advertiser. She blamed Dickinson for glorifying women in police work to the thousands of little girls like Rory, who watched *Police Woman* weekly when they were coming of age during the tumultuous 1970s. Of course, she could complain about being lured into police work by Dickinson, but inwardly, Rory knew her career had been predetermined by the law enforcement familial gene. Besides the lack of a boyfriend, the only thing she had in common with Angie Dickinson was a partner named Bill.

***

The restaurant was not as bustling as it was when she'd left for the bathroom. The lunch rush was over, and Bill wasn't at their table, which was now glistening with disinfectant and set with silverware wrapped in fresh white napkins. Rory stepped out into the sunlight and a wet blanket of humidity.

Bill was leaning with his back against the driver's door of their marked Dodge Durango, tapping the face of his watch. "Are you *finally* done?"

"Yeah, yeah, let's go," Rory said, walking to the passenger's side.

"I wish I understood why it takes you so damn long." Bill clicked the remote and turned to open the driver's door.

"I can't decide if I like this lipstick," Rory said. She leaned forward slightly, so Bill had a direct line of sight of her through the Durango's cabin. She put an end to their Female Police Officer's Bathroom

Process discussion by rubbing her swollen bottom lip side to side with her extended middle finger.

***

Two hundred yards away in a wooded area, Richard Broussard lay prone, toes pointed out, his legs forming a wide "V". For stability, he pressed his pelvis and belly to the grass. He arched his back and propped himself up on his elbows, letting his natural bone structure support his weight. Broussard shouldered and steadied his weapon, his arms and hands providing the third leg of his shooting tripod. He sighted through the scope and expelled a slow breath, relaxing his diaphragm. His intended target's head filled the viewfinder, and Broussard centered the crosshairs.

"I got you, bitch."

He willed his muscles still except for his right index finger, which hooked the trigger. He blinked.

***

Bill's face exploded, and the driver's side window shattered as the .223 rifle round exited and tumbled. It continued its murderous path, traveling through the Durango's interior and taking out the passenger window, ripping through Rory's right collar-bone.

Bill was dead before the shot's crack and echo could register in his brain. He was dead before he could remember the curve of his wife's hips and her inexplicable tenderness when they first made love as twenty-somethings. He was dead before he could remember the overwhelming love and weightless responsibility he felt while stroking his son's forehead as the boy slept.

There was no traveling towards the light or "tell Maureen and Connor I love them," and Bill never saw the horror on Rory's face.

But, as she cradled his devastated body and sobbed, Rory couldn't shake one thought. The last thing Bill Landry ever did was fuck with her, and the last thing he ever saw was her flipping him off.

For the second time that day, she pressed her portable radio's emergency button.

***

The elevator chimed as it descended each floor, and the doors slid open at the Acadiana Behavioral Health Center's lobby with a mechanical whoosh. Rory spotted Mark Bergeron right away. *Bastard!* She scanned the elevator control panel and punched the button to close the doors, but Mark rushed forward and sacrificed his arm. The doors ground to a stop, then opened wide again.

"So much for patient confidentiality," Rory said, her face reddening. She felt exposed and vulnerable, but found her legs and stepped from the elevator. She blew past Mark, so close their shoulders touched.

Mark groaned and watched the elevator doors slide shut. He closed his eyes and forced an exhale. Rory's heels click-click-clicked on the hard tile floor behind him, and he took off after the sound.

"How are you, Rory?" Mark asked, trailing her, breaking into a jerky walk-jog like a toddler trying to keep pace with an older sibling.

"Learning to be a southpaw."

"I should try that. I hear it increases your brainpower, keeps you from getting dementia. Something like that ..."

"I'd be happy to shoot you in the shoulder, but they won't let me carry a gun right now," Rory said, focusing straight ahead. Her heartbeat rushed in her ears.

"Seriously, Rory," Mark let out a nervous laugh. "Fuck. Can you slow down? Are you doin' okay?"

Rory wheeled around. Her face was a dark, deep auburn like her hair, and pain had settled in her blue-gray eyes. Not a new, fresh pain. But lasting. Permanent. Mark saw it and braced himself.

"Not *once*," she said. "Not once did you call to check on me, ask if there was anything I needed. Matter of fact, I haven't seen or heard from you in months, not since Bill's funeral. Not a card. Not an e-mail. Not. One. Single. Call." Rory delivered each word like a finger poke to his sternum.

"I know. I'm sorry. I didn't know what to say." Mark's body sagged with the truth. "I failed you ... as a friend."

"So, why are you here now? You must need something." Rory wanted to run, escape the confrontation, but she did what she always did. She was a pain in the ass.

She pressed close to Mark and grabbed his tie, inspecting the pattern. She winced but held it out taut at the bottom with her shaking right hand, and she slid her left hand up, fiddling with and tightening the knot around his neck, nearly choking him. Mark let her.

"And to think I had feelings for you."

"Rory, we went on *one* date!"

"I bought Class A lingerie for that date, Mark. The good stuff."

"You can't possibly still be mad about … "

"About you telling me I was emotionally unavailable?"

"I didn't know you had feelings for me."

"I still do."

"Really?"

"Yes. I feel like punching you in the face."

She smiled a false smile and dropped the tie, patting his shirt collar flat with her fingertips. She brushed imaginary dust off the shoulders of his suit jacket, then opened it, exposing his short-sleeved dress shirt.

"Who do you think you are? *NYPD Blue*'s Andy Sipowicz?

"Rory, I'm sorry."

"I don't need friends like you, Mark. So go fuck yourself."

She left him dumbfounded, like a stopped clock, in the center of the lobby, and she stormed off towards the doors.

"We got a lead on Bill's killer." Mark had reached for the only thing that would keep her from leaving.

"Yeah?" Rory slowed, pressed her hips against the door's crash bar, then stopped. Her ears screamed. "I'm sure I'll hear about the arrest in *The Daily Advertiser*."

Rory tried to swallow the lump in her throat. Tears filled the corners of her eyes and began spilling onto her cheeks. She turned around and leaned against the door. Holding her arm across her stomach for support, she wiped her eyes and cheeks with the back of her left hand.

"What do you need from me?"

"Let's take a ride. I'll fill you in on what we got."

***

Mark told Rory to leave her car in the parking lot and walked her to his black, unmarked Crown Vic. They took Congress Street to Johnston Street, then headed south. Mark activated the wig-wag lights, and the late afternoon traffic moved out of their way.

"Isn't this against regulations? Or do you homicide detectives get to transport civilians in unmarked units?" Rory asked.

"You're not a civilian," Mark said. "You're on medical leave."

"I go to physical therapy three times a week and a shrink once a week. Have been for four months. And I hear things I shouldn't, constant ringing. So, I'd say I'm damn close to being a civilian."

"Yeah, that's nice," Mark cut Rory off. "Look, this guy out in Milton contacted us late this morning about a rent house that one of his tenants vacated without any notice. Guy says the renter was a real oddball."

"Oddball in Milton? Shocker."

"He says there's something we need to see in one of the bedrooms."

"You get a search warrant just in case?"

"Jeff Ortego is at the Judge's house getting it signed right now."

As they approached the Acadiana Mall, Rory said, "On the way back, we can stop and get you some long-sleeved dress shirts."

"Jesus, Rory."

"You know everyone calls you Sipowicz behind your back."

"Except the ones who call me Sipowicz to my face," Mark said, picking up his phone.

She stared out the window while Mark drove and fielded calls from Ortego and the Crime Scene Unit supervisor. It was sugar cane harvesting season, a twenty-four-hour-a-day controlled burn operation resulting in thick layers of smoke and plumes of floating ash. Rory watched as a cattle egret, backlit by the setting sun, perched itself on a grazing cow whose back was peppered with sugar cane ash.

"Everything's all set," Mark told her. "Jeff has the warrant and will meet us there. The landlord says the house is completely empty, so we only need a couple guys from Crime Scene."

Mark turned the Crown Vic east on LA 92, a two-lane state highway littered with fast-food wrappers and flattened sugar cane stalks. He switched on the headlights as they crossed the metal drawbridge at the Vermilion River and passed NuNu's Grocery Store. NuNu's was famous for its boudin and cracklins, and older shoppers still spoke Cajun French, a language Rory's parents were mocked for speaking when they were in school.

About a quarter of a mile past the drawbridge, Mark turned onto an unmarked private road and continued south along the river. The gravel road was turtle-backed, higher in the middle to promote drainage and prevent flooding. The wig-wags bounced off the tree canopy, making it difficult to see, so Mark deactivated them.

"Dammit, it's pitch black out here. Wish we could've done this in the daylight," Mark said.

"I can't hear," Rory leaned over and turned down the radio and the air conditioning.

Mark slowed and scooted forward in his seat, his elbows and forearms wrapped around the steering wheel, and looked left and right down each opening in the trees. The gravel crunched under the tires.

"We should be close," Mark said. "Look for an old trailer house on piers."

Rory looked in the side-view mirror and saw another dark Crown Vic and a van approaching from the rear.

"That's Jeff and a guy from Crime Scene," Mark said.

The three pairs of headlights settled in, and the convoy led by Mark and Rory came to an opening marked by a battered and leaning wooden mailbox post. A plastic mailbox rested on the ground next to two empty aluminum garbage cans lying on their sides.

"I think this is it," Mark said, turning onto the single-lane drive, braking, and steering around deep potholes.

The drainage coulees on each side of the road were layered with palmetto palms and chicken trees, then large live oaks with long, knotted branches weeping with greenish-gray Spanish moss.

They came to a circular clearing a few hundred yards in and a 1970s house trailer raised on concrete piers. The floor sagged between the pyramid-shaped piers, and rotted wood and insulation dripped from the trailer's underside. A flimsy structure with a tin roof and a carport had been built over the trailer. The trailer wore it like a hat. A work truck was parked in the carport, and a man sat on the pre-formed concrete steps that led to the porch and front door. Mark positioned the Crown Vic so its headlights illuminated the porch. The man raised his arm, using his palm to shield his eyes.

"Is that the landlord?" Rory asked.

"Yeah, his name's Robert Trahan," Mark said. "Rory, you're gonna hate me even more for saying this, but I need you to stay in the car until we clear the trailer. We're gonna do this right, but quick. This place is givin' me a *Deliverance* vibe."

Mark exited the car before Rory could argue, and he met with Jeff, who handed him a manila legal folder. They walked up to Trahan. The men huddled and shook hands. Mark opened the folder, pulled out a sheet of legal paper, and handed it to Trahan. Rory watched Mark as he stood next to the landlord and pointed out the specifics of the warrant.

Trahan wore work boots and a uniform shirt with an oval company patch above the left breast pocket. A thick chain with keys was clipped to his Lee jeans. All the men had dark wet spots on their shirts between their shoulder blades, where sweat ran down their backs. A stepladder was propped up by the porch beside a cardboard box of light-bulbs.

Trahan grabbed the stepladder and the box of light-bulbs, and Rory watched as the men climbed the porch steps and disappeared inside the trailer's front door.

***

Once inside, Trahan led the way down a short hallway into the main living area. The trailer was dark and reeked of mold and cigarette smoke.

"You work at NuNu's?" Mark asked.

Trahan patted the patch on his shirt. "Yessir, for tirty-tree years, me," he answered in a thick Cajun accent.

Trahan unfolded the stepladder and placed it in the middle of the room, directly under an exposed light fixture. He pulled a bulb from the cardboard box and climbed the ladder. He screwed in the bulb, illuminating the bare room, then climbed down.

"He paid rent for another tree monts, but you kin see he took evertin'." Trahan climbed back up the stepladder, unscrewed the light-bulb, then climbed down. "I'm a show you da kitchen."

"Mister Trahan, where's the room with what you wanted to show us?" Mark asked.

"Oh. Da bedroom. Back here."

The men followed Trahan into a bedroom. He repeated his stepladder routine but, when he screwed in the light-bulb, nothing happened.

"Can you flip dat switch?" Trahan asked, jutting his chin towards the wall switch.

Jeff Ortego flipped the light switch, bathing another empty room in 60 watts of soft white light.

"Mister Trahan?" Mark asked.

"Look here, look here." Trahan walked to an outward-opening door leading to a dingy bathroom. A faucet dripped water into a sink with exposed pipes. He closed the door, revealing the side that had been hidden from view.

It was plastered with *The Daily Advertiser* newspaper clippings of Bill's murder. The articles were slashed and ripped. In the middle of the door, about eye level, with red circles drawn all around it, was a photograph of Rory, posing with an award for the department's most DWI arrests.

"Holy shit," Jeff whispered. "He meant to kill Rory."

"Everyone glove up and get this processed." Mark stepped forward and studied the door. "Mister Trahan, you have a phone number for this guy?"

"Yeah, but he don't answer."

"Any idea where he might've gone?"

"No, sir, I never came here 'til dis mornin'. Rent was paid, so I didn't have no need. A lady live down da road complain about him not pickin' up his trash cans. She tol' me he been gone two monts."

More light shone into the room, and Mark and Jeff took positions on each side of the lone window, peering out. A Ford F-150 pick-up truck pulled parallel to the trailer, then skidded to a stop with its headlights directed at Mark's Crown Vic.

Trahan stood in the middle of the window, oblivious, and crossed himself, "*C'est lui!* Richard Broussard!"

"Shit! Rory's outside in my unit!" Mark said, running.

Mark burst through the front door to see Rory outside the Crown Vic, arms raised, pleading with Broussard. "I'm sorry. Please ... please. Don't kill me."

Broussard turned his head to Mark's noise, then raised and leveled his rifle at Rory.

The single gunshot scattered birds from the trees, their wings fluttering frantically. A perfect stillness set in, and moths danced with sugar cane ash in the F-150's headlights.

***

Sitting on the sofa in Dr Blanchard's office, Rory looked out the window at the neon ribbons of traffic on Pinhook Road.

"I used to like this time of year when the sun sets early. It's cooler in uniform."

"At some point, Rory, you have to tell me what happened in Milton."

"I know."

"The Sheriff tells me you were brave."

"I was scared to death."

"Tell me what happened. Just start wherever you'd like."

Rory took a deep breath. "Richard Broussard drove up in his truck while everyone else was inside the house. I didn't know anything about what they'd found."

"You recognized him?"

"No, I don't even remember arresting him. His hair was matted, and he was barefoot and filthy. He looked crazy."

"I know he'd been in and out of Tyler Mental Hospital."

"Maybe I'll get his old room."

"Rory, stop. You're not crazy."

"He got out of his truck with a rifle before I could get my door open. I had trouble with my right hand."

"You've made remarkable progress."

"I was mad that Mark made me wait in the car, so while they were in the trailer, I snooped around and found his backup weapon. A Smith and Wesson thirty-eight snub-nose revolver. I thought it was the same Detective Special model that my dad and grandfather had, but I laughed because it was a woman's gun, a LadySmith model. It had *LADYSMITH* engraved on the frame."

"What did you do with it?"

"When Broussard ordered me out of the car, I slid it behind my back, in my waistband."

"Okay."

"Broussard laughed at me and said, 'I knew you'd show up.' He railed on about me arresting him for DWI, causing him to lose his job, his family. I knew he was going to kill me."

"Okay."

"The others inside saw the headlights from his truck, and they came running out the front door. He turned his head to look at them. It was just a split second. When he turned back to me and aimed, I drew the LadySmith with my left hand and fell backward. I shoved my left arm in between my legs and pressed my knees together to hold my arm steady. I hit him in the forehead."

"That was quick thinking. You saved your own life."

Rory said nothing. She looked out the window again. Blanchard waited.

"The top of his skull cap floated in the air, then fell and made a thudding sound." Rory stared at the drops of condensation on the window that reflected the traffic lights like beads of mercury and wondered whether she had spoken out loud. Blanchard's silence confirmed that she had. Eventually, he cleared his throat.

"The Sheriff told me he's offered you a plain-clothes position in Homicide when you're ready."

"I'm going to take it. When I'm ready."

"Then we'll work towards that goal."

Rory turned her attention back to Blanchard. She was sure of only one thing at the moment.

"Mark doesn't know this yet, but I'm keeping the LadySmith."

* * * * *

RIOT IN THE MENTAL INSTITUTION

Ryan Sayles

2127 hours, Carcasa PD

"PD, three-zero-three."

Unit 303 was driving north on Rainbow Boulevard, the smell of a roadside pizzeria coming in through the air vents and stirring its fingers in their stomachs. Corporal Seaton leaned back in the passenger seat and watched as his trainee, Officer Day, snatched the mic off the bracket and took a breath before responding.

"Go ahead." Her voice was the kind of calm and monotone, as if nothing surprised her anymore.

"Three-zero-three, we just received a nine-one-one hang-up call with shouting and screaming in the background. It traces back to Bat Hovno Blazon Institution. The caller said, 'riot at the mental hospital' and hung up."

Day allowed herself a look at Seaton, her eyes an ethereal gray as the dusk shadows passed over her face. But the shadows were all that moved on her. No twitches, not even the nearly imperceptible pump of blood beneath her skin. "In route."

She hung up the mic and put both hands back on the wheel. The shadows, made by passing street-lights, crawled along her skin at forty miles per hour and she struck Seaton as being at home playing in the dark. Any call involving the words "riot" or "mental institution" always seemed to stir an extra nerve in a cop, but Day was placid. Unperturbed.

"Giddy?" Seaton asked, his tone mostly a joke.

She shrugged, eyes on the road. "Just got one more thing to do before getting off work, is all."

"Had any other calls like this before now?"

Day shook her head. "My second night with Corporal Wahlski we had a disturbance call to a house that turned out to be a domestic violence with, like, four participants. I learned pretty quickly there."

"He was your Phase One trainer, correct?"

"Yup."

"So, second day on the job you get a rare sighting of a four-way DV?"

"Yes, indeedy." She smiled, another rare thing for her. "We charged them all. Four dominant aggressors. It was pretty cool."

Seaton was still getting used to Day. This was their third shift together and he was her final trainer; two weeks with him and he would determine whether she would become an independent officer or get bumped back into remedial training. He had no doubts thus far. While Corporals Wahlski, Cohen and Ambrose gave him their notes on her – "she's squared away, all-business, don't let her go," said Cohen – one must always find out for themselves.

Day was an Afghanistan combat veteran who earned a Commendation Medal with a "V" device authorized. The "V" was for valor, something not all Commendation Medals received. She earned it during a fire-fight where she and two others actively moved against the enemy, pressing and holding them back so a group of injured civilians – elderly women, clutching closed the scraps of their Chador garments, torn and bloody, after being caught in an explosion – could get behind American cover and escape.

Her husband and children would brag about her actions. Seaton was impressed. He had never been in a fire-fight. Didn't want to be, either.

"You ever been to the BHB Institution?"

Day shook her head. "No. I've driven by it a lot. Cohen said it was an in-patient crisis center?"

"Yes. Addiction and psychiatric emergency stuff." Seaton said. "They'll take junkies and the folks with psychological problems so the hospitals and jails don't have to. They'll help them come down or sleep it off. They also keep patients who need a few weeks intervention, some court-ordered stuff. Yadda yadda. I'm surprised you haven't transported anybody there yet."

"Cohen and I were going to, some career drunk the whole PD knows, but at the last minute he changed his mind."

"Probably Rodney. Big white guy, vulgar?"

"Red hair."

Seaton smiled and snapped his fingers. "Yes. At some point, you'll fight him. He's an asshole like that. Just be ready."

"Not a problem."

The silence in the car spread out the way a grumble of thunder will roll across the skyline, taking its time to stretch across the horizon. A harbinger.

"Well, let's land at the Hovno place and see the lay of the land. If it's bat-shit crazy in there, we can call for back-up." Seaton said. He shrugged and put a piece of gum in his mouth. "You know how it goes, though. People exaggerate when they call nine-one-one."

***

"Well, maybe they weren't," Seaton said, standing on the sidewalk next to the Bat Hovno Blazon Institution, staring at a reinforced window that had the wooden leg of a chair stabbed through it as far as it could go.

Inside, people were still shouting.

Day walked right past him, taking in the window as she went. "Looks pretty dead-nuts on to me." She keyed her mic. "PD, three-zero-six. Go ahead and start two more units."

Karl in Dispatch came back across the air, saying, "PD copies. Break. Three-zero-four, three-zero-five, be en route to three-zero-three and three-zero-six's location." They both copied and off in the distance a siren began wailing, then two.

Seaton caught up with Day, who had gone to the front entrance where a slim man in jeans and a button-down shirt was waiting in the doorway. He kept looking back over his shoulder, a key-ring in his hand. The key-ring, something comically stereotypical of a janitor's ring, was large enough to fit a fist through and held a collection of keys so thick the odds were against anyone actually knowing what all the keys were for.

Day walked up, easy in her demeanor and pointed to the keys. Smiled, said, "All you're missing is a mop bucket."

The man's eyes flicked up and down her as if he'd developed the skill to size someone up in the same amount of time it took a snake to strike its prey. He looked back to Seaton, who was no titan. "There's plenty to mop up." He said in a dismissive voice.

"What's going on inside?" Day asked.

"C'mon, you need to speak with the Charge." He turned around and started walking inside. He shuffled like he was older than he seemed.

Seaton propped the door open with a rock. Keyed his mic and said, "Three-zero-four, three-zero-five, come around to the east side main entrance. The door is open. We're going in with an employee."

The hallway was slender, plain and long. Here and there the painted cinderblock wall was broken up with a steel door. Day and Seaton walked with the man, came to a T-intersection in the hall and turned left.

They passed by a door with a small glass window in it. A woman stared out from it, her eyes wide enough to fit posts inside. She was on her cell phone. As the officers passed by, they heard the deadbolt disengage in the door and she stepped outside. Dressed in nurses' scrubs and comfortable tennis shoes, her short hair tightly wound in a bun. "I gotta go, I gotta go, the polices is here. Finally." She hung up her phone and started walking the way they came.

"I guess she's not the charge nurse, eh?" Day asked the man over his shoulder.

"Patricia? She's an idiot."

Day and Seaton looked to each other and Seaton asked, "What the hell is going on here?"

"Right here." The man turned another corner and opened a door and the shouting came full-on. The man stepped out of the way and tried to say something, but he couldn't be heard over the noise. Day screwed her face up into the disapproving look her children would recognize as the first signs of her steam escaping her tea spout. She walked past the man and Seaton kept close.

The door opened into a patient area – another hallway with an activities room on one end – and several patients filled the space. Agitated, the hallway was hot with human body heat and smelled.

Day saw a chair nearby and jumped on it. Now looming over the crowd, her head rubbing the ceiling, she shouted, "Police! Everybody shut up! Now!"

Seaton stood there, impressed by her command voice. The patients responded, quieting down. One patient, a scowling woman, crossed her arms defiantly and said, "I ain't takin' no orders from no white bitch." And she walked off down a side hall.

Day, still on the chair and noticeably losing her cool, looked back at the man with the key-ring and said, "Now, what in the hell is going on here and where is this charge nurse we're supposed to be speaking with? Answer me."

Down on the opposite end of the hall another deadbolt clicked open and a steel door opened. Another spooked woman stepped out. Same scrubs, tennis shoes. 1980s reading glasses and bouffant hair. She waved her hands in a nervous manner and said, "Okay, so, tomorrow I'm putting in my two weeks, but tonight, I guess I'm the charge nurse."

Seaton zeroed in on her. "What do you need done, here?"

"I need everybody to go back to their rooms," the Charge said.

"You heard her," Day said. "Go back to your rooms."

The finality in her command was only enough to send about half the people wandering off. The other half did begin to clear out of the hallway just enough to cut a path down to the activities room. Like the Red Sea parting, revealing an angry young white sitting on a couch in the room, fuming, shirt torn, staring daggers down the hallway right at Day.

"I need help with her," the charge nurse said. She nodded to the young woman, who nursed her exuding fury like a volcano whose top is cracked open and the lava inside is just beginning to surge.

The charge nurse started walking towards the activities room. "Her name is Katlyn. She's a brand-new patient, here to wean off her cocaine addiction. She got into a fist-fight with a woman named Shanice. Shanice went into her room when we called you, but Katlyn has steadfastly refused. Their fight greatly disturbed the rest of the patients and they got out of control as well. Beating the walls, screaming, running up and down. At least two other patients were trying to start fights. This has been an incredible nightmare; I just can't believe it. I can't. I can't believe it. This is not what I signed up for."

The Charge purposefully sealed her lips shut and took a long breath through her nostrils. Day could see her hands trembling. She smoothed her scrub top and said, "Everyone else seems to have calmed down when I called you, but I need Katlyn to cooperate. I have ordered her to go to the seclusion room, but like I just told you, she has steadfastly refused."

Day got down from the chair and stared at Seaton for a moment. The look of amusement on his face was infectious to her. "You're enjoying this." A statement more than a question.

Seaton couldn't hide a smirk. "I enjoy anything steadfast."

The charge nurse, whose name tag read "Tina", said, "So, we obviously need her to go to the seclusion room. I've already said so."

"Obviously," Seaton said. "Okay." He motioned for Day to take the lead and she stepped forward. There were still patients in the hallway, and as Day set a straight line to the activities room and marched it, they responded out of some subconscious respect for the woman who was cracking her knuckles.

Day entered the room and said, "Get up, Katlyn. We're going down the hall."

"Oh, fuck you, bitch."

"I don't ask twice."

"Did Tina even tell you what that nigger whore did to me? Look at me. Look at my fucking shirt." She grabbed the large tear from her neckline down past her breast and yanked at it. The fabric floated and fell. Along her chest were red streaks like finger scrapes. Her hair was in a ponytail, flyaway strands hanging down over her cheeks. The same red finger streaks went across her neck.

"That kind of language doesn't make friends," Day said.

"Fuck friends, fuck these people, fuck niggers and fuck you," Katlyn said.

"You wanna press charges against her?" Seaton asked as he came over.

"Why? Is Shanice going to charge me?" Katlyn snapped out of her stewing fury just long enough to be concerned about going back to jail. But people did that; most times they didn't want to press charges unless it was in retaliation. It told the cops how they felt about their own actions. Maybe Katlyn started it. Maybe once they spoke with Shanice, details would come out that Katlyn wanted to keep in.

"Haven't spoken with her yet," Seaton said. "Why? Should we?"

"You tell that little nig … "

"Shut up with that word," Day said. "You're surrounded by blacks in this place and we're not going to be here the rest of your stay to take your lumps for you."

"Yeah," Seaton said. "You are going to get your ass kicked if you keep that up."

"Oh, fuck the both of you," Katlyn said with true vitriol. "Look at me. Just look at me."

"Already have," Day said. "Lemme guess. You called this Shanice the N word and that's why you fought ... "

"That filthy little bitch wanted to keep needling me all night. Talkin' shit to her friends like I wasn't even there in the same room with her. I gotta a lot of shit goin' on right now, okay? I don't have the patience for some dirty cunt who's only in here because *she sucks dick on the street for crack* ... " Katlyn yelled around Day, down the hall, " ... who thinks she's better than me. Ghetto fuckin' street trash."

"Okay."

Seaton rolled up next to Day. Started to say something as both their radios blared. Officers Maurin and Bethune arrived on scene. He looked at Katlyn, her body still tense from the fight and ready to fight again. Her left arm went along the back headrest of the couch, her hand gripping the fabric like it was the one thing keeping her from sinking and drowning. Both her legs bobbing up and down with excessive energy. She stared intently.

He turned to Tina and said, "Would you go get our other officers from the parking lot please?"

Tina turned to obey, but the man with the key-ring was there. "I'll get 'em." Without waiting for a response, he went back through the door they came through.

Day never moved her gaze from Katlyn. She took in how the young woman's right hand seemed to be the only thing on her reacting to when Day moved. Day shifted her weight from one foot to the other. The hand twitched. Fingers half-curled into a fist every time. At the ready.

The cops looked at each other and huffed. Day looked down the hall, saw four or five patients milling about, clearly upset by the fight that took place before they arrived. Tina walked past them, saying something to them in whispers but not a single patient acted like they heard or cared.

Tina came up to the police, looked at Katlyn. "Well, Katlyn, as we discussed in your treatment plan *and* as all of this was happening, there are consequences for your aggressive behavior."

"Ma'am, give us just a minute," Day said.

"No," Tina said, trying to take the authority back from the police she'd given them when she called 911 and then hid in a room. "Katlyn, you need to stand up right now and go with us to the seclusion room or these officers will arrest you and make you."

Seaton leaned over. "We've got two more officers coming and then we'll … "

"I think she'll go now," Tina said, her chin jutting out. "Yes. Yes, I think she'll go now."

"Fuck you, Tina. Go suck a dick with that nigger Shanice."

Day clenched her teeth and touched Tina's upper arm. "This is going to be a fight, so stop making promises on our behalf."

Tina looked at Katlyn. "Would you like to be transferred to another clinic that is stricter on its addicts? We're very good to … "

Katlyn's face contorted like all the thunderstorms inside it were ready to come rolling out. "I fuckin' told you I'm not an addict!"

She kicked out from the couch, catching Tina in the gut. Feet out from underneath her, the charge nurse collapsed back. Behind her, the man with the key-ring appeared through the door with Maurin and Bethune, and Day and Seaton were on Katlyn, dodging her kicks and knees. Day got the arm reaching down the back of the couch, clutching for dear life and for all her efforts could not break her grip but she remembered something from the academy defense tactics where when that happens, the instructor – who was probably overzealous – said to concentrate one finger at a time like you were starting a lawnmower.

Day grabbed one of Katlyn's fingers and yanked. The grip broke. She got the second one and Katlyn threw a knee across her body at Day's hip while Seaton was wrestling with her and Maurin and Bethune came rushing over. Second finger came loose.

Day took a knee to her side and got the third finger. Katlyn's grip lost the couch and they got her up. Katlyn jerked her body, writhing against the struggle as an officer took each limb. Katlyn seized and yanked like she was possessed by the devil, screaming and cursing, trying to bite whichever officer was nearest. They carried her to the middle of the room, stutter-steps and nearly tumbling over each other, holding her about waist high. She screamed at the ceiling, floating in the room.

"Let's get her cuffed," Seaton said over the racket.

And in a moment of perfect orchestration, all four officers let go. Katlyn hit the deck and they were on her, flipped her over. Yanking her arms behind her, one cuff and then two. She continued to scream, curse. Thrash and roll. She had on jeans, and Seaton grabbed the hems of her legs, gathering up all the fabric he could and twisted his fist into it. She had a hard time struggling against that.

They picked her up again. Maurin, who was all of five foot four but with the shoulder span of a titan, grabbed her legs from Seaton and stacked them one top of the other. Clamped them between his arm and his body. "I got it, Corporal. You wanna clear our way?" he asked.

Katlyn was now upside down with Day holding onto one arm and Bethune the other. Seaton looked down the hall, seeing Tina back on her feet examining the glasses that must have fallen off her face. "Yup. Let's go."

They started walking, the first patient just standing there with a blank look. Behind him an entire herd of dumb sheep, mesmerized by the sights and sounds of the struggle that was coming their way. Katlyn never gave an inch, and if the cops were going to toss her around like a sack of shit, she was going to make them earn it.

"Tina!" Seaton said. "Get us to this seclusion room, now."

Tina looked up from her glasses, a scowl embedded in her face as deeply as hate for the whale was embedded in Captain Ahab's heart. "In just a minute. I'm fixing ... "

"Get off your ass and do it now or we're letting her go and leaving," Seaton said. With that, Tina huffed in such a way as to cuss at the man and turned around.

"C'mon." She settled her glasses back on her nose as best they would and made her way through the thickening crowd of patients. That same nose stuck up, she offered nothing except to walk off at a pace it was obvious the cops would struggle to keep.

"Boy, somebody's pissy," Bethune said as he heaved up on Katlyn's arm.

"Yes," Day said, grunting as their addict twisted and flexed. "She lost control of her facility. Now it's our problem."

"Let's get this done," Seaton said. "Knuckle down. I want to get off shift some time tonight."

"Fuck all you pigs!" Katlyn punctuated into the conversation.

They struggled against Katlyn and shouldered their way past the patients who refused to move. Katlyn never stopped her charade, gnashing with her entire body. Vulgarities spewing like a hose with no one holding it. Down the hall, past what looked like the front door and foyer, and down another hall. In a fight, a few seconds is an eternity. Distance was no different. In that moment the facility had miles of corridors, endless and snaking through its interior. Finally, there was a single, dark room down the hallway and that is where Tina stopped.

"Oh, I see a light at the end of our tunnel, here," Maurin said over the bray of Katlyn's screaming.

"I have to get the restraint board," Tina said flatly as she walked back the way they came. Seaton saw the door, a heavy wooden thing with a door handle on the exterior only, was labeled "seclusion" and he led them into it.

"Just set her down," he said and this time they lowered her down on her side. He took a deep, cleansing breath and pointed to Maurin and Bethune. "You two, go find the Charge and light a fire under her ass. This is ridiculous."

"Yup," Bethune said as they walked out.

Maurin turned around and motioned to the door. "Want it shut?"

Seaton was about to say "no" when he looked down at Day. Day was on a knee, pinning Katlyn in a spot to be still, examining her wrists. They were just bloody. Day had on a pair of disposable gloves they all carried, turning her arms.

She looked up from cuffs to Seaton. "All that thrashing, I bet."

"Oh, sure," Seaton said. "She was going hog wild." He nodded to her and then looked to Maurin. "Yeah, go ahead."

Maurin shut the door and Seaton knelt down beside Katlyn. He motioned to her wrists again and said, "Lemme see."

Day manipulated Katlyn's arms, all the while the woman crying and screaming and threatening. The woman was tired, breathing heavily. It didn't stop her from sporadically thrashing, flexing and rolling. Cursing that was becoming background noise. Day grabbed one of her arms and squeezed, held it still. "Knock it off, girl. You've already rubbed your wrists to the point where they're bleeding. You've got to calm down."

"Oh, shut up, twat. I fuckin' hate women cops. I fuckin' hate 'em."

"Yeah, sure," Day said.

Seaton huffed out. He wanted the cuffs off her: they were loose to begin with, and not only was she still able to cut herself on them, but any looser and she'd slip out of them. He didn't want to lose physical control over her. "Settle down."

And just like that, Katlyn did. Her body relaxed, tension coursing out of it the way hot steel will lose its heat when plunged in water. Her limbs went slack. Seaton actually looked over her to make sure she was still breathing. There her reddened face was, blinking back tears, spittle and snot down her cheek as she breathed in and out, raspy and heavy from the fighting.

Katlyn began to moan and mewl. Then she said in the same kind of whine one would hear from a child with a scraped knee, "They hurt. I promise ... I won't do anything. Please."

Junkies in withdrawal had a way they said "please" that sounded the same the world over. It was like smelling a human being burning: once you experienced it, you never forgot it, and others with the same experience just knew it too.

Seaton and Day looked at each other, shared a groan. Seaton nodded, reluctant. "If we let you out, are you gonna be cool?"

Katlyn seized on the moment. "Yes! Yes yes yes yes."

"You only get one shot at this."

"I promise. I promise. I swear I promise."

Day, her key in her hand, made eye contact with Seaton. He nodded and she unlocked a handcuff. Snapped it close again as soon as it came off her wrist. Katlyn moved her other arm to better accommodate Day as she took off the other cuff.

Seaton and Day stood, instinctively took a step back. Katlyn jumped up, pointed to the tear in her shirt. "Look at what that nigger did to me!"

Her bare breast hung out, escaped from her bra cup. It too, was scratched and red. "Look at it!"

Seaton made a scrunched-up face. Day simply reached out and pinched a grip on her bra, tugged it up to re-swallow Katlyn's breast. "That word, honey ... you gotta stop ... "

Katlyn became reignited, screamed, "I fuckin' hate women cops!"

And then she spit on Day.

Both officers were on her. Katlyn struggled and screamed and then the door opened, Maurin and Bethune and Tina with the restraint board. They all tackled Katlyn in round two fashion, dragging her down to the ground.

Tina said, "First, roll her over. I need to give her a shot." She pulled out a needle and an alcohol swab. "Somewhere in her love handles or her butt. I don't care."

"Keep your fuckin' needles outta me, bitch! I'll kill you."

"Oh, be quiet," Day said as she dragged Katlyn over on her side by the arm she was controlling. "You're not killing anyone."

Maurin, who had a leg, grabbed Katlyn just above the knee and pushed to help Day.

"Next time I spit on you, you fuckin' bitch, it'll be fire! I swear to God!"

"Which reminds me ... " Day mumbled as she used Katlyn's arm to wipe off the gob of spit on her uniform shirt.

Tina flipped up the bottom of Katlyn's shirt and tugged down her pants just enough to expose a plump section of skin suitable for the shot. She tore open the alcohol wipe and hastily rubbed it around the skin, pressing down. She uncapped the needle and grabbed a wad of flesh, squeezing it into a taller mound, deeper than the needle could go.

Like a drunk throwing darts, Tina jabbed the needle in. Katlyn screamed about being murdered and whatever else she could think of, jerking in spasms like she was being electrocuted. Tina depressed the plunger, going at a snail's pace because the medicine was in an oily suspension and therefore injected slower. Plus, it went into the fat as opposed to a vein.

As soon as her thumb reached the end of the syringe's barrel, she pulled out the needle with a flick of her wrist and snapped on the spring-loaded sharps cap. Tossed the whole mess over into the far corner.

"Get her on the board," Tina said, over the ruckus of Katlyn still screaming.

The officers slung her over and worked to pin her back down as Tina moved the board underneath the fight to try and line it up to Katlyn.

Each officer took a limb and Tina went around her, using the built-in straps on the board to tie each one. When Tina reached Katlyn's bloody wrists she uttered, "Ugh." And without gloves she gingerly worked around the mess. Who knew what Katlyn had or could transmit? Tina, now a professed short-timer, wasn't going to leave her job with her 401K and a nice case of Hep C.

"Okay," Tina said, standing up and backing off like she'd just dug up something unsettling.

The officers each were more cautious, making sure the restraints didn't fail somehow. When they did not, they backed off and regrouped nearer to the door. Breathing heavily, they stood in a tight cluster, staring at the woman withdrawing from cocaine.

"It's still pretty crazy out there," Bethune said. "This crowd gets riled up easily."

Seaton looked at his watch. "I've got a beer at home that I need to be drinking, so ... "

The others laughed and Tina stood there, stone-faced. Day looked down at her spit-slimed uniform. Saw some blood from Katlyn there as well.

Katlyn jerked and fought her binds, still shouting vulgarities and her favorite racist word. She was still crying, red and puffy from all she'd been through. The scratch marks on her chest were glowing red with the exertion. Her breast had escaped again.

Maurin opened the door and the hooting and hollering of so many uncontrolled patients came to them. He shook his head. "What now?"

Tina huffed a sardonic, bitter laugh. Finally, she said, "We're just getting started." And removed four more loaded syringes. The cops stared at them, fanned out like a hand of cards in Hell's poker room.

She nodded to Bethune, "Like he said. It's still pretty crazy out there."

* * * * *

THE SNUG

Keith Wright

Detective Bill Derbyshire was feeling a little woozy. He had done since the arrest. He was alone in the locker room and stared at the mirror, his greying temples and laughter lines still gave way to the hint of a younger Bill: the idealistic young fellow who could change the world. Remember him? Scarcely. Bill was just relieved to have completed his final shift safely, particularly when his last arrest was an armed criminal. He remembered approaching the guy after he came out of the convenience store and getting him handcuffed without too much problem. Then he started feeling nauseous and clammy. It was probably because it was such a big day: his last day, after thirty years on the job. It was good to finish on a high and charge his last prisoner with robbery. It felt good.

He sat down for a couple of minutes on the wooden slatted bench to take it all in. So, it was finally over. It had passed him by so quickly. Thirty years. Gone. Just in the blink of an eye. It was a huge chapter of his life that was coming to an end. All the big moments came flooding through his brain, the pain and death, the humour, the sadness. His marriage had failed many years prior. Sissy had wanted children, and because of the job, that became impossible, and so inevitably they drifted apart. He would be going home to an empty house.

Bill was glad there was no fuss. That was how he liked it. Bill had said his goodbyes over the last two or three days to his friends and colleagues in person and made it plain he didn't want any fanfares. He just wanted to get home and get his fishing rod out.

It was time for Bill, he'd had enough: all the hatred and abuse for decent people trying to look after their community was wearing everyone

93

down. Him included. He had never known such a time. The so-called leaders were spineless, and Bill and his mates all knew they would be thrown under a bus if something went wrong. You can't work like that, it was untenable. He didn't use to think like that. He hated the prospect of retirement, once upon a time, but now, not so much.

He stood to get his gear out of the locker, the memories now fading away. He was tired, and he closed his eyes momentarily.

He was startled by the hands smacking on his shoulders as he emptied his locker.

"Bill! My old mucker."

"Jesus H Christ! Don't do that, Howard."

"Come on, are you ready?" His colleague was prematurely balding, but still had the zest that perhaps Bill had lacked these last few months.

"Come on where? Ready for what?"

"We're having a little drinky-poos next door for you." Howard was smiling, and he seemed pleased with his surprise. He had his "going out" clothes on.

"Ah, man, do we have to?" Bill suddenly felt anxious.

"That's nice, isn't it? Come on Bill, all the guys and gals are waiting."

His shoulders dropped, and he sounded like a petulant teenager. "You know I don't like a fuss."

Howard faced him and took hold of the tops of his shoulders. "You have given your life to this job, Bill, you need a decent send-off. Do you think we would just let you walk off into the bloody night? No chance."

Bill wiped at his brow, he was a little light-headed, and this news didn't help. It was probably the stress of it all. He didn't want to appear ungrateful; it was just that he hated being the centre of attention. It was kind of them, though. He would probably look back on this and smile. Anyway, he dutifully followed Howard to The Gateway pub, conveniently located next to the police station. It was a beautiful old pub, one of the oldest in the country and went back centuries in different forms as an inn and staging post, originally located at the entrance to the city. Once outside the police station, the two friends began to jog, as a light rain trickled down from the heavens.

Bill saw the crowd through the open door as soon as he burst into the lounge area. He was almost physically knocked back by the wall of sound that met him.

"Surprise!"

There was around fifty or sixty of them. Colleagues old and new. Some he thought had been dead and buried years ago. It warmed the cockles of his heart to think that people had made an effort just for him. Bill was always unassuming: there was no swagger to him. That was why people liked him so much.

Bill's face reddened, and he smiled before mopping his brow. His vision was murky, a little meandering, like looking across a dusty savannah seared by the baking sun. There were children there, and young James came running up. He was holding a slice of a meat-feast pizza. "Do you want some pizza, Uncle Bill?"

Bill laughed. "No, thank you, I think I will pass. I'm not a big fan of pizza anymore. Thanks for the offer, though, kiddo." It was all one big blur.

Howard was given a microphone, which not only amplified his voice, but also distorted it slightly.

"Ladies and gentlemen ... there must be at least one lady, surely? I'm not sure about there being any gentlemen, ahem."

There were cries of "Oi" and "Behave."

"Our dear friend, Bill, will be joining you very shortly, but first there is one very special surprise for him which has taken a lot of arranging, which cannot wait. I'm afraid."

There were cries of "Boo, get him a drink" and "he's only just bloody got here."

"Come on, Bill," Howard whispered. "Follow me."

"Now, what? Howard this is great, but ... "

"No buts, this is something special. It doesn't happen every day now, does it?"

He led Bill through the crowd by his wrist. Sharon, from Traffic, leaned over and kissed his cheek. Frank reached through the mob and tousled his hair as he rode through the wave of excited friends. Near the door, he saw Sissy. "Congratulations," she said with that lovely smile.

"Thanks, Sissy, you didn't have to come."

"It was the least I could do. I've only got an hour before ... " She hesitated, but was committed, " ... I have to pick the kids up from karate."

Bill smiled thinly and nodded. "I don't know what the hell is going on, but I'll grab you in a bit for a chat."

Sissy hugged him as Howard dragged Bill away. "Come on, we can't be late."

"Late? Late for what, for heaven's sake?"

It was cold in the old pub stairwell as they began to climb the stone steps. After four flights, Bill was puffing and panting, gasping for air. "I am so unfit." He muttered, wiping sweat away. He looked down between the bannister and felt giddy. "Christ, I hate heights." His friend was ahead of him. "How many more, Howard?"

"One more."

At the top, there was an old oak door with an ancient sign above it saying "The Snug". This was old expression for a smaller room in a bar where you could have a bit of privacy. Usually used by couples, the snug had a frosted glass window above head height so that outsiders could not see inside. Modern pubs didn't have them nowadays. Howard heaved open the heavy door for Bill to step through. A handful of people shouted, "Surprise!", as he walked in. It surely was a surprise.

The room was lovely and warm. There was a fire in the hearth, and it was calm and welcoming, not like the madness he had endured downstairs. There were half a dozen tables, but only four were occupied. At each of the four tables sat a familiar face. Apart from the guy with the messy beard, at the back: he was reading a newspaper and seemed disinterested. Perhaps he was one of the locals, pissed off that his hideaway had been disturbed?

Bill was smiling but still felt a tad queasy, although it didn't seem as bad as before. He was still struggling to catch his breath from the stairs. Once all of this calmed down and he got home, things would improve, he felt sure. Bill just didn't like all of this attention, although his face lit up as soon as he saw Delottice Brown who was beckoning him over. They had long since made their peace, but she had something new to tell him.

"Missus Brown, how nice to see you. What is going on? Thank you for coming."

"Sit down, Bill. I don't mind giving my time for you, you know that."

Bill's mind went back to that horrible day when he killed her son. He had only been on the Firearms Unit eighteen months. It seemed to be the perfect department for a young buck to ply his trade. They were desperate for people like Bill: fit, strong, intelligent, but level-headed.

"Tango papa two nine, no change. Hang on, stand-by, stand-by. Target in view and is approaching BMW. Money exchanged, and contraband received."

"Strike, Strike, Strike," Sergeant Meadows bellowed over the airwaves.

Bill was closest. He was out of the car in a second and aiming his pistol right at the chest of the known criminal. "Armed police. Stand still!" he shouted authoritatively, but calmly, fighting the adrenaline coursing through his veins.

Courtney Brown was in jeans and a loose-fitting top. He didn't stop. He kept on walking right towards Bill.

"Armed police, get on the ground!"

Courtney reached behind him and pulled a gun from his waistband at the pit of his back.

"Don't be stupid, Courtney," Bill shouted.

The problem was that Courtney was indeed stupid, and Bill fired twice as he saw the kid's arm rise in his direction.

"I didn't want to kill him, Missus Brown, if he had only done what he was told." Bill shook his head. "I think about him every damned day."

"Hey, Bill, come on, this is a celebration. I'm here to thank you."

"Thank me? I'm confused. Why would you thank me?"

"Because I know my boy. Courtney was buying drugs that day, and he was going to give them to his brothers, to get them addicted. You know how addicts work, the more they recruit, the more they feel their lifestyle is validated."

"True."

"I know these things, Bill. I ain't nobody's fool, and you know that."

"I sure do."

"When I heard it was you that shot Courtney, I did a lot of praying and thinking. You were just a kid yourself when your skinny white ass showed up on our street back in the day, with your shiny shoes." She giggled.

Bill flushed a little. "I have put a bit of weight on, granted."

"You played the boys at basketball every damned week, and they bust your ass every time, yet you still came back for more."

"I did improve a little ... "

"But when I got to thinking, you never really lost a game, now did you? 'Cos every hoop you missed, my boys felt good about themselves. That was true kindness, Bill. I ain't nobody's fool. I'm on to you." She laughed.

Bill laughed too.

"Don't forget, I've got four boys, Bill. It wasn't just Courtney I was trying to raise by myself."

"I know."

"But, because of what happened that day, my boys never got hooked on no drugs. Better yet, that fool boy of mine was going on to kill some people. You didn't know that now did you, Bill?"

"Go on to kill? No. What do you mean?"

"He had sworn vengeance on Michelle's family. His girlfriend's dad had banned them from seeing each other. He was a racist, but that's another story. I didn't know this until after the Coroner's hearing. That crackhead son of mine was heading off to kill the whole damned bunch."

"Oh, wow. My God."

"So, you see, you did not take a life, as everybody claimed, even them fool demonstrators, you saved several lives. Goddamit, you even saved my other sons. Without Courtney leading them away from Jesus, they all thrived, they became good citizens, Bill."

"I knew that Denford was in the church, doing well for himself." Bill smiled.

"He sure is, and Lenton's a lawyer. Who would have thought?"

"That's great, Missus Brown. I am so pleased you took the trouble to tell me all of this. It helps, no doubt."

"I thought you should be made aware, so you can enjoy your time not fretting about it, you know."

"Thank you. That is very kind."

The young, slightly unkempt young man, a couple of tables along, was waving Bill over towards him, excitedly.

"Excuse me, won't you, Missus Brown. We can chat downstairs, in a minute."

Bill stood up and spoke to the room. "Thank you so much for giving your time everyone, this is amazing." He was feeling better already. He had known many retirement "dos", where cops and civvies were present, but it was a touch of class to get members of the public involved.

They nodded and smiled in return.

Bill went to the table of Clarence Bignall. This was a face he would never forget, despite it being partly covered by straggly blond hair; nor could he forget the day they met.

Bill sat next to Clarence on the rooftop. There was a drop of 800 feet below, and his heart was firmly placed in his mouth. Cops are not immune to fear.

"Sup, dude?" Bill said as if they were meeting in a park rather than the top of a multi-story car park. There was a hint of irony in the greeting. This kid looked like a "dude", a hipster.

"Sup?"

"What's troubling you, kiddo?" Bill asked. He had both hands on the concrete of the wall. It was gritty and merging with the sweat on his palms. The wind seemed stronger at this height, and it was blowing his hair, and forcing him to shout, more than speak. He did not feel safe. Maybe he should have waited for the fire brigade, but then it could be too late.

Clarence was tearful, and he sobbed. "Nothing."

"Nothing? Oh, okay, I didn't realise it was just a bit of sightseeing you were doing. I'll leave you to it."

The faintest of smiles ran across the young lad's face. It didn't stay long. "What's the point?" he said.

"What's the point? Hey, man, how long have you got? There are a million points. I can go through every damned one if you like." Bill smiled at him reassuringly.

The young man sniffled. His anguish and tears were corrupting his voice. "No, there ain't, not for me."

"Listen, relax, and … let's just talk a bit, yes? What's your name?"

"There's no point." He hutched forward slightly. He was shaking his head.

"Hey, don't go doing anything daft, now. Okay? You promise me you will tell me first, yes?"

"I don't know, man."

"Yes?"

"Sure, whatever. Just leave me alone, will you?"

"What is it that's troubling you, my friend?" Bill offered the youngster a cigarette, which he took. Bill lit it for him with great difficulty in the wind and then lit his own. Lighting cigarettes always put the world on hold momentarily. He thought it might help break up the youth's frame of mind.

"Everything."

"No, come on, what is number one on the list?"

"My dad, for a start."

"How old are you?"

"Eighteen."

Bill shrugged out a laugh. "Christ, I wish I were eighteen. I would do so many things differently."

"That's what everyone says."

"Why didn't you do this last year?"

The young man looked at him sideways as he blew out a cloud of smoke. "Do what? I don't get you."

"This, rather exotic gesture, and ridiculous decision, by the way, of harming yourself. Why didn't you do it last year?"

"I ... well ... it didn't feel that bad, then."

"And next year?"

"There ain't gonna be no next year."

"But do you see my point? Things change, kid, all the damned time. This isn't the solution. There are lots of other solutions, but this isn't it. This is a permanent 'solution' to a temporary problem." Bill even did that shitty thing with his fingers to emphasise the speech marks of the word "solution". "Do you understand what I mean by that? Do you see how things have changed this year and they just as surely will next year."

"I get what you mean, I think. You mean if I jump, that's it, but things can change and even get better."

"Not *can* change, *will* change. What's your name?" he asked again.

"Clarence. Clarence Bignall."

"I'm Bill, Bill Derbyshire." Bill offered his hand, and Clarence shook it. Bill leaned in and used his other hand to grab around Clarence's neck and rolled them both backwards. Clarence had been duped, and Bill quickly handcuffed him behind his back for his own safety.

Clarence raised his glass to Bill as they sat at the table. "Thanks for saving my life all those years ago, Bill, and for coming to see me when I was getting better too. That meant a lot. You didn't need to do that."

"It was my pleasure. I'm glad things worked out. I told you they would, now didn't I?"

Clarence lowered his gaze. He seemed thoughtful. "I went into teaching in the end, can you believe that? I've got three children, all of whom wouldn't be here if it wasn't for you, Bill."

The cop smiled. "Thanks for coming, Clarence. I'm grateful." Bill offered his hand to shake it.

"Hey, last time we did this, I was in handcuffs a few seconds later." Clarence laughed.

"Not this time, I promise." They shook hands and briefly embraced. Bill could not help noticing that Clarence had scars on his wrists.

The detective could see Charlotte Baker blowing kisses over to him at the end table, and he walked over, grinning.

"I can't believe that you guys would do this for me." Bill said as he sat down. He felt dizzy again and nearly missed the wooden chair as he clumsily dropped his backside onto it. He had to steady himself and almost knocked Charlotte's drink over.

"Are you okay?" Charlotte asked, concerned. She wore a summery dress with quite a bit of cleavage on display. She was tanned and had a toothy grin.

"I'm fine. I think it is all the bloody excitement. I'll be fine when I get a drink."

"Do you want a sip of mine? It's Bacardi and Coke."

"Do you mind? I'm parched."

"No, of course not, fill your boots. There's plenty more where that came from."

"I can't believe they didn't get me a drink." He sipped at the glass just to wet his whistle.

"You would think, wouldn't you?"

"This is amazing, thank you so much for coming, Charlotte. You're looking well."

"Thanks. I'm just happy that you are finally going to get some peace, away from all the madness out there, Bill. You've earnt it."

"Thank you, but you didn't have to do all of this, honestly."

"It's the least we could do. You are an incredible guy and a wonderful cop. You have changed all of our lives. You need to know how your brave deeds saved so many more than first appears. If we don't tell you, who will?"

"Don't be daft." Bill said. "It just happened, that's all."

He caught a glimpse in her briefly sombre expression, in the shadows of her eyes, of the eight-year-old girl, so frightened, twenty years before.

He had been the only negotiator on duty at the time, and when he saw the dilapidated house with the curtains blowing through the smashed windows, he knew exactly what he would be facing. Every cop's heart always sank when they saw those billowing curtains.

As Bill walked towards the house through the unkempt garden, a man with a large knife appeared in the window. Bill stopped about ten feet away. He knew him instantly.

"Let the girl go, Jacko, I will take her place, no problem."

"Fuck you!"

Bill wanted to be cavalier, diffuse it, play it down. "That's a bit rude, isn't it? Let me help you out of this mess, Jacko. Come on, you know me, I'm not going to fuck you over."

"I don't trust pigs. Read my lips. Fuck you." Jacko was sweating, and it merged with the dirt on his face. Hygiene was never number one on his "to do" list.

Bill was doing his utmost to be calm, and front him out, even though the adrenaline was making his legs tremble a bit. He hoped the dangerous and excitable criminal could not see that.

Bill folded his arms. "I've known you a long time, Jacko, and if you think your best option is getting me out of the picture, then you're dafter than I thought." He got no reply, but Jacko scratched at the mess of grey hair: it seemed to have registered. "I can make all of this go away. Look, you've made your point. It will be over, dead easy. But if I go ... who knows which cop turns up? Who knows how this ends?"

"It's already over. Back off or I'll stab her. I've got Charlotte in here you know."

"Okay, I'm going." Bill turned and headed towards his car as soon as Jacko mentioned harming his daughter.

"Oi, stop! Hang on."

Bill stopped and smiled to himself. He turned. "What?"

"Bring me a beer."

"I can't do that Jacko, but I can get you a pizza. The only condition is, I come in, and we sort this mess out. Agreed?"

"Just bring the fucking pizza."

Thankfully there was a pizza shop across the road and, within five minutes, Bill was chewing at the "Mighty Meaty" alongside Jacko and his big scary knife. The pizza was good, though maybe a tiny bit too spicy. "The longer you are in here mate, the longer time you will serve, that's all. You need to let your daughter go, and that will do you a load of good further down the line. Trust me, you're not helping yourself."

"She's all I've got." He shouted over to her, "Ain't you, sweetheart?"

Charlotte was sitting on the floor, crying, her back against the wall and her knees brought up towards her chest. Bill winked at her, but her face didn't acknowledge the friendly gesture. It was frozen in fear, the fear of her crazy, unpredictable father.

"See. Even she fucking hates me!" Jacko threw the pizza across the room. Some landed on Charlotte, and she jolted. Jacko's agitation came in waves. Spittle came out of his mouth as he screamed at her. "I'm the fucking reason you're even alive! You ungrateful little bitch!" He started throwing cups at her, which smashed on the floor. The shards were hitting her knees, exposed above her white school socks.

Bill stood up. "Jacko, sit down," he ordered.

Bill's colleagues had moved closer to the house, and their faces peered through the filthy windows to try to get a view.

Without warning, Jacko charged towards Charlotte with the knife raised, as if to be used in a chopping motion. Charlotte screamed.

Bill made his move and barged into the madman in a rugby-tackle-style move, which he made a complete mess of, but it was enough to knock Jacko off his feet, and the two of them ended up in a heap. Jacko still clung on to the knife.

"Run, Charlotte!" Bill shouted.

She ran for the door. Jacko tried to get to his feet, but Bill blocked him and felt the knife slide into his groin. He fell backwards but was relieved to hear the door bang shut behind Charlotte. His colleagues ran inside and managed to subdue Jacko, by weight of numbers. The man was clearly in need of some sort of mental health intervention.

Bill had been hurt. He was hospitalised, but his life was never in danger. It did mean, however, that his dreams of a family were over. The stabbing injuries meant that Bill was now unable to father any children.

"Thank you for putting your life before mine, Mister Derbyshire," Charlotte said, holding his hand.

"Call me, Bill, that's okay. Anybody would have done it, trust me."

"No, they wouldn't, I know he would have killed me that day if it wasn't for you."

"How is he? Jacko, I mean." Bill rested his elbow on the table. He seemed genuinely interested.

"He's fine. Just as grumpy as ever, but because of you he has been on the right medication for years, and he's just a typically normal, miserable old bastard." She laughed.

Bill laughed too. "That's the club I'm joining."

"He helps folks with mental health problems now. He gives talks and everything."

"No way."

"He does. He always says to people that if he can sort himself out after what happened on that day, then anyone can. So in a way, you have helped all the people Dad has helped, just by getting us through that day and helping dad get back on the right track."

"I'm amazed."

"I'm so sorry for what happened to you, Mister Derbyshire, you didn't deserve that."

Bill sighed. "You're right, I didn't, but it's life. I couldn't let it destroy me." He thought of Sissy waiting for him downstairs, and what might have been.

"I'm just thankful that it was you who showed up that day, Mister Derbyshire, he would never have let any old cop in the house with bloody pizza. It could have ended way differently. He trusted you."

"That was his first mistake." They laughed.

Behind Charlotte, the man with the beard gestured an invite for him to sit in the chair opposite him. Bill kissed Charlotte on the cheek and headed for Mr Beard, whoever the hell he was. Bill sat down. There was something about this guy, but Bill couldn't put a name to the face. So why was he here?

The man had a beige suit on and rounded glasses perched on the end of his nose. His beard would have been magnificent if he had run a comb through it in the last month, which he had not.

Bill reached over to shake hands and the man responded, but he continued to read the paper, which seemed somewhat disingenuous bearing in mind he had invited Bill over in the first place.

The detective motioned to get up. "Anyway, I won't keep you. Sorry if we have upset your peace and quiet. I've got a party waiting for me downstairs."

The man finally averted his gaze from the newspaper. "There ain't no party, Bill."

"Sorry?"

"There is no party downstairs."

"Is this a joke? There is. I've just walked through it. It's downstairs."

"There is no downstairs."

This was freaking Bill out. "What do you mean?"

"This is an interesting article." He handed the newspaper over to Bill who read the headline: "Cop Killed in Bungled Heist."

He shrugged. "What's this? Do I know him?"

"You know him, alright. It's you, Bill. I'm sorry."

"Me? I don't think so. I've just charged the guy with robbery. This doesn't make sense."

The man pointed to some text part way down. "Detective William Derbyshire sadly lost his life when the gunman ... "

Bill put his hands on his head. He looked distressed. "This is one sick joke. I've just bloody charged him, at the police station next door, less than an hour ago."

The man sighed. "You haven't Bill, that's continuum psychosis. It happens to everyone, don't worry. It's just a transitional thing. Your mind is living out what it thinks should be happening. But, in reality, unfortunately you are just in the process of dying. In the latter stages, you will have had the flashbacks and all of that good stuff."

Bill remembered his thoughts in the locker room, all of the memories which came flooding into his mind. "This can't be."

"I'm afraid it is, Bill. Your final moment was when Howard slapped you on the shoulders. That was the moment when ... how can I explain it? Your existence jumped into another groove. You had moved from one reality into this ethereal one."

"This is a wind-up, yes?"

The man was shaking his head. "No wind-up, Bill. Sorry, old chap. It happens to us all when the time is right."

"It can't be my time? It can't be. All these people have come to see me."

"Have they?" The man indicated to the tables behind him.

Bill turned around, and different people occupied the tables. People he didn't know.

"Who are they?"

"You spoke to the essence of Delottice, and Charlotte. The part of themselves that they keep in this realm. Clarence passed away last year, however. Everyone does their bit here. They were sincere, though, I hasten to add. Everything they said was true." He smiled.

"So, that's it. Just like that."

"There one minute, here the next. That's how it works, Bill. Did you expect a warning? Some kind of notice, perhaps?"

"No, but why bother with this so-called party?"

"We like people to get a glimpse of how much they impacted peoples lives, the change they made by living their lives well. You should be proud that you got three tables: most only get one."

"Right." Bill was stunned. "Any chance I can go back down?"

"Sorry, Bill. You will be fine here, don't worry, once you shake off your transition confusion. You're a young soul, so it takes a little longer. You will be moving on soon."

"So, now what? What am I supposed to do?"

"You're at table three, Bill. The next one will be here any minute. It's Terry Downs, Mister Downs, your old teacher. Remember him? He's had a heart attack. Sorry, no, not *had*, he is *having* one right now, actually. He won't survive. Don't you want to thank him for listening to you when your dad died? Nobody else did. He was your favourite teacher, tell him so. Thank him for easing your pain and for urging you to join the police. He changed your life, Bill."

"Yes, but, how do you know about ... "

"Table three, Bill. They're coming up the stairs now."

Bill was shaking his head as he moved over to table three. Suddenly the door opened and in walked Mr Downs.

Bill heard himself saying, "Surprise!"

* * * * *

THE OLD LADY

T.K. Thorne

It may be a mistake I'll regret, but I pull over onto the side of Highway 11, a back road somewhere between the city of Trussville and Argo, Alabama. Not much traffic this time of night. This is a crazy move. I'm not a cop anymore. I'm an old lady with osteopenia, for God's sake. I could break something.

I hear this voice every time I step onto the mat for training or swing a leg over my horse. For thirty-odd years, I listened to that voice. Playing with martial arts and horses was an over-and-done part of my life. But here I am. In fact, I'm on the way home from jujitsu class, and I'm dead tired. All I want to do is eat dinner and crash.

But I saw something. Correction: I thought I saw something, but I'm not sure what to do about it. I don't even know where I am except I'm pretty sure I haven't passed Argo yet. I look around for something familiar. Two nights a week I drive this stretch of road. I should know where I am. But I am not particularly observant when I'm driving. Especially when I'm tired. And to be totally honest, that part of being a police officer was never my strong suit. I looked out the window a lot and daydreamed. Dealing with people was a better skill, and it got me through most situations.

But if something is wrong. If I saw what I thought I saw, I need to be able to give a location. Wait. That old barn up ahead. I do know approximately where I am, and all I need to do is call 911 and report it. They can check on the radio and make sure he is okay.

This is actually a decent idea. I pick up my phone. "Damn it!" It's

107

stone dead. I plug it in every night, but the charger end must have been loose again.

I should go home and forget about it.

Stubbornly, I twist in the seat and back my pickup carefully along the dirt edge of the road. I can only see a few feet behind me at a time. Thankfully, my truck has four-wheel drive, so if it's muddy, I won't get stuck, but I hate backing and doing it with mirrors just makes it worse.

"Steady, don't over steer."

I can't remember when I started talking to myself. Somehow, as I grew older, it got easier and easier to get distracted. I often can't remember why I walk from one room to the next. My thoughts skip like a skimmed stone over still water. It helps focus if I talk out loud.

"I'm going to the kitchen to get my water bottle. Don't forget the water bottle. Pay no attention to the cat litter box that needs cleaning … or that jacket on the chair. Aim. Kitchen. Water bottle … "

It seems forever until the front of the white car I had passed is a dim pink in my backup lights. Behind it is the marked car, lights flashing. I grab a flashlight and purse, my chest ticking like a grandfather clock on steroids, and do the body slide that brings my feet closer to the ground with less jar before dropping. Trucks are made for men, not short old women. But I do love the feeling of all that steel around me.

The white car's headlights and the flashing blue lights behind it hit my eyes. The trooper is probably sitting in his car writing a ticket and approaching him at night is going to make him go for his gun. I can see the headlines: "Crazy Elderly Woman Shot by State Trooper."

I flatten against my truck as the vehicle parked just behind me switches the headlights to bright, blinding me, and takes off in a spray of mud, missing me by inches. Out of reflex or maybe out of pique, I aim the flashlight into the driver's face. Only a brief glimpse – white male, scruffy beard – as he gives me quick hard stare and then he's gone.

"B-three-nine-six." It's all I could see of the tag. I repeat them to myself to keep from forgetting.

"Three-nine-six. Three-nine-six." Smallest first (three), then triple (nine), then double (six). I have never been good with identifying vehicles, which all look alike, but it is a four-door, white sedan, and I recognized the Chevrolet "bowtie" emblem. I turn back to the trooper car and the flashing blue lights. Something about that intense color has such allure for me. It's the same blue as airport runway lights and the "on" of a Bluetooth device, a siren-song blue you could get lost in, float away in. Maybe when it's time to go, I could get one to stare into to escort me to the Darkness. That and the hypnotic sound of ocean surf. Then I'm set to meet my maker … or whatever.

I pocket the flashlight, which could look like a weapon in the dark, step to the side of the truck and keep my hands up, palms forward, waiting politely for the trooper to open his door and ask what I'm doing.

Nothing happens. I wait more seconds. Nothing. I can't really see inside because his headlights are on in addition to the blue lights. Careful to keep my hands up, I step around to the passenger side, not too close. If he's concentrating on writing that ticket or whatever, I don't want to appear suddenly in his space.

Maybe I should just back up, get into the truck and go home.

"Yeah, maybe," I mutter. "But I'm here, so I might as well make sure … "

I see the body now, crumpled beside the front tire. *Oh my God … the blood.*

***

"Coffee?" The plain-clothes detective asks.

I shake my head. "Can't drink caffeine after three PM, and I'm wired plenty." What I don't say is my body is harboring all this stress, and I'll probably be constipated for a month. That would be TMI: too much information. I have become my grandmother.

He grins and nods, putting his mug on the table between us and taking a seat in the tiny interview room. To be honest, I'm a little surprised Argo has a Black detective. It's a tiny town in St. Clair County, which is mostly rural.

I eye the steaming cup, probably left over from the day shift and reheated in a microwave. I heard it ding. The miracle of hearing aids.

Focusing on details helps keep emotions stuffed into the box created so many years ago when I needed not to feel things no matter what was happening. That's the only way you can do your job when someone is screaming at you or shooting at you or you have to deal with a dead body. The box is located in my gut, just out of reach. Probably why I have to eat prunes.

"Thanks for coming to the office," the detective says. His eyes are dark with crinkles at the edges. Maybe in his twenties or early thirties. Who knows? To me, he looks like he just graduated from high school. Did I ever look that young? How does a criminal take him seriously?

We've been over what happened several times, but now he hits me with what he's been wanting to ask. "I listened to the tape of the call. You sounded very calm on the radio, considering … "

Oh crap. He thinks I'm a suspect!

I take a breath, wishing I had agreed to the coffee, if only to have something to do with my hands. It never occurred to me that I would be a suspect. When I found the trooper's body, I automatically shoved down the panic into the box, checked for a pulse, and crawled across the front seat of the patrol car to the radio.

"Most people would have called nine-one-one on their cell phone," the detective says casually.

"My phone was dead."

"Really?"

I dig into my purse and hand it over to him. "Radio is quicker, anyway. Anyone close by could have started that way."

"Good thinking, just … unusual."

You are a suspect! Ask for an attorney. Now.

"Am I a suspect?"

"I never said that."

Then it hit me. He has no idea who I am. I'm a short, somewhat dumpy, gray-haired old grandma, but I could be a little shorty, dumpy, gray-haired grandma that killed a trooper or I could be connected to the killer. It's just my word that I'm a witness.

"I guess I went for the radio out of old habit. I'm a retired police officer."

His eyebrows rise. "Really?"

He's not believing me. I'm used to that. I never looked like a police officer, whatever that means, even when I was one. The first time I appeared at my sister's house in my uniform, she laughed. I don't blame her. My hat was too big and fell over my eyes. Every inch of my several-inches-smaller waist was occupied by a piece of equipment. My gun was twice as big as my hand. And God knows, the silver hair and turkey skin under my neck don't help make it more believable.

"How long were you an officer?" he asks.

110

I know this actually means he is trying to wrap his head around the absurdity and hopes for a mental escape hatch from the idea, that maybe I tried it for a little while and it didn't work out.

"Twenty-nine years."

His mind is spinning again, trying to decide whether to believe me or call me out. After a long pause, he leans back and nods. "That would explain why you went for the radio instead calling it in."

I let out a breath. Maybe I don't need the lawyer.

"Tell me one more time why you stopped."

I am tired. I want to go home and drink a glass of wine, but I know the drill: ask the same question different ways and see if there is a hole or something the witness forgot to say. At least I'm a possible witness now and not a probable suspect. Maybe.

"I slowed down when I saw the blue lights," I repeat. "A flash of movement between the trooper car and the sedan caught my eye."

I don't tell him that I always do that: slow down and check when I see a patrol car on the side of the road. It's something buried into who I am. If a fellow law enforcement officer is in trouble, you do not pass by without giving aid. If the situation just looked hinky, I would hang back and call 911 for backup. That would be the safe and sane thing to do. If my phone wasn't dead.

But if something were going down, I know myself well enough to know I could not just sit, even if I get so old that it amounts to bopping somebody with a cane or throwing my false teeth at them.

"It was so fast," I say, "just a blur of movement, but it worried me, and I pulled over. I should have just called, but my phone was dead, so I backed up to check on him."

"It was a stupid thing to do," I say out loud and bite my lip. "And it didn't make a difference." I don't want to think about that trooper who gave his all, whether he had a wife, children. I can't think about that or the walls of the box might dissolve. I sure as hell don't want to start crying.

"It might have made a difference. You didn't know. And it might still make a difference in finding the bastard who slit his throat." He hesitated. "We have a name."

His attitude has shifted. I feel it. And he wouldn't have said "bastard" otherwise. I'm not a suspect anymore.

"The trooper," he says, "the victim ... called in a driver's check before things got nasty."

"Good." That is a relief. "It's just a matter of finding him then."

"Unfortunately the tag on the car was stolen and it looks like it might be a fake ID."

Back to not being good.

He sighs and sips at the coffee crud. "So, all we really have at the moment is you."

"And hopefully something from forensics."

He nods. "Hopefully."

***

Mucking out a barn is not something I thought I would still be doing in my seventies. But it's not unpleasant. Horse apples don't stink like meat eaters' poop. In fact, it's a comforting smell, earthy. And there's an art to working the rake under the apples and lifting them in a smooth movement that keeps them on the tines until you dump them in the muck bucket.

I like being outside and working with my hands, though there are some mornings when I need a hot shower and some aspirin to be able to move without pain. But today wasn't one of those.

At least a couple of hours of daylight remain before I need to head to class, though the sky has grayed over, and the wind is suddenly speaking of rain and a summer storm. I worked in the city for decades, but up here on my mountain is where I truly feel alive, with cows and tall pines for neighbors. If I can't have blue lights and the sound of an ocean in my ears when I die, the tease of wind and pungent smell of horse will do. I've thought about simplifying my life since Five died. That's what I called my last husband. It would make sense to move into a condo in town where I wouldn't have to keep up a yard, much less forty acres. But I keep putting it off. And where would I put my horses? Some fancy-ass barn I'd have to drive fifty miles to get to?

Through the open stall door, I can see my three horses grazing, keeping me in visual range in case I decide twice a day is not enough to feed them. Hope burns eternal. I take a moment to admire my latest treasure, Nickie Jones, a rescue off the track, an old lady like me. She ran until she wasn't winning and then was sold to the Amish, who worked her until she was too old for that and then sold her at auction. She was in a kill pen in Louisiana, headed for dog food in Mexico when I bought her sight unseen right in the middle of the Covid pandemic. All she needed was good food and attention, and now her black coat gleams, and although she's a little stiff in the right hip, she no longer favors her back leg. She's the bottom rung in the horse social ladder, but she is happy, and I'm happy to have her.

I'm about to go for the last pile in the corner when Nickie Jones jerks her head up, ears pricked toward the road. A horse has a wide range of vision, but to focus on something in the distance, she raises her head. That movement also signals as a warning that a predator might be in tall grass beyond the herd, and the other horses go on alert. I smile. It's likely a stray dog or a fox or a coyote, even though it's early in the day for them. No one ever comes down my dusty road.

I go back to the horse apples. My back is turned to the stall door, so the first time I'm aware that I'm not alone is when a man's gravelly voice speaks.

"Well, there you are."

My head jerks around, as startled as Nickie Jones had been. A burly man stands in the doorway, an open knife in his hand. It's not a pocketknife.

My heart goes into accelerated percussion, the demand of blood from my extremities making me momentarily light-headed. I am back in the night on the side of the road, pressed against my truck door, a face illuminated in my flashlight. Scruffy beard, hard eyes, the same face and hard eyes considering me now. I got a partial tag number from his car as he sped away, but he had plenty of time to see mine when I backed toward him and, if he had connections, to trace my address.

It's hard to breathe.

He takes a step into the stall.

Lights flash. *I am kneeling beside the trooper, his skin chill under my fingers.* My knees weaken. They will bend to the ground when the steel slices.

Why didn't I bring my gun to the barn?

But I didn't. If I am not going to go down to the Dark, I better get with it. The study of martial arts is the study of violence, but the key is intent. We learn principles of the human body, where the weak points are to disable, how to take someone off balance, how to use a wristlock or an armbar. The aim is to defend. But there are two kinds of attack. One, the more likely, is at heart a social message: the establishing of who's the tough guy, the top dog, usually mano-to-mano or gang-to-mano. The intent is to brawl or prove bravado, or maybe even to rob or maim in anger.

This is different. The intent here is to kill. Me. I must meet that intent with a total commitment to violence. Anything else and I lose. I die.

He takes another step forward, the knife lifting waist high, the grip easy, confident. He sees a short, slightly dumpy, old lady trapped in a box far from witnesses or help. He sees prey.

I see death.

My old *sensei* was shorter than I and was still teaching at eighty-plus-years. He understood he would always be the prey unless … he wasn't.

A loose grin on his face, the man comes for me. As I step forward to meet him, I flip the grip of my right hand on the handle of the muck rake, jabbing the end of the stick hard into his throat.

***

For the second time in a matter of weeks, blue lights play on my face. This time in my pasture. I know the officer walking toward me is going to have a hard time believing who killed the man that lies sprawled in my barn. Certainly not me. I'm just a little old lady.

* * * * * *

THE TRANSLATOR

James Ellson

- 1 -

In the middle of the night, under a sliver of bone-coloured moon, the translator and his family were extracted.

The department always used a specialist team. All ex-military. A woman with a Belfast accent in charge. They carried silenced Glock 17s, wore infra-red goggles, and, apart from the woman, said nothing.

The translator carried his daughter down to the scruffy white Transit on false plates. She wore her hooded dressing-gown, and smelt of sleep. He'd promised a pet for her birthday, and mentioned a tortoise. His wife grabbed kitchen supplies and their holdall that always sat packed in the hall. He returned once, argued with the woman, and won. In his daughter's bedroom, he unscrewed the false socket. Pocketed the cribs.

The three of them waited in the rear of the van. The translator stroked his daughter's long flaxen hair as she slept with her head on his lap. Through the one-way glass, a bat arced. Next door's dog remained unusually quiet.

"I'm tired of all this," said his wife. "It's our fifth house in as many years."

The translator felt for her hand.

"You said we'd settle here. Make proper friends." She uncurled her fingers and turned away. The moon had disappeared, and the silvery clouds were dark again.

After staying in a hotel for three nights, they were transferred to a new house. An alarm had been fitted, and their possessions, including his wife's dusty-leaved banana plant and his daughter's handmade

115

dollhouse, had already been moved. The new rental was semi-detached. A couple of retired teachers lived next door. There was a small garden with a trampoline, and along the back fence, laden fruit bushes. The neighbours opposite and two sets either side had been vetted to scale six, the whole street to three. Even at work, only his boss and the big boss knew the address.

The teachers had taught in the local school for over a hundred years between them. Both had signed the welcome card that arrived the next day.

The translator studied the locality on his phone. While his wife and daughter went food shopping, he checked the exterior doors' security, the window-locks, and the gate in the back garden.

In the afternoon, the other neighbour knocked on the door. He was a tall thin man with a pudding haircut. His olive coat was made of gabardine. He brought a bottle of wine and homemade biscuits that smelt of cinnamon. The translator's wife asked the neighbour inside which was annoying. He looked up and down the street, but there was only a fish van making a delivery.

His daughter sipped orange squash and the three adults drank tea. They ate some of the biscuits, the translator unsure how many he'd eaten. He wondered why their new neighbour hadn't taken off his coat.

"What do you do?" asked the neighbour.

The translator glanced through the hatch into the kitchen where his wife was refilling the teapot. "I'm a translator."

"You don't look like a translator."

The translator forced a smile. "I keep myself trim."

"I'll say. I'm an engineer. My sister Jan who lives with me is a swimming instructor at the local pool. She's there now, otherwise she'd have popped round, too."

The translator was given a week's leave. He remained at home, watching and listening. He tested his mobile, the land line, and the alarm. He scouted the fields at the back, checking the drainage ditches and advancing up the dead ground. Noted the arcs of fire. At night he peered out of the windows and recorded details of vehicles driving past. Occasionally, he padded around the house to check the doors and windows. He looked in on his sleeping family, his wife's pale cheeks, the gentle snuffling of his daughter.

When the seven days were up, the department demanded him back.

- 2 -

His boss's door was closed, and the PA, a stupid woman and plain as a cupboard, was away from her desk. The translator knocked, and opened the door. His boss put the phone down without another word. He was a large balding man with cauliflower ears.

"So?"

"I don't know."

The translator went over to the dirty window. He parted the blind with two fingers. A van with flashing hazards had stopped a little way up the road. The driver wheeled sacks into an alleyway. They begged the question. He turned back.

"You do know, but won't tell me."

"I don't know."

His boss took out a pack of cigarettes. The translator pulled the blind. His boss flicked his lighter. The translator opened the window. Like chess, but quicker. Draughts.

"What can you tell me?"

His boss inhaled deeply. He stood, and lumbered to the window. Cold air battled with the smoke that rose in fits and starts like a Native American's signals. His boss stood there smoking, then flicked out the half-spent cigarette. The translator dropped the sash, and half-pulled the blind. His boss returned to his chair, unlocked a drawer, and took out a file.

"I'll play mother."

In the street, the delivery driver wheeled another sack, shunting it up the kerb. The sack was heavy, and bulged as if it contained a body.

"Your address was in a notebook. The notebook in a rucksack. The rucksack in a takeaway raided by immigration. Thirteen people have been interviewed, and thirteen people have made no comment. The notebook was negative for DNA, fingerprints, and impressions. The handwriting expert got nowhere. The notebook is sold in supermarkets, the bag was empty and new. In the notebook, only your address and a coded number."

The door opened, and the big boss walked in. She wore a black trouser suit, and red high-heeled shoes. She was tiny and without a curve in her body. The basement thought she was related to the PA.

"Is he behaving?"

117

"So far."

"Listen. No one's died, and no one's been injured. Leave it with us."

The translator felt for the keys in his pocket and jabbed himself in the leg. They talked about his family as if they were people in a distant land. In a way, maybe they were. Everyone was.

His boss proffered his cigarettes, but the big boss shook her head. She took out her own pack, and lit up, the smoke pluming forth like tusks. They did it on purpose, the translator was convinced. She held it in the side of her mouth and ripped a page from the desk-pad. She tore off a corner, and resting it on hand, wrote something down. She folded it several times and handed it to the translator.

"Your next assignment."

The translator started with the dry leads. First, the rucksack. After bribing the pimply property clerk, he booked a meeting room and locked the door. He set to work. The empty pack weighed more than the online specification. It was a start. He pressed and prodded, and slowly cut it up with a pair of scissors. A razor blade and two tablets with a faint J on one side were sewn into the shoulder straps. It wasn't much, but it was something. He trawled the *modus operandi* database, and came up with three hits. He wasn't convinced, thinking they were probably a smokescreen. Next, the code: *101149145N*.

It meant nothing to the department's experts, and nothing to him. His cribs included an old friend from school who'd been the further maths geek. It was a risk, but a low one.

"Course I'll have a look, T. We should meet up for lunch some time."

"We should."

Which left the notebook. Mass produced, and sold by three supermarket chains. The serial number narrowed it to one chain, and to the north of England. One store had sold seven to a customer at the start of the year. The cashier had left, but there was CCTV and they'd email it over. The translator watched it several times. The camera covered twenty-five tills, and even with enhancement, the picture quality was poor and the audio indecipherable. The customer wore a hat and common clothing, but she was white. It all helped.

He drove home.

As he pulled off the road, his neighbour's sister, Jan, also returned home. She drove a light-blue newish hatchback. It was clean, and from the little he could see when he climbed out of his car, the inside tidy. On the backseat was a string-bag of floats, and in the boot, coils of white rope with red marker buoys. She parked, and they met at the fence.

"How're you settling in?"

He smiled. "Fine."

She wore a pale-brown cardigan and jeans. She smelt of pine woods, and looked everywhere but at him.

The translator heard his front door open. His daughter rushed out and grabbed his leg. He mussed her hair and dangled a dog lead. She screamed and ran off back to the house.

"Mummy, Mummy!"

"Maybe I could teach her to swim?"

The translator nodded, then followed his daughter back to the house. In the kitchen he poured a glass of water and drank it at the sink. Upstairs his daughter was running around and shrieking. He watched Jan put on sunglasses and position her garden chair so she could see their house. The day was warm, but the pearl-grey sky was cloudy.

His wife entered the kitchen. "I've been thinking. You said this job, this role, this whatever it is you do and won't tell me, was only for eighteen months." She closed the door, but it opened again so she slammed it shut. "Then it was extended by a further twelve." She folded her arms. "It's now been five years. I want out."

The translator refilled his glass. "What about seeing that woman?"

"We've only just arrived. I'm having a break."

The translator swirled the glass of water and looked at the bubbles. "I'll finish this assignment, then we'll sit down and talk."

"You promise?"

"I promise."

He drank the water, and felt it sloshing around in his stomach like waves in a small harbour. A whole city could be poisoned by contaminating the water supply.

- 3 -

His assignment could wait. The wet leads couldn't.

The drawback of teaching hacking on the training courses meant the department was vulnerable from within. The translator waited until

America came online, then found a vacant office, sat down, and tapped on a computer. There'd be tripwires that he couldn't avoid, and an enquiry, but by then it would be too late. He downloaded the thirteen interviews into his phone and left for the day. Banged the fire alarm on the way out.

He drove to a deserted viewpoint overlooking the city, and parked between broken chairs and a soggy mattress. There was litter everywhere, like a covering of volcanic ash. In the hazy distance stood castellated grey blocks.

He listened to all the interviews, although he knew the thirteenth was his only hope. Twelve people had said nothing, not a single word. Only one person had spoken, part-time cook and student, Wu Ling. He'd confirmed his name and date of birth, his national insurance number and immigration status, and then like a prisoner of war, repeated it over and over until they'd given up. The department's advanced interviewers, too.

His wife phoned. "You'll think I'm being paranoid." Her voice went up and down. She took a deep breath. "I went next door to introduce myself to the teachers. There was no answer at the front door so I walked down the side to the back. I peered through the windows, and knocked. Got no response."

"They might have gone away."

A car drove onto the viewpoint and parked on the far side, next to a sea of nettles. It was a dark-blue saloon with a dog grille. Even with the grille, it looked like hundreds of others. A man in an olive parka climbed out of the car and walked round to the boot. He'd parked so the translator couldn't see what he was doing.

"Have you seen either of them since the day after we arrived?" said his wife on the phone.

The man in the parka closed the car boot, and hefted a long black sports bag. Supplies and spare clothes for a long walk; bolt croppers and a balaclava; a sniper's rifle? Where was his dog? Was it his car?

"I've heard the TV."

"You're just saying that."

"Make an appointment."

"I don't want an appointment with her!" Half shout, half wail. His wife sniffed, then blew her nose. "I don't want to have to. I want a normal life when I'm not always looking over my shoulder." She blew her nose again. "I went round to see Jan, our neighbour. She was really nice, said there was probably nothing to worry about. You know she hasn't lived here long?"

"How long?"

"I don't know. She didn't say exactly."

"I'll come home."

The translator tapped a series of numbers into his phone, then entered the index plate of the dark-blue car. The result came back negative, but in itself it didn't mean anything. There was no sign of the driver. The wind was picking up and next to the blue car, the nettles swayed like dying soldiers. Black birds wheeled round and round the same small patch of sky as if they were disorientated. The city was disappearing in the gloom.

The translator's route home took him past Ling's campus. He drove for a half mile, then turned back. It wouldn't take long, and it might solve everything.

He sat in the campus canteen and waited. He wore a fluorescent jacket and scuffed boots that showed the metal toecaps. His yellow construction hat was on the table. The camera in the ceiling corner, and the cashier were dealt with. He drank some water, and opened the packet of club sandwiches. Students flowed in like a burst river. Ling entered by a side door. The translator checked the photo on his phone, and waited until the student was at the till with his tray.

"This man has paid for your meal."

Ling glanced up. He wore earphones, and a small rucksack not unlike *the* rucksack. He pushed back the earphones.

"Are you one of them?"

"What do you think?"

They sat down at the translator's table. Ling studied the items on his tray as if his life might depend upon it. He was thin, and smelt of hair grease and body odour. He needed a shave. Badges of merit down one arm like a boy scout, but post-modern, ironic. *We've been here before. Today is tomorrow.*

The translator deconstructed a sandwich, pushing aside the salad and peeling the ham from the cheese like sticky-backed plastic. "Do you want it?"

Ling shook his head.

The translator held the slice of cheese up to the light. Thin as a garrotte. "You know cheese?"

Ling looked at him blankly.

"On the Isle of Man they make a halloumi with hallucinogenic properties. They call it the Big H."

Ling backed out his chair but didn't move fast enough. The translator shot out his foot and hooked his toe around a chair-leg.

"I don't know anything."

"What don't you know?"

The translator grabbed Ling's phone from the tray.

"Nothing there."

"It doesn't matter."

The translator went onto the dark web and downloaded a three-minute home-video involving a young girl and a dog. He sent it to ten of Ling's contacts, picked at random. He ate a sandwich. Drank some water.

There was no response, so he sent another ten messages.

A minute passed, then a gangly Korean-looking youth stood up from a nearby table and walked over. "Wu, you sick fuck!" He spat in Ling's face, and returned to his cackling mates.

The translator passed Ling a serviette. He played him the video while he ate the second sandwich. "Over fifty contacts in your phone have your surname."

"There's a man who lives above the takeaway. Fat. Chinese."

The translator stood up. He opened a clean serviette and wiped his fingers, then screwed it into a ball and threw it at Ling's face. He finished the water. His mouth tasted bitter, from the sandwich or the water, he wasn't sure.

- 4 -

The takeaway was in a parade of shops at a busy road junction. There was parking for thirty cars, and a constant flux of vehicles and people. The takeaway sold chicken and chips, and the smell of cheap frying oil billowed out from a vent above the signboard. There was a barber's, a chemist, and a small grocery store. Traffic clamour never ceased.

The translator sat in the back of a van, and looked out through one-way glass. He ate cheese sandwiches, drank black coffee, and pissed in an old milk carton. He took photos and noted car plates, considered his cribs. He saw drugs and counterfeit clothing being sold. He saw drugs being inhaled, and injected. He saw misery, and poverty, and boredom.

After a few hours, Jan parked her hatchback in the parade, and entered the chemist. She walked round the aisles, looking out more than at the shelves. She queued, and spoke to a white-coated assistant. She exited, paused on the threshold, looked up and down. A stretch limo purred through the junction. His neighbour stared at the van, then drove away.

An overweight Chinese man walked out of the takeaway. Shoulder-length hair that fell from a central parting. He climbed into a small brown car, and pushed a chocolate bar wrapper out of the window. He reversed out into the traffic, the bar sticking out of his mouth.

The translator pulled on a cap, and followed in the van. The fat man stopped at a betting shop, then a petrol station. He drove east, and parked near the football stadium, on a quiet dark street of terraced houses with patches of wheel-marked grass.

The translator waited further up. The fat man slopped up to a front door, and knocked. He rang the bell. If it was a shudder and jerk locale, then the translator didn't know it. If it wasn't, then evens it was the fat man's closest relative. If it was a laundry, the translator would look for another job.

And maybe he should anyway. His wife already appeared to be on the brink, and he had said the last place would be the last. But if he got to the bottom of it, finally found out who was responsible, he wouldn't have to.

An old Chinese woman opened the door. She held two walking sticks. The two of them embraced, and disappeared inside. On the windowsill was a pot of flowers: hydrangeas, the translator guessed.

He listened to music on the World Service and drummed his fingers. He translated some of the lyrics.

The fat man opened and closed the front door, and drove away.

The translator put on a postman's jacket, grabbed a delivery bag. He walked up to the old woman's front door and posted a bundle of pizza flyers. The smell of cheap cooking oil wafted out. He took scissors from his pocket and cut the flower heads into his bag.

He drove back to the takeaway, and waited. He ate more cheese sandwiches, translated more foreign music.

At midnight, the takeaway closed and the lights came on in the flat above. The translator locked the van and walked down an alley to the back. He climbed an external flight of stone steps to the backdoor. A figure moved behind frosted glass. A foul smell leached through an air-pellet hole in the glass. The translator pulled on a balaclava, thinking he should have brought a nose peg. He fiddled two wires into the lock, and poked around. Twenty seconds, not quite a record. He pushed open the door and slipped inside.

The bedsit smelled like a disturbed grave. A TV blared in the front room. In the bedroom a mattress lay on the floor next to an open suitcase filled with DVDs. A black sheet hung over the window. The smell emanated from the kitchen, and he peered around the door. A mincer was screwed to the table, and a heap of dead pigeons lay alongside. Cleavers of every size, and a mallet. A blackened drip-stained vat sat on the stove, and mouse droppings littered the floor.

The translator crept along the hall.

A bare ceiling light revealed a large front room. The TV stood in the corner showing a western. Newspapers, fast food trays, and bottles lay strewn. Sat on an armchair, the fat man was taking off his shoes. He'd rolled up his trousers and wore no socks. His feet were dirty and swollen. Bunions protruded. They presented what the induction course, all those years ago, had called an opportunity.

The translator stepped behind the fat man. He felt down the side of his neck and pressed down hard. The fat man twitched. On the TV a lone gunfighter rode into a whitewashed town. The translator took a coil of rope from his bag and tied the fat man to the chair, ankles tight to the chair-legs.

In the kitchen, unscrewing the mincer made him gag. He filled a bucket with water, and carried it with the mincer, the mallet and a selection of cleavers into the front room. He turned up the volume on the TV. The gunfighter was in a bar, eyeballing a table of bandits.

The translator tipped the water over the fat man. He came to, and rocked the chair. He looked at the mincer and the cleavers and the TV.

"I was expecting you."

The translator sighed. He hefted the mallet, and with an admittedly ostentatious backswing, whacked the fat man's bunion. The fat man screamed. On the TV the gunfighter drank a whisky. The translator swung again. He swapped sides. He varied his swing. The fat man pissed himself and dribbled. Then vomited down his front.

"What do you know about the rucksack?"

"Nothing."

The translator swung again, and again. The fat man passed out.

On the TV, the shooting started, and bandits fell out of windows into water troughs. The translator filled the bucket and doused the fat man.

"My life means nothing."

The translator nodded. He delved into his bag and removed the bag of hydrangea flowers. They were squashed and broken, but the point was made.

The translator waited until the gunfighter rode out of town. Then he turned off the light and went with him. The hero had won, but that was a film. The fat man didn't know. It was a problem. Outside, the black night pressed down.

- 5 -

The translator stopped at a petrol station and bought a packet of cheese sandwiches. A bollard light flickered, and a keen wind bent the spindly trees. He removed the slices of tomato and cucumber, and buzzing down the window, skimmed them onto a patch of scrubby grass. He closed the window, pressed the bread back together and took a bite. As if by magic, a pigeon appeared out of the gloom, and pecked at the brightly coloured splodges.

Maybe he should find another job. He couldn't do it forever and at some point he would have to stop. Why not now? Go before he was pushed under a bus.

His phone buzzed with messages. Nothing from his wife, but she could be moody like that. Seven missed calls, all except one from withheld numbers. The translator pressed redial.

"Sorry not to have got back to you sooner." The maths geek from school. "Anyway, it was easy. The N, I'm presuming, stands for name, but the numbers refer to letters. Spells Janine. Sure it's that … "

The translator dumped the sandwich and reversed out of the space.

The pigeon took off into the murk. He slammed the gear lever forward and accelerated hard. He called his wife but there was no answer. He called and called, drove faster and faster. He knew there'd been something wrong: his neighbour hadn't smelt of chlorine.

Outside their new home, there was a jumble of vehicles caught by blue flicker. The car screeched to a halt, and he climbed out.

Paramedics were wheeling a gurney with his neighbour to the ambulance. Jan's right shoulder was bandaged. They loaded her into the back.

The translator felt a tap on the arm.

"She's one of ours," said his boss. "Meant to be watching over you and yours."

"Janine?"

"No ... Janet." His boss kicked away a stone. "I'm sorry."

His boss handed him gloves and a pair of overshoes. "Don't touch anything."

The translator ducked under the tape and went into the house. He dumped the forensic garb and climbed the stairs as if they were the Hillary Step. Their bedroom was empty. He took a deep breath and went into their daughter's room. The two of them lay on the bed, his wife cradling their daughter. Blood on the headboard. They'd been executed, one bullet in the head apiece. He shuffled forward, and sunk to his knees. He picked up his wife's hand and stroked it. He wept. He stroked his daughter's hair, kissed them both.

He picked up a framed photo of his wife in her wedding dress. Inset was a second photo of the three of them at the zoo. They were standing in front of the monkey cage, all acting the fool. As he took a tissue out of his pocket to wipe the glass, a piece of paper fell to the floor. His next assignment. He opened it up.

Janine.

He screwed up the paper and tossed it away. He polished the photo-frame and set it down, then plucked out the photo at the zoo.

Through the window a scene tent was being erected. Nearby stood a scrum of people in forensic suits.

The translator looked down at the photo. They'd fed the penguins, seen aardvarks, and learnt about African painted dogs. Eaten fish and chips for lunch, and candyfloss for the first time. His daughter had her face painted as a cheetah. In the car on the way home, she said it was the best day in her life. His wife had leant over, and whispered in his ear, "See, you can do it."

There was a cough behind him. He turned.

One of the paramedics stood in the doorway. "Belfast accent? Your neighbour said you'd know what she meant." The man clomped back down the stairs, and moments later, the ambulance drove away with sirens wailing.

The translator took the new dog lead from the back of the bedroom door, and went into the hall. He popped the loft hatch and rigged up a cinching loop. He fetched a chair, stepped up, and kicked it away. He twitched and twisted. One way then the other, slower each time, and finally came to a stop. The photo of his wife and daughter at the zoo fluttered down, and the last thing he felt was the tips of his fingers.

* * * * *

THE CARPENTER'S SON

Mark Atley

Angelo's in town to take care of a problem because that's what hitters do, and right now, Angie's in a car, a Toyota, white, non-descript. Something that doesn't stand out. Something no one remembers. Parked under a highway bridge in Saint Louis, outside Bush Stadium. Here to take care of Darla's problem: a guy that won't pay up on a thing Darla's got going. In Angie's world, there are earners and hitters, and Darla's an earner – he's the hitter – they're on opposite sides of this, with different skills.

Angie's father was a hitter: The Carpenter. He moved to California from out east to work on movie sets doing construction and carpentry. His father wanted to get in good with some of the unions, said he wanted a steady paycheck for his family. His father had backing, which helped him escape The Life, almost, but being a Made Man means there's no leaving The Life. There's just a transition to something new, with fewer jobs and higher risks. His father went from an earner to a hitter, but it was the nails from a nail-gun that earned his father the name The Carpenter.

And in this world, you do what your father did, meaning Angelo's a hitter, but that doesn't mean he likes being what he is.

Tired of waiting in silence, Angelo says, "I should've been an actor," and looks over at Darla, who's sitting in the driver's seat of the car, clipping her toenails. "Like that'd been something. I'd not be here, waiting like this, you know? I could be at home. Could be all sorts of places. Be on my own time, be my own man, you know? Have a normal life."

Darla won't know what he means, because she doesn't know him. Not really. No one does, but that's not the point. Being normal was his father's dream and Angelo's adopted it, but that doesn't mean he can reach it any more than his father did. But still, he's got loves, music, movies, even thought he wanted to play baseball at one point. It was acting in high school, what school he attended, that fostered his love and dreams of working in the movies. He fell in love with it, being someone else, pretending.

But there was always something special about movies and he figures it started with his father taking him to the movie theater, whispering in his ear, telling him he'd worked on this set or that set. Always saying it with a sense of pride. Like he liked knowing that his creations were immortalized on film, telling Angie, "Most things built get torn down."

What Angie doesn't love is killing people, but what's he going to do about it? He's in The Life. It's not like he can leave it now. No one leaves The Life.

But he's still got those loves.

Right now, Angie talks to Darla to pass the time as he stares at the walls of the stadium. The glow of the lights peeks over the rim of the red-bricked building and his eyes track the world around him. People are everywhere, walking, talking, yelling, running, and all sorts of things, giving the whole place a sense of energy, it courses through the air. Home games do that: bring the noise, the whistles, yells, horns honking, general commotion. There's even a quartet of drummers on the sidewalk beating on plastic buckets. They sound good so he cracks a window to let the percussive rhythm into the car.

Darla tells him to put the window up, but Angie doesn't. She says she's afraid the rain might get in the car. He says, "It stopped raining a few minutes ago." She tells him the noise is giving her a headache. Angie just looks at her in response.

They're waiting for Darla's guy to show up. The guy works in the ticketing office at the stadium and earlier Darla texted the guy, saying they needed to talk, telling the guy to come out to the parking lot. The guy texted back saying, "Wait, the game's about to start."

So they wait and Darla does her waiting clipping her toenails, with her foot propped up on the dash, body bent forward, her fingers holding the clippers and toes. "What'd you mean about the acting thing?" Darla asks while studying her handiwork.

He means a lot, but he doesn't say that.

The nail clippers click and a nail from her little toe, a fragment, flies his way, landing on his thigh. He brushes it off. "Do you have to do that here?"

She glances at him.

Angelo says, "The clicking's giving me a headache."

"I have to do it somewhere," Darla says, focusing on her foot. She adjusts some in the seat to switch feet. She leans back, dropping her right foot to the floorboard, and brings up her left foot.

"Yeah, but like, do you have to do that, right now? Like here in this car now, because you know we got something to do?"

His way of reminding her to stay focused, it's her problem he's here to fix.

Darla shrugs and surveys her left foot. "I can't stop now that I started," she says, her tone saying she doesn't care too much about Angie's thoughts. "It would bug me all night, it wouldn't be even. It'd feel wrong." She clips a nail. "What makes you think you should have been an actor? You're good at what you do. That's why you're here, right? I mean if you can't do this, I need to know now. It's about to happen. I can't have it not happening. Crenshaw doesn't like problems."

"Not a problem, I'm going to do the job," Angie says to reassure her. She's right. Crenshaw doesn't like problems, but waiting's got him thinking. "But yeah, I am good at what I do, but that's not a marketable skill outside my social circles," talking with his hands. "I mean, it's not like I'm a plumber or a carpenter. Not like I could walk up to some office recruiter, say, 'Hey there, I'm Angelo Castello and I kill people.' Like that's going to make the job core happy about anything. That'd send them into a tailspin. Have them choking on their coffee. No one likes hitters, including the families. We're that girl no one wants to see, but you call when you're drunk. Even the military don't like having killers. No one does — that's why they come up with all those fancy words, all them about the same thing — killing people."

And Darla obviously doesn't like being in the car with a killer either, especially one talking freely about killing people: he can tell by the way she shifts away from him uncomfortably, but there's a lot of things she seemingly doesn't like about this. She doesn't like having problems; doesn't like that this guy, Phillip, put her in this situation; doesn't like dealing with Crenshaw; and she sure doesn't like having this car in her name. She's bitched about it since she picked him up from the airport.

But here she is, in a rented car, resenting being told what to do, her eyebrows creasing any time Angelo offers her a suggestion, which she takes as an order, but it's not like she has a choice. What's she going to do about it? Complain to Crenshaw? That'd make her a problem for him, and she knows how he deals with his problems.

But what Darla doesn't like most about this whole thing and what she's bitched the most about is having to drive Angelo around, telling him how much she hated having to pick him up from the airport, drive him all over, put him up for the last five nights, everything, going on about it nearly non-stop about how he's depressing her mood. But again, what's she going to do about it?

Nothing.

"This is what I get for staying too long in a thing that was too good," Darla says. "It was good, this thing, but it went too long."

Angelo glances her way.

"That's the first rule of the street: know when to walk away," Darla says. "The second rule, don't take help from no one. But I didn't follow either. So I'm a two-time fuck-up, I had to call for help."

"And Crenshaw's not one to offer help easily."

"Yeah, but it wasn't supposed to go this way. Life's taught me a lot of things: being a sucker isn't one of them."

"What happened?" Angelo asks.

"This was supposed to be a simple thing that ended up not being simple," Darla says.

"So what's the problem?" Angelo asks, except, he knows what Darla's problem is: she doesn't handle complications well and she's not patient. So it got to the point where Darla needed capital and protection to keep her scam going. Her mistake was outsourcing the problem-making to a local. The local did her dirty work for a piece of the action and protection, but his prices increased, putting her in debt. And not a monetary debt, but one of favors for favors. Then the local sold her debt to Crenshaw like banks do mortgages.

"Phillip," Darla says, "he skipped on the last three payments, which I feel like I've been awfully understanding about, but then he threatened to expose me. Crenshaw's people, your people, told me that couldn't happen. Told me, 'We'll send someone to you.' Then explained to me what I needed to do. Told me, 'Crenshaw will take care of the problem.

But you've got to be involved because he wants his people cleaning up their own problems.' I know what that means: help kill Phillip."

But she doesn't want to help kill Phillip, Angie can see it in the way she shivers every couple of minutes.

She doesn't want to be in the car with him, but she can't not be around him either: he's going to fix her problem.

So Darla bites her tongue, concentrating on making sure she doesn't clip too much of her nail or go too deep on the cuticle, and pretends Angelo doesn't bother her even though he sees he does.

Trying to change the subject, Darla says, "If you don't like it, killing people, why do it?"

Angie tells her it's because his father did it. He didn't have much of a choice. "It's not that I don't like it, just wonder what would be different if I did something else." He pauses, taking a breath, which causes Darla to look up from clipping her toenails. He says, "I mean, with where I grew up, it wouldn't have been that big of a stretch, you know, to break into something. It's not that big a deal. Commercials, walk-ons, hell, I see guys getting extra gigs all the time. All they got to do is just stand there in the background. Get paid for it."

Darla points out the front window at the stadium with the clippers. "You know I read somewhere you'd have better luck playing professional baseball, have a better chance of breaking into that sport than anything else. The thing I read was talking about other professional sports but included acting. Singing too."

"I like baseball," he says. Then shows her he's wearing his red Cardinals jersey, a proud souvenir. He says his father loved the game, telling her his father said it was about patience and skill.

Darla rolls her eyes and sighs like Angelo didn't understand what she meant even though he did. "I'm saying, most people, they don't get to be what they want to be when they're young," she says. "They dream about it, but those dreams go to shit, you know? Besides, what are the odds that you would make it big in movies?" She turns to look at him. "Can you even act?"

Angie nods his head. "I can act some, but you got it wrong. I don't want to be a star, just an actor."

"What's the difference?" Darla asks. Then drops her foot from the steering wheel, rotating her body in the seat some to look at him, pointing the clippers at him. "You're good at what you do, right? You come highly recommended." That's a lie, she doesn't know anything about him, but Crenshaw did send him, which means he comes with a certain understanding. "That's why you're here now with me because I need something done."

"You're right, you do need something done, need your problem fixed," Angelo says. "And I'll fix it, but we have to wait."

"Why do we have to wait?" Darla asks. "What we should've done was just drive over there and you ring the doorbell and do your thing. Why wait?"

Angie smiles. "You said that at the airport and we can't do that."

"Six days is too long," Darla says. "I'm running out of espresso. You've been here six days, waiting for this gig at my apartment, telling me how to do things and I don't like it. Not to be rude, but I don't want to know nothing about you or why you would want to be some pompous actor."

Angelo says, "I don't want to be a big-name jerk off," correcting her as he turns and slips his arm around the driver's headrest. "Not like those guys you see on-line and in magazines and things, where people follow them around taking their pictures and shit. I don't want that. I want to be that bit-part guy. Small-time, you know, do it like it's something respectable. I'd like to have something like a steady paycheck and be normal. I'd live like acting wasn't that big a deal. Do it like a craftsman does his thing. My father was a carpenter. I'd do it like that. Be like a carpenter. Wear sensible clothing. Have a marriage that lasts. Maybe one that don't. You know, be like those guys you forget are in your favorite shows, but when you see them, you love seeing them. I want to be that guy. A normal life."

Darla tells him, "You're too good-looking for that. If you were any good at it, that'd be an issue for you, too memorable." She points at his head. "Couldn't have that ponytail."

Angie nods because he gets what she's saying: the hair would have to go. "Yeah, but the ponytail hasn't been much of a problem in this job. I'm sure I could make it work for me in the acting thing."

Darla nods her head like what he said makes a lot of sense. She reaches in the back seat and comes up with some rubbing alcohol in a small travel-sized bottle, a thing of nail polish, and some cotton swabs.

"You're going to do this now?" Angie asks, motioning to the nail polish.

Darla says, "You said wait, this is me waiting."

And waiting's difficult for her.

Crenshaw told Angie to take care of her problem and he told Angie how he should handle the problem. Angelo says, "I don't like these lights."

"What lights?" Darla asks.

Angie points out the window at the overhead lights looming over the parking lot like inverted spotlights. "These newer lights make everything white and bright. The parking lot's lit up. It'll complicate things."

Darla leans over and looks out his window. Her face says he's right, but wishes he wasn't.

"That's a dangerous thing," Angie says, meaning the lights. "That'll make what I have to do harder."

"That going to be a problem?" Darla asks.

Angie shrugs.

"You don't know if that is going to be a problem or you don't care?"

He shrugs again. "It is what it is."

"Can you do this or not?"

"That's not the question you should be asking," he says.

"What the hell does that mean?" she asks, "What question should I be asking?"

"If we're going to do this tonight, or not?"

"No, we're doing it," she says, "because I don't want you staying at my place any longer. You've got to go so I can get things back to normal. You're too particular, wanting to make sure no one knows you're staying at my apartment. Wanting me to hide you from my neighbors like I'm not an adult woman, can't have a man around. Like that's weird. But it's not like I'm going to tell anyone you're here anyways. Why would I? At least you clean up after yourself. But you picking up all the dishes and washing them and cleaning the apartment so rigorously has me thinking you might have a mental problem about dirt. Makes me feel like I'm a slob. We're doing it because we have to."

"Yeah, but you don't want to rush it," Angie says, head still against the window looking out into the parking lot. He pauses. Then, he turns to look at her. "That's when mistakes happen."

"We're not rushing anything, we've been waiting for a couple of days."

"We have," he says, leveling his hands like scales, "What's waiting a few more?"

She huffs, saying, "Whatever," and settles back into her seat, bringing up her right foot, placing it on the steering wheel. She turns away, mumbling, "I'm tired of waiting."

But waiting's easy for Angie, it always has been. It gives him time to think things over, and silence helps with that. Doing what he does for Crenshaw means he does a lot of traveling because Crenshaw doesn't leave California. He sends Angie and a few others to take care of problems, and the travel gives Angie time to think, which he does best in silence.

But doing these types of jobs means thinking about his father. He used to tell him the reason he picked up the nail-gun was, in his humble craftsman's opinion, it didn't make a mess. There weren't any loud bangs or flashes to worry about. There weren't serial numbers to track. Nails were cheap and no one notices a pocket full of nails, but they'll take note of a pocket full of bullets. Besides, it's not like he wasn't familiar with the nail-gun.

His father told him the best piece of advice he heard about doing this job was about using the tools you have. He said Jimmy Momo told him that on his first job in California. Said Momo wanted a union president dead for holding up a movie production. Happened to be his father's union president and it happened to be a movie his father was working on. So his father got the hit – for convenience to hear his father tell it.

Momo told him, "Use what you got."

And what his father had was a nail-gun, cordless, because transportation's easier. Just snuck into the guy's office, and put the nail in the back of his head … and The Carpenter was born.

What Angie has now is a Browning .22 caliber target pistol. Lean, with a small frame, good for target shooting, doesn't make a lot of noise. And his ability to wait. The gun's in the door pocket. Magazine's full. He'll need most of the bullets. He's a good shot, but what he has to do, he's got to be close. Good thing he's good at killing.

Down here by the stadium, there's still a sense of history and with history comes red bricks covering about everything, which makes the sound bounce off in every direction. That'll help.

Darla doesn't wait well, applying a coat of nail polish to her toes, hot pink. The polish won't do her any good, though. It won't have time to dry.

Her phone buzzes in the center console. Darla picks it up and reads the text message out loud to him, "Phillip's going to be out in a minute."

Angie nods. "You ever want to be something that you're not?"

Darla says. "I told you, I didn't have the luxury of dreaming growing up."

"So you're like a shark, swimming, breathing, and living?" he asks.

"Yeah, that's the idea."

"That doesn't sound very fulfilling."

"Coming from you?"

He's not sure what she means by that, but he lets it go. It's almost time. No reason to get upset. Angelo says, "I wanted to be an actor. I shared that with you. I mean I don't get much time to talk to anyone."

"Because when you see them you have to kill them?" she says, letting out a nervous laugh.

A figure appears in the distance. Must be Phillip, gray-headed, old, losing hair, wearing a Cardinals shirt, bright red over tan pants, with old man tennis shoes on his feet. This'll be easy.

Angie looks at Darla, swiping polish on a toe, and he can see she is shaking so bad she can't get the lines right. He says, "You never ask yourself what if? Like what if this happened or like what if this other thing happened? Never dream about what could have been? You know they say there might be universes for every decision we've made in our lives. Think about that. Think about all the people in the world and all the decisions you have to make throughout your life. That's a lot of possibilities."

Darla stares at her toes, taking a deep breath. "No," she says. "I've never thought about it."

Angie looks out the passenger window. "I've thought about it."

Darla looks up, notices Phillip walking toward the car, and drops her foot to the floorboard. She's going to screw up the polish. She only has half of one foot done.

Angie figures that will bother her, not being even, but maybe he should remind her about priorities?

Darla screws the lid back onto the polish and drops it in the cupholder.

The time before a hit can be stressful. The key, what his father said, was Angie had to be patient, not anxious, and wait. Angie squeezes his hands together, checking the tightness of the batting gloves, which go with his Cardinals shirt.

Darla observes him doing this and asks, "Wait, where'd you get gloves? Should I have gloves?"

Angelo doesn't say anything.

"And how can you sit there looking so calm?"

Angelo sees she can't keep herself from shaking.

"What's the plan?"

As Phillip draws closer to the car, Angelo says, "The plan is I'll take care of the problem, it's what I do," but Darla doesn't know what that means. He tells her, "Point to the passenger side, please."

Narrowing her eyes in a questioning look, Darla complies and points Phillip to the passenger side, signaling Phillip to go to Angie's window, which is cracked because he wanted to listen to the drummers, who are still beating away on their plastic buckets in the distance.

Angie uses his left hand to roll his window down as Phillip appears at the window, breathing heavily, face red. He leans into the window, pointing a finger at her, saying, "Listen, I told you, I'm not paying. I don't care who you bring here to try to intimidate me. Leave me alone."

But before Darla can respond, Angie sticks the barrel of a long silver handgun to Phillip's chin. The barrel is skinny for a gun. Angie puts it to the underside of Phillip's chin and pulls the trigger three times. No warning. No hesitation. Just like that. The gun's quiet, barely making a noise, and what noise it does make gets lost in the drumming.

Out of the corner of her eye, the whole thing makes Darla jump in her seat.

Phillip's eyes flash confusion like he doesn't understand what just happened. He looks down at Angie, who acts like he didn't hear anything and doesn't even look at Phillip, stares straight ahead. Then, in reflex, Phillip's hands snap to his throat and grab at the underside of his chin as the idea of what happened crosses his mind, but it is too late. The tang of blood and rain hangs in the air as Angie places his gloved hand on Phillip's forehead, and ever so softly pushes Phillip out the window as Phillip's body starts to bleed. A drop of blood lands on the seat between Angie's legs.

Outside the window, Phillip stands straight, mouth open, trying to scream, but can't, blood trickling out from between his fingers. Wild-eyed, Phillip collapses and falls out of view.

Angie turns in the seat.

Terror flashes across Darla's face as he turns the gun on her.

He places the barrel against her left eye, holding it there, making sure his placement's good. He notices her eyes are green, didn't think about that before, the hot pink would have worked well with them. He pulls the trigger twice: the Browning coughs.

The placement's good: in the eye through to the brain. Darla's body slumps and falls against the seat. It's not like the movies. That's something his father told him: people don't go flying around when they're shot.

Angie checks the car one last time and doesn't see anything he might have left behind. He takes a moment to double-check. The guy didn't bleed too much, but Angie remembers to be careful getting out, blood did drop on the seat.

No worries about the girl, though. He cleaned the apartment, erasing any evidence he might have left behind, but it all depends on how well the cops look. Time will tell. It'll give him a day or two for sure. That's all he needs.

Angie exits the car, careful about not touching the blood on the seat, and shuts the passenger door. Looking down at Phillip's feet, he shrugs and places the Browning in Phillip's hand, not the one around his throat. That'll be a problem, three shots to kill oneself, but he can't fix it. It won't sell what he's trying to do, but oh well, what's done is done, after all, it's Phillip's gun. Angie stole it when he arrived in town. He didn't tell Darla about that. She thought he'd been lounging around her apartment waiting, and in a way, he was, because he figured the best place to do this was in the parking lot at the guy's work. No cameras down here and home games bring a lot of traffic. So he waited for the next one, knowing how to make this look, and nature worked well today, the rain. There's a puddle, so no unnecessary shots for gun residue. Angie drops Phillip's gun hand in the puddle.

Stepping back, he studies his work. It looks natural. That'll work. He stands, checks himself, and fixes his shirt, no blood, that's good, but if there was blood, the shirt's red so it would be hard to spot anyways.

Angie walks away from the Toyota, removing the batting gloves because they hold sweat and fit tight. He'll throw them away somewhere else. Right now, he puts them in his back pocket. He'll dump the shirt someplace else when he's done.

At the crosswalk outside the stadium, he reaches in his pocket and removes a dollar, dropping it in a drummer's bucket. Four drummers look at him, but only one says thank you, none stop drumming. An off-duty police officer, working the crosswalk, waves him forward and Angie crosses the street.

The game's in the second inning, which means there is enough time to catch the Cardinals play Cincinnati. It should be a good game. His father loved baseball and used baseball to teach him patience. Angie enters the stadium and passes through the checkpoint, handing his ticket to the attendant to be scanned, and wishes his father could be with him to watch the game.

* * * * *

WAITING

Lisa Cutts

I would do anything – absolutely anything – to avoid giving evidence in court. I mean anything. I'm used to getting my own way: it's part of my charm. It had worked for me as a child, as a teenager and as an adult. Very few people ever turn me down or give in when I push against them. I suppose it's part of the reason I'm here in the first place. I'm used to getting my own way, regardless of what others think and say.

My mum used to call me defiant and willful, at least until she met an untimely end, then she couldn't call anyone anything. Her words couldn't get to me after she drew her last breath. Well, what I mean is that there were no new insults to crawl into my head and worm inside my brain, making me believe that I truly was worthless.

Now, here I was waiting to go inside the court and tell them all about that most terrible of crimes – murder.

They told me that they couldn't coax me in any way – no telling me what I was supposed to say – but it hadn't stopped them from dropping a hint or two. I suppose they didn't want me to get into the witness box and go off on a tangent. Never ask a question that you don't know the answer to. Isn't that the rule the legal professionals are supposed to live by? I wouldn't know, as I've never got all that close to any of them. It's difficult to mix with their sort in my line of business. Our worlds don't easily collide, although we have crossed paths from time to time. That was always inevitable. You can't make an omelette without breaking eggs is another of the old clichés. Court is surely the place to wheel out overused adages.

As I sit waiting my turn, I think back over the endless police interviews and questions about what had happened and what I could remember. I can only hope that the answers I give to the court today, are the same ones I'd supplied all those months ago. I don't have the best memory, although thinking on my feet is one of my many better qualities. That was what my mum had always said, and I tend to agree with her on that point. There were many things we rowed about, even came to blows over, but not that one. It certainly paid dividends when her time was up.

I can hear footsteps coming towards me, the sound harsh along the empty floor, echoing along the corridor. I could look up, but I don't. Whoever it is can call me, wait for me to respond in my own time. It's not as if I want to be here, they know that well enough after all the waiting. For months they've been bothering me, asking me this, asking me that. Why can't they leave me alone? It's not as if any of this is my fault. That's what I tell myself.

Trying to make it feel like it was my fault was one of the tactics they employed, obviously. They got very little reaction from me going down that route. "Don't you think you could have done something, *anything*, to stop this?" they had asked me more than once. I had stared back, knowing whatever answer I'd have given them, it would have been the wrong one.

I shut my eyes and remember the screaming, the blood, the total chaos of what was happening. It's ricocheting around in my brain. It haunts my every thought, both the waking ones and the terrors in the middle of the night.

This shouldn't be happening. *It* shouldn't have happened.

Sweat runs down my back. I can feel it soaking into my shirt and know that beads of perspiration are breaking out all over my face. I mustn't show weakness, I have to do this, despite every single part of me wanting to get out of here as fast as I can. Only I know they won't let me. They'll bar my way and I'll be in so much trouble. I don't want to be here. Anywhere but here.

The footsteps have gone now, left me alone again. My nerves settle down to somewhere between panic and fury. The question I have asked myself over and over is the same one the interviewing officers had asked me: could I have done something to stop this?

The warning signs were there. I can see that now. Lack of eye contact, withdrawal, a refusal to talk about anything of actual importance. And the naked truth was that I had recognized what was going on, but failed to believe it would happen. That's what I tell myself at three in the morning when sleep has evaded me again. I had known really, hadn't I? Did I choose to ignore it or to deny what was going on before my eyes?

I'd watched the sun edge around the curtains every morning for the last four months, two weeks and three days, sometimes managing to convince myself that I genuinely hadn't seen the cries for help masquerading as bravado. With increasing frequency, I have to surrender to the thought that I was fully aware of where this was heading.

Ignoring it seemed so easy, you see. I was busy. We were all busy living our lives, running from one insignificant point to another, surrounded by people, but so alone. Everyone in their boxed-off compartmentalized world, oblivious to the pain and hurt around us, or so weighed down trying to cope with our own, we fail to pause and take a moment. We're always in such a hurry.

I take a breath, and then another, stealing myself for the onslaught of questions that are about to follow, only to be hit by the all too familiar feeling of self-loathing.

The phone interrupted me that morning, I remind myself. I was in the middle of something and I couldn't get to it before it rung off. A few minutes later, I glanced at the screen and thought any minute now, *I'll return that call.* Except I hadn't. Not only my failure to return the call disgusts me, but my reaction to it. I hadn't told a soul that I had been in a bad mood. I had my own problems to deal with and the sound of the phone chirping at me, annoyed me. When I saw who was calling me, I'd rolled my eyes and tutted. Yes, tutted. Now I have to live with that.

It wouldn't have taken much to work out that he needed someone to talk to, especially at that time in the morning. It was so early, that I'd barely had time to get dressed. We had agreed to meet for breakfast: an artery-clogging fry-up of epic proportions. It was our regular Friday treat when the shifts allowed time, along with a couple of swift pints at the other end of the working day. It was our way of setting ourselves up for the weekend, with hours of joking in between that neither of us would make old bones with all the fatty food and booze. None of that's relevant now.

If I'd have answered the phone, returned the call, today would have started with a full English, two mugs of tea and a plate of toast. I glance at my watch. In less than five hours, the two of us would have been on our way to the Druid's Arms, moaning and muttering about how the week had gone. Complaining and swearing about our workloads and why there was never an end in sight. Our usual Friday ritual.

I wipe my hand across my face, close my eyes and wish I was a better person. Any minute they'll call me inside court number six and a jury will stare at me and see the fraud and disappointment that I am.

My mum had known it. That's why she waited until I'd gone out for the day and swallowed handfuls of pills she had been storing up. We had spent most of the previous night rowing, her screaming endlessly abusive words and insults at me. It wasn't the first time I'd walked out on her threats that she was going to end her own life and that I'd have to carry the guilt for the rest of my days. Once more, she had been right. I did carry it with me, from the morning of my sixteenth birthday when I found her body, right up until today, over twenty years later.

My mouth feels dry and my tongue thick. If I didn't know better, I would say this is the start of a panic attack. I had them a lot when I was a teenager, something that everyone put down to the shock of finding my loving mum's body. I had never told anyone that guilt would do that to a person, especially one who wasn't completely blameless.

Here I am again, having to face the consequences of my actions, or rather, the lack of them. This time it's different: if I'd had known the outcome of this one, I would definitely have answered the cry for help. I should have been a better friend.

More footsteps, only this time there are two people walking towards me. From the corner of my eye, I can see the black uniforms and bulk of stab-proof vests, radios, handcuffs, other police clutter adorning them. I should have been wearing mine today, just like any other day on duty. Under the circumstances, I didn't even ask. I suppose I'm a disgrace to them.

They stand a few feet from me, not wanting to approach me too quickly, I suppose. I can hear their whispered conversation, the shuffling of their boots. I think they're here to make sure I'm not by myself, that I'm going to go through with giving my evidence and not end up the same way as Clive. Thinking his name is enough to make me cry.

We had joined the police together – two fresh-faced new recruits. He always took things to heart and stressed over the daftest things. I was always the one who forced him out of the police station well after our shifts had ended, prying paperwork from his fingers or threatening to unplug the computer if he didn't stop working and come and join me for a late-night drink, game of cards or dirty kebab. I took my job seriously, but he lived it day and night. I suppose events of my sixteenth birthday shaped me. When you live with knowing your depressed mother had enough medication hidden away to kill a herd of rhinos and then you give in to her pleas and tantrums for you to go out and buy her a bottle of vodka, leaving her all alone with nothing but suicidal thoughts, you process thoughts a little differently than other people.

Clive often used to call me late at night or early in the morning telling me that he couldn't sleep because of a call we had attended. Usually he worried about something that wasn't even in our power to do: sometimes, we had to do the best we could for people and move on to the next one.

That is exactly what the two uniformed officers sidling up to me outside the court are doing. They were sent as part of their tour of duty with no idea of what the next ten or twelve hours were going to look like. For their own sakes, I hope that they hadn't been warned they would spend their shift treading on eggshells, all the while making sure I did as was expected.

One of them calls my name. I blow the air from my cheeks and hold up my index finger. I have to build up to this.

It's my final chance to think what I'm going to say to the court, how I'm going to present myself. I don't want to come across as uncaring, but I'm not sure breaking down in tears is the right way to go either. If I cry, it's because I'm an emotional woman, yet if I don't, I'm a hard-faced bitch. I remind myself that I'm still here as a professional, however much that feels fraudulent. If I'd been as dedicated to the job as Clive, this wouldn't have happened.

The last call we were sent to that day was a domestic violence one. There was only an hour to go before the end of a very long and unrelenting shift. I was due to go on annual leave, you see. A whole nine days to myself without the radio sounding in my ear to send me off again to sort out the ills of the local inhabitants who always seemed to want to beat one another, steal from each other and tirelessly cause aggro to stop me getting home on time. What exactly did I have to rush home to? Very little, but that wasn't the point.

Clive was always the one who answered the operator and actually sounded cheerful about taking calls. He almost seemed to be grateful that we had been especially chosen to race off to other people's homes, wade into their crises and take care of everyone else's lives. Except when it came to it, he couldn't take care of his own and I couldn't take care of him.

I should have known how he was feeling when we left the house after fifty minutes of talking to the jittery young woman whose boyfriend had left her with a black eye, bruised ribs and terracotta plant pot through the living room window. We were no strangers to distraught victims of crime, nor to being on duty hours after our scheduled finish time. I had a fridge full of beers and several hours of action movies to watch to kick off my holiday. Getting home on time was my priority. Finding the violent boyfriend before he came back was Clive's.

I let out a sigh and feel the cheap plastic bench move as one of the police officers sits down beside me. I prepare myself for trying to get my act together and manage some coherent sentences. Anyone can see what a mess I am. Only I know it's not a new feeling. I hear my name again and something about being the next to go and give evidence. I nod and mumble my understanding, staring straight at the court door. The next time it opens, I know the wait is up.

The thing that eats away at me the most is how I persuaded my crew-mate to leave the scared and battered woman in her insecure two-bedroom house. I reminded him that she wouldn't cooperate with us and refused to tell us what had happened. There was every chance she knew where he'd scurried off to, but refused to help us in any way. The irony of that statement was that we weren't the ones who needed assistance: the petrified woman with bruises on her face had that covered all by herself. As it had approached midnight, I'd made a point of looking at my watch and shaking my head. I'd already primed Clive by telling him that I had to get home before the bewitching hour to spend the whole of my mum's birthday in quiet contemplation. I had known that nothing else was bound to get him back outside and in the patrol car.

The door across the scruffy court hallway opens, the draught pushing a ball of hair and fluff towards my feet. I know the usher is seconds away from taking me to meet my fate. I would do anything to avoid what's coming next. They'll make me tell them what happened.

Clive had called me several times while I was on leave. Mostly, he had chatted about work, sometimes about himself, more frequently about me. That was typical of how he was: he had really cared about other people, whereas I tend to use them. It's my nature, which I'll admit, isn't an attractive trait. I've never really hurt anyone. Even my mum's death wasn't something I actively caused – providing you don't count failing to act and giving in to her demands for alcohol. It's not as if I actually killed her. Besides, I was sixteen and was left alone with her and her drinking. How else was I supposed to cope? For all these years, I'd kept it together: knowing it was my fault and that I could have helped prevent it, only I didn't know how to. What was my excuse this time around? Two decades on and I really had no excuse.

With less than twenty-four hours of my holiday remaining, Clive had called me for the seventh time in as many days to let me know the news: Lola Turpin was dead. More accurately, Lola Turpin had been murdered. It took me longer than it should have to remember who Lola Turpin was. The last time we'd seen her was in her modest but cosy two-bedroom home as she nursed a black eye and tried to clean glass out of the living room curtains. Her angry boyfriend, with a propensity for violence and a penchant for punching women in the face, had returned one last time. Only this time, the beating was the last she would ever endure.

The usher is in front of me now, long black robe flowing behind her, questions about whether I want to swear on the Bible or affirm. Does it matter? If there is a hell, I'm going there. I had ignored the signs from my friend and colleague who really couldn't live with what had happened, feeling – as he explained in his suicide note – that this was his fault. We had left without arresting the boyfriend who had successfully enlarged his skillset from an upper cut or two, all the way to making sure his victim was dead.

If I'm to be shown any mercy, the courtroom dramatics will avoid the part where I went to Clive's house when he failed to come into work that morning. He was never late, and, of course, I knew that he wasn't sick. He had called me, interrupting the menial task I was doing at the time, and I hadn't telephoned him back. A quick text from me would have done it, I'm fairly sure of that. We talked about everything, and I can say with a fair amount of certainty that had we spoken that day, he would be here with me now. The pair of us would have sat waiting to give evidence in the trial of *R v Stoneman*. The arrest and subsequent multiple murder charges against Adrian Stoneman would have helped Clive sleep at night, if only he had lived long enough to see it.

As I take a deep breath and follow the usher into the court, I know I'll not only have to live with having told Clive a total lie about why I wanted to get away from work on time – it was months before my mum's birthday and I had never marked it in any way – but I would have to process finding my best friend's body in the bath, razor blades besides his severed wrists. I could try to blame him for what he'd heaped upon me. I could never blame anyone else for not protecting Lola Turpin and her two young children.

* * * * *

RIGHTS AND WRONGS

A.B. Patterson

- 1 -

"You're a dinosaur, Harrington. Whilst you've been hiding in your Jurassic swamp, the Police Force has progressed."

The smug, superior stare rained on me across the desk like rancid urine. I needed a shower.

His lame effort to echo a Dirty Harry script, absent of irony, was risible. It was an insult to the film, as well as real police work.

The new divisional boss, Detective Inspector Mal Royd, looked about sixteen, but we all knew he was early forties. His CV had been widely circulated when his appointment was announced. All these rapidly rising show ponies seemed to feel the need to market themselves. I guess it makes up for their lack of genuine policing credentials.

Whilst it was Monday, I was still shabby from the old boss's send off on Friday night. Actually well into Saturday morning: we made it to a greasy breakfast before crawling off to our respective hovels. Yeah, exactly what a send off for a stellar bloke should be like. We gave DI "Bomber" Black a hell of a farewell. It had been a real old-school affair, including two hours at a superb strip joint. The Vice Squad boss had been with the troupe, so we got deliciously well looked after at The Purring Puma, the city's finest titty bar.

The younger demons always wanted to know the origin of "Bomber", but it was never shared. Some things are best left that way. And it had never been solved, either.

Twenty years ago, two young constables were gunned down in an ambush. It had been in the midst of Mafia turf wars, with each other, and with us coppers. Not that the boundaries were always textbook clear.

149

Don Alfonso Fucile had given an interview to the ever-hungry media with not-too-veiled references to the two young cops getting what all of us deserved. He then made a not-at-all veiled call to the Detective Commander to tell him to call off the dogs, or else.

Wrong move. So wrong. You know, one of those classic monumental misjudgements, like the Japanese thinking they would get away with Pearl Harbour.

Wallis Black was then a detective in the Special Branch, now disbanded. Of course. These days the public wanted police results, but without having the stomach for what that entailed.

Anyway, our Commander, a man who was renowned for his way with words, told Don Fucile to go fuck his ugly, syphilitic whore of a Sicilian mother. Shortly after, that Oedipal opportunity was forever removed from the city.

The Don got into his black Bentley to go to mass one drizzly Sunday morning, turned the ignition, and was promptly dispatched in tiny pieces across the suburb. A waste of a fine motor car. The blast was so strong that twenty-two houses in the street lost their front windows. Fortunately no one else was seriously injured. Forensics couldn't even find the Don's fingerprints or teeth. But the ID could be positively made courtesy of the Special Branch surveillance video from over the road. It cut out in the split second of the blast, its covering window being one of those decimated, but a surly faced Don Fucile was clearly the only person in the car when it blew.

And so Detective Black became "Bomber" Black. Discreetly at first, but then more openly as time passed. Like I said, it was never solved. Of course. And like I said, old school.

I drifted back reluctantly to the promoted-on-merit useless cunt sitting opposite me. His CV read like a roll call of bureaucratic wankfests: Force Policing Directorate, Commissioner's Secretariat, Personnel, Academy Curricular Development Unit, Systems Transformation Project Command, Office of Strategic Policy, Diversity Consultation Team, and the obligatory stint in Professional Standards. So, a fine career of anything and everything except actual police work.

As for the dinosaur line, if he'd been remotely old school I might have credited him for knowing the Dirty Harry film it was used in.

But I knew better than to think these newer uber-ambitious types would ever watch any hard-core police films. Getting too dangerously close to a reality check.

People like Royd are an offence to the uniform they parade around in. Every payday they ought to be charged with obtaining a benefit by deception, section 137 of the *Criminal Code*.

I did my best to appear as contemptuous as I was, short of giving him the bird. "Whatever you say, boss." I loaded some scorn onto that last word. I could see the loathing rise in his eyes. I continued, "But, if I can draw on your deep well of experience, are we still supposed to be locking up criminals?"

"Harrington, it's not all about arrests. Can't you get up to date?"

"My apologies, boss. I've always thought being a detective sort of revolved around solving crimes and arresting those responsible."

"Are you being sarcastic?"

"No, of course not. I would never be disrespectful to a superior officer, boss. I aspire to rank myself, and your fine example gives me inspiration to become a senior officer of the future." I swallowed hard as I struggled to look earnest. Plus it helped keep the vomit down.

He stared at me, the faux stroking of his ego leaving him torn and confused. His ego won out (it usually does) and his face relaxed, resuming its supercilious mien. What a dumb wanker.

"Take it from me, Harrington, it's all about politics and perceptions. And the perception problems created by your methods, and your fellow dinosaurs, are a headache the Force doesn't need."

"With all due respect, our methods do get results. I rather thought parents would be happy to see us locking up the paedophiles who rape their kids."

He stared at me coldly again, with all the humanity and warmth of a tiger snake. His type was just as dangerous, too, but only to the likes of me. The violent criminal scum out there had nothing to fear from the new police.

"But perhaps, boss, I'm just being old-fashioned. Nostalgic maybe."

"More like out of date and rotting in the bottom of the cupboard, Harrington."

Ouch. I felt like pouting at him and saying, "Ooh, you bitch, slap me harder." I resisted the temptation.

He droned on. "And your latest complaint, for arresting and torturing that suspect a few weeks ago, has now landed. Internal Affairs spoke to me this morning. Quite a brutalization session by all accounts."

"You mean that fucking ped's account, which, by the way, isn't true. And might I remind you, with all due respect of course, that we got a little eight-year-old girl back to her family. Alive, remember? She'd be dead without our work."

"Which would be a damned sight easier to do the PR for than another sordid episode of police brutality."

"Alleged brutality," I corrected him. "And I'm so proud to be sitting in front of a senior officer who'd prefer a dead child to bad publicity for the police." I didn't bother veiling the sarcasm this time. I badly wanted to show the cunt what brutality really was.

"Whatever, Harrington. Not my job to deal with the complaint anyway. But I'm confining you to desk duties until IA have finished and done with you. And then hopefully I'll be done with you, too." One of those memorable expressions, perfected by the righteously arrogant, oozed over his face, involving a smooth hybrid of a sneer and a grin: what I call a "grineer". I'm sure his breed must practice in front of the mirror. Well, I suppose they spend a lot of time admiring themselves anyway.

I pictured smashing the cunt's face into the corner of the desk, but I guessed that wasn't what he meant by "desk duties". More's the pity.

- 2 -

It was the Azalea Quinn case, one of the nastiest I'd ever had to work on, which led to my desk confinement.

Little Azalea was eight-years-old and had never arrived home from school. So her father, social justice campaigner and prominent lawyer, Richard Quinn, told me on the doorstep of their expensive inner-city terrace house. Being a woke warrior obviously paid well.

We'd got the call shortly before the end of the shift. My offsider that week was a new arrival in the Squad, Detective Kellie Hanssen. Her genes had carried those blonde, Scandinavian good looks perfectly: picture Agnetha from ABBA. Aside from being easy on the eye, she was also good company as it had turned out over the last few days together. She was intelligent and eager to learn more of the detective trade.

On the sterile, gentrified threshold, I introduced us and then made the traditional request in these circumstances, "May we come in, please?"

Not much surprises me these days, but it turned out there was always the possibility.

"No, officer, certainly not. We can discuss this perfectly adequately without you coming inside our house. We have no time for the police and their fascist attitudes, as I'm sure you're well aware. If you actually read the news at all. If you can actually read, that is."

In other circumstances I would have given him a juicy expletive-laden piece of my mind. But I reminded myself the little girl was missing and bit my tongue.

He continued, "I only called because my wife insisted. I'm sure Azalea will turn up, probably just hanging out at a friend's house."

Ms Quinn was standing slightly behind him to one side. Her mean, hatchet face was a conflicted mixture of contempt for us and anxiety for the missing Azalea. She said nothing and just grimaced, albeit half-heartedly.

The knob of a father gave me Azalea's details and a photo. Part of me wondered if little Azalea had run away to escape the suffocating wokeness at home. But she was a little too young to recognize sanctimonious bullshit and virtue signalling.

As he went to shut the door on us, I had to make a comment.

"Thanks Mister Quinn. Despite what you think of us, we'll work our arses off to find Azalea. Because that's what we do. For everyone, regardless."

The snarky, self-righteous face stared at me, mouth half open, but no words were forthcoming.

I'll chalk that one up on the board: detectives one, social justice wankers nil. But point scoring wasn't the priority, Azalea was.

When she hadn't turned up twenty-four hours later, we knew she'd been taken. Kids running off to friends' houses unannounced always resolved themselves in the first day or so.

On the morning of day three, I got a call from a snitch who told me he'd seen the news bulletin with Azalea's photo, and he had some drum for me.

Kellie and I met the sleazy Nathan in an adult shop in Northside.

"Who's the bitch?" was Nathan's opening line as we sidled up to him in the B and D section.

Kellie bristled next to me. I raised a hand to calm the pressure and I pointed at sleazebag.

"She's my offsider and don't talk like that."

"Whatever, DS, but just lose her. I only talk to you."

Kellie's agitation radiated heat. She looked at me as if to say, "Are you going to punch this fucker, or shall I do it myself?"

I lowered my voice. "I know this grates, but wait over by the cashier. I'll be done in a minute."

Her look said she wanted to challenge me, and fair enough, but needs rule. I gave her my sergeant look in return. She scowled and walked off.

I turned back to Nathan.

"You didn't need to call her that. And I don't want to hear it again."

"Whatever."

"No, not fucking 'whatever'. You won't speak to her again like that, understood?" I glared at him.

"Mmm, okay."

"What have you got, Nathan?"

"DS, I can't stand female cops. Call it a mummy issue, or something. More to the point, what have you got for me?"

"That depends on the quality of the drum, as you well know."

"I got a chat group on the dark web. Little Azalea getting done over, and I mean really fucking done over, by this ped. It was pay per view. A lot of coin changed hands. And she had cock everywhere, believe me."

"So, the details?"

"Cash first, DS. I reckon it'll be days before your lot find what I've found, so this is a five hunge tip-off, for sure."

"If it's good drum, yes."

I pulled out my wallet and extracted the five hundred. I'd visited the informers' tin before we left the office. I folded the money and handed it to Nathan discreetly.

"Okay, here you go, but if your drum is bum, then I'm coming for the money back. And I won't be in a good mood. Clear?"

"Relax, DS. It's totally kosher. You'll see." He handed me a folded piece of paper. "All on there with names and passwords for the group. Your cybercrime boys will know how to get into it."

He walked off.

Kellie glared at him all the way out of the shop, as I walked over to her.

"I do not like being called a bitch, Bruce, especially by scum like him."

"And fair enough, but we needed the drum, and we are not going to change the cunt's personality. So sometimes you gotta suck it up. I read the riot act to him."

I told her what I'd got from him and her look mellowed, ever so slightly.

"And, partner Kellie, I'll buy you a drink to make up for it."

She smiled, finally. It was like the sunrise after a stormy night. "A bottle, Bruce, of champagne. And then I might call it a deal."

"You're on." Yeah, a bottle of champagne with her was going to be dangerous, but bugger it: here for a good time, not a long time. And why did my hook-ups always drink champagne?

- 3 -

Watching the sexual assault of little Azalea was stomach churning and would be an appalling memory forever. No amount of time or booze or degrading sex erases those images, believe me. But watch it we had to, part of the job. The one we do for society. We have to live with those things for the rest of our days, but all the do-gooders out there couldn't give a fuck about that. Way more interested in the rights of scum like the molester doing Azalea.

As the online bids rose higher, so did the depravity. Kellie began playing with her phone, obviously looking for a distraction. I let her, as only one of us needed to watch the whole thing: so we knew it backwards if we ever got to interview the offender.

By the time the video feed faded out, Azalea looked catatonic and there wasn't any possible way left to violate her that the scumbag hadn't performed for his dark web audience, and the sordid satisfaction of his own deviant predilections.

The geek from the cybercrime unit was taking us through it on a laptop in the Ops Room. Young Chad Tranh didn't look like a regular detective, at least not from my vintage, but he sure knew his stuff. Times change.

"So, Chad my little genius mate, we've found the footage, how about a location?"

"That's much harder, Bruce. Like all these fucks, he's using a proxy server offshore. This one's in Tuvalu. So no IP tracing of any use. And there's no distinctive background of any use in this footage either, at least without finding the room used."

"You're right there. Just a bedroom and furniture. Could be anywhere."

Kellie put her phone down. "Chad, are there any other posts or whatever they're called on here from this fucking sicko?"

"This is the most recent, and a lot of stuff gets deleted real quick from these sites, once the money stops."

"He's still a ped," I said. "They love their souvenirs and sharing with their ped mates. It's their version of a pissing contest. If he's true to form, there'll be other stuff."

"Okay, I'll start trawling more. This'll take a while."

"Cool. We'll go grab a coffee. Can we bring you one back, mate?"

"Love one, Bruce. Long black with two, please."

"No worries."

I was out the back of the building having a smoke when Kellie texted me to come back upstairs.

Chad was sparked like a child on a sugar high and Kellie was looking happy for the first time in hours.

"Got a lead," she said.

Chad pointed at his screen. I could see an image of a park. Chad pressed a button and the image became a video. The footage panned around to a kids' playground. A shrill, almost falsetto, male voice suddenly came over the top of the background noise of traffic and children shrieking.

"Yum yum, fellows. My local delicatessen. A fine range of little virgins."

The footage zoomed in on the play area, lingered, and then cut out as a phone ringing could be heard.

"Okay," I said, "fairly typical ped happy snaps."

Chad looked at me. "True, but he was careless."

"Probably too busy barring up," said Kellie.

I chuckled. "Careless how so? I don't see his face, and he's not doing anything illegal anyway. We haven't criminalized deviant thoughts, yet." That was a good thing as I had had some sordidly dissolute daydreams about young Kellie over the last week working with her.

"It's posted last month by the same user as the rape video," said Chad. "So it's more than likely him for both."

"And we didn't see his face in the rape video, either."

"A whole load of ped penis, though," said Kellie. "Along with some distinctive scarring."

"Yes, but we need to find him before that's any use."

Chad was busting to jump back in. "But, like I said, he did get real careless. Unlike the rape video, for the park one he forgot to turn off his location services."

"Meaning?" I asked. This area was so not my strong suit.

Chad flicked his screen onto maps and pointed. "Meaning I could extract the GPS coordinates. And it's that park there."

I leant in and read "Acacia Reserve" on the screen.

He tapped the mouse pad and up came street view. Chad panned it and there was the playground.

I slapped him on the shoulder and winked at him. "You geeks really are useful."

We all laughed.

"Okay, Kell, let's get a list of all known sex offenders in a two kilometre radius and we'll start with them."

- 4 -

Adding the phrase "Urgent – child's life in danger" to every data request elicited a level of efficiency we weren't used to seeing, either from our own people or from the telcos. By the time the civilian office staff were heading home for the day, we had our target.

Ronnie Redlin, or "Rotten Ronnie" on the street, lived two blocks away from Acacia Reserve. His house was an unrenovated 1930s bungalow, which would tally with the old-fashioned wallpaper style on display in the backdrop to the rape of Azalea.

Ronnie had four priors for various molestation offences, and he had served time for the last three. He was still on parole from the most recent stretch.

Parole for such predatory scum never ceases to dismay me.

His last little victim had survived, but she had permanent injuries. She'd never be having her own little girls, let's leave it at that.

"Why do these fuckers ever get released?" Kellie almost shouted, looking over his record.

"An eternal mystery, Kell. But the irony here is that Azalea's father is exactly the sort who'd be campaigning for early releases. He was in the news last year whingeing about those ISIS terrorist arseholes getting indefinite detention, the ones who blew up the bus full of kids from that Jewish school."

"Karma's a bitch today, then."

"Yep. And it's a bitch for Ronnie, too." I held up a telco data sheet. "His phone registered on the cell tower on the edge of that park at the same time as that video of the playground."

"Hang on a sec, Bruce." Kellie rifled through some printouts in front of her. "Yep, the device that made the playground video is the same model as his phone."

"Okay, I reckon we've got enough to convince a Justice to give us a search warrant. Plus we'll bung in there the playground video as a breach of his parole conditions to stay away from kids."

"Like your style, boss."

"Look and learn, Kell. Free tuition." I winked at her. "Lessons from the old school."

"Do they come with a drink? I heard that was old school, too." She grinned at me. "And you did agree to champagne."

"Do bears shit in the woods?"

She laughed, as did Chad.

"I don't know where you older guys get all these one liners from," she said.

"Yeah, they broke the mould after us. It's the new Police Force, and all is well on the Earth. Another reason us old blokes drink so much."

"Well, I'm happy to have some tuition there, too."

"Work, then play. Let's catch this fucker first." I tried not to fantasize about playing with Kellie.

- 5 -

There are two sounds intrinsically linked to high-priority (i.e. no genteel knocking on the door) search warrants, and both of them get my loins moving. Yeah, we've already established I'm old school, so get over it.

The first is the sound of the twelve-gauge Remington pump-action shotgun being cranked up by the junior detective as the raid team assembles a couple of doors away from the target house. It's always the junior guy who has the shotty and who is first in the door. Just the way things are, although I guess that'll go down the drain soon enough, like everything established (i.e. that works). So that's the rule, unless the junior guy is also the biggest, in which case the second-most junior has the shotty and the biggest lad has the ten kilogram front door key, otherwise known as a sledgehammer. Which brings me to the second sound I get off on: the splintering of wood as the key opens the front door.

Joining myself and Kellie for the raid on Rotten Ronnie's dosshouse of depravity were Chad Tranh to deal with the computers, Erik "The Fridge" Salenko on the front door key, probationer Gavin Arnott on the shotty, another Detective Sergeant, Frankie "Hollywood" Savage, named for his love of acting, and his offsider, Ahmed Khoury, another probationer. Frankie and Ahmed were allocated the back door, in case of a runner as the front door gave way. Not that Ronnie looked like much of an athlete, but you'd be surprised how fast some middle-aged sex offenders can run when the motivation is pressing. All eventualities had to be catered for. It was what us old timers called, with pride, "contingency planning". These days all you hear about is "strategic planning", usually uttered accompanied by some discreet stroking in the nether regions. Increasingly the stroking isn't so discreet, either.

We crouched at the front door as Frankie and Ahmed scooted along the side path to the back garden.

Big Erik was 195cm and 120kg, hence his white goods moniker. Watching him take down the front door with the key was sheer fucking poetry in motion. He swung that sledge as if he were twirling a cocktail umbrella.

Young Gavin, shotty to his shoulder, screamed, "Police, search warrant!", as he stepped over the remnants of the door and into the hallway. He moved quickly along as we checked the rooms on either side.

"On the fucking floor, arsehole!" I heard him roar as he reached the lounge room.

Frankie and Ahmed appeared from the other direction, pistols levelled.

I stepped around Gavin and shoved Ronnie onto his face on the floor. I cuffed him.

"Hello, Ronnie, you filthy piece of shit. You're coming with us for a friendly chat."

There was no one else in the house, anywhere, and we looked hard. We found the bedroom that was an exact match for the scene of Azalea's defilement. I called the forensics team in from their van in the street. They got to work.

I went back to Ronnie, now sitting on the floor against the couch.

"So where's the little girl?"

"Fuck you, pig. I'm not saying nothing."

Kellie shot her toecap into his ribs and he shrieked.

She leant towards him. "That's for the double negative, you ignorant cunt. Oh, and for being paedophile scum. Where's Azalea?"

"Fuck you, bitch. That's police brutality."

I grabbed his jaw. "Brutality? Really? You haven't seen anything yet, cunty. Wait till we get back to the office."

- 6 -

Kellie and I did the interview with Ronnie. And it was a short one: Ronnie was a fan of succinctness. Truth be told, we didn't lay a finger on him. We didn't need to in order to get his confession to the abduction and rape of Azalea. It came out of his mouth as an announcement of pride in his perverted achievement. He was no doubt barring up as we showed him the video footage from the dark web forum. When he said how "lovely and tight" Azalea had been, Kellie looked as if she was going to take a swing, but I settled her down.

"Ronnie, where is Azalea now?"

He cackled like a demented witch. "Ooh, the sixty-four million dollar fucking question, that one, detective."

"You're on toast for raping her, Ronnie, but at least do yourself a favour and let us get her back to her family."

"My heart bleeds. Maybe she's dead already."

"Is she?"

"Again, good question, detective. But you'll never see her again. Maybe I sold her, to be enjoyed by others. Or maybe I locked her in a small, confined space, to slowly starve to death. Or maybe I buried her with enough air for a day or two, then to slowly asphyxiate. So many delightful possibilities."

He grinned maniacally as a rivulet of drool trailed out of the corner of his mouth.

160

"Where the fuck is she, Ronnie?" I almost yelled, conscious of the video still recording, as this was the official interview. And I badly wanted to belt him, but no. At least the jury would get to see what a sick fuck he was and how he was getting off on his own depravity.

"I'm not saying anything more, detective." He looked directly at the small window shielding the camera lens and then looked at his watch. "So, detective, at nine thirty-seven PM my interview is over. Anything after this is inadmissible. Ha, I do so love that word."

I turned to Kellie. "Go and turn off the recording please, detective, the interview is terminated."

"No worries, Sarge."

She left the room and half a minute later I heard a tap on the camera window and the indicator light went out.

Ronnie sneered at me. "Fuck you, pig."

I sat there silently, which surprised him.

Frankie and I had made a contingency plan, of the old-fashioned type, for this particular dilemma.

I looked at the window and lit a smoke. We weren't supposed to, but I knew at this time the boss and the admin staff were all long gone. I leant back and pushed the switch for the extractor fan. A muted humming started and a gentle draught flowed across the room. The smoke drifted towards the vent.

Ronnie looked hungrily at the glowing cigarette.

I smiled at him.

"Got one for me, Sarge?"

"To use your words, Ronnie, fuck you."

He glared at me. "So what are we waiting for, detective?"

I smirked. "The second fucking coming. You'll see."

He looked a mixture of confused and anxious.

Suddenly, the Mickey Mouse Clubhouse theme tune blared from outside the door. Frank living up to his Hollywood moniker. He had style, did Frankie. I couldn't help laughing out loud.

"Act one, scene one, Ronnie. *Mate.*"

The door opened and accompanying the Disney song was a 180cm Mickey Mouse and a 185cm Donald Duck with a large clutch bag. The pair did a dance holding hands on their way into the room.

Ronnie's jaw dropped as the door closed.

Mickey and Donald cavorted around the room and the giant mouse gave Ronnie a pat on the head, followed by putting him in a headlock and dragging him backwards still on his chair.

The oversized duck punched Ronnie full in the guts and resumed his dance routine.

"Where's the girl, Ronnie?" I glared at him, as his eyes radiated a befuddled fear. "It'll go easier on you if you talk. Believe me, it'll be a lot easier."

To reinforce my point Donald belted him in the guts again.

"Last chance, Ronnie," I said.

"Fuck you, pig," he wheezed in a pique of stupid bravado.

I shook my head. "Okay, fucktard, have it your way."

I nodded at Donald who pulled a spare chair out from the table. He dipped into his bag and spread a plastic sheet over the chair.

A life lesson here: whatever the context, when the plastic sheets come out you just know it's about to get messy.

Mickey lifted Ronnie by his neck so he was more or less standing and Donald moved in. Ronnie tensed for another gut punch, but it never came. Instead the duck's white, cotton-covered hands deftly undid Ronnie's belt and trousers, and pulled his clothing down to reveal his genitals. I could see the familiar scarring along the side of his penis, even in its flaccid state. Mickey plonked Ronnie onto the plastic-covered chair.

The Disney tune blasted again and the door flew open. Goofy skipped in, did a twirl, and slammed the door. Out of the dog's blue pants appeared a compact cattle prod.

Ronnie's eyes widened until they looked like saucers.

Goofy stepped over to Ronnie, tipped his little green hat, and zapped Ronnie's penis with the prod. The molester shrieked into Mickey's white fabric hand clamped over his mouth.

"So, Ronnie, where's the girl?" I was trying not to crack up at the pantomime unfolding before me. It'd been well back in the old days since I'd seen this performed, and even then it was strictly reserved for dire straits.

Mickey took his hand away from Ronnie's mouth, but the ped said nothing.

Goofy looked at me and I nodded.

The man-sized dog lunged in and zapped Ronnie's junk again.

After a third and fourth electric assault, the last accompanied by the evacuation of his bowels, Ronnie spilled his guts.

I left him with Mr Disney's creations and escaped the stench of runny shit in the interview room.

Kellie was sitting at her desk. "I don't want to know, do I?"

"I like you, you're a fast learner. And no, you do not. What you don't know can't hurt you. But I have a location, so let's move."

- 7 -

Little Azalea was naked and semi-conscious when we cut the padlocks and chains on the old shipping container on a deserted, overgrown industrial block behind a disused rubbish tip and recycling centre. Her injuries, whilst not life threatening, were serious, and those were just the external ones. The paramedics reckoned another day and she would have been gone from dehydration.

We arranged a high-speed police escort for the ambulance to get her to the hospital. We followed and I rang the father en route. Not even a "thank you" from the self-centred, sanctimonious wanker.

At the hospital he was even ruder. The hatchet-faced wife was again wordless, exuding her silent vitriol into the sterile air outside the treatment room.

Wankstain husband sneered at me. "No point you hanging around, officer, I'm not going to let you speak to her. The social worker can do that in due course, and she'll be far preferable to you."

"Yeah, that'll be really effective."

"Get out of my face, officer. Go back to your cave. The sooner we defund the bloody police the better."

I smiled as obsequiously as I could. "No problems, Mister Quinn, it's been a pleasure as always to serve the public, especially someone with such heartfelt gratitude." I followed up with a little mock bow.

"Piss off, you prick."

Good, at least I'd got under his skin. Didn't compare with punching the fucker, but that wasn't going to happen. At least not here and now.

"With pleasure, *Sir*. I need to rush back to the office and get to work on my recommendation for the parents of the year award. I'd hate you to miss out."

Kellie sniggered. "Yes, see you later, *Sir*." She followed my lead and did a little curtsy.

We turned and headed back out into the sultry evening.

- 8 -

Rotten Ronnie put in an early plea of guilty, indeed the earliest possible. Smart prick. His lawyer asked for the commensurate discount on his sentence, since Azalea didn't have to testify at a trial, since Ronnie was truly remorseful, since Ronnie had had a traumatic and abusive childhood, and since blah, blah, blah.

And we thought that was an end to it all, that we'd never hear Ronnie telling his jury of peers about his Disneyland experience.

Myself and the team all glared at Ronnie as he was led away to start his twelve-year stretch, nine if he behaved, which he would. These pricks know how to play the system. I estimated nine years and one week before the next child was raped by Ronnie.

So not long enough. Never is, for these scumbags. Peds have the highest recidivism rate of any criminal type. Great argument for life imprisonment, and I mean the whole of life imprisonment. But the social justice wankers have ensured that never happens. Seems to me the only social justice available is for the filthy paedophiles.

We finished the day early at the office and headed for the local pub to toast putting another piece of shit behind bars, even if it was for too short a time.

The pub, with the champagne promised to Kellie (just as well I'd picked up some overtime on this job), was followed by a taxi ride to my place, at her suggestion. Yeah, they can take their new non-fraternization policy and stick it where they don't want people fraternizing. But no lube, not for them.

In my spartan bachelor studio, three hours of delectable depravity ensued, with plenty of lube. It was the sort of wild, lustful sex that makes you feel deeply alive, and the sort that you know you'll probably never have again.

I duly had my session with IA, those prissy, self-important, shiny-arsed clowns with badges. Never met an angry man, any of them. Never done any real fucking police work either.

I sat there with my union rep, who was also a lawyer. We didn't have the right to silence, that's reserved for criminals, so I was ready to give the bare minimum of answers required of me.

The more senior of the poncy pair started the recorder and gave the usual spiel.

"Now, Sergeant, Ronnie Redlin states that he was beaten up and tortured when you interviewed him. What do you have to say?"

I was itching to correct him and say, "Detective Sergeant", but I restrained myself. My union man had spent twenty minutes beforehand stressing to me to keep my mouth workings to a minimum. Yeah, this IA wanker wouldn't want to use the title "Detective" because it was one he'd never achieve.

I looked the fucker straight in the eyes. "I never laid a finger on him in that interview room. And that is the absolute truth."

"He says a stun gun was used on his testicles. What about that?"

"Really? Well, as I said, I didn't touch him, with my hands or anything else, including this stun gun."

"He says you sat there, smiling and smoking, whilst other people assaulted him. What about that?"

"Really? Who exactly?"

"Answer the question, Sergeant."

My union lawyer fired up, right on time. "Inspector, he's answered in relation to his own actions, and he said he didn't do anything to Redlin. Now, if you want to ask him about the actions of other people, you need to specify who. Otherwise it's merely a fishing trip, and he doesn't have to answer any of that. So, Inspector, who are the other officers alleged to have been involved in this assault?"

The prissy idiot swallowed hard. The other one couldn't even look at me. I tried not to smile.

"Well," whimpered the Inspector, "they were disguised in costumes. Mickey Mouse and Donald Duck."

"And Goofy," muttered the offsider.

I made my deliberate snort especially loud.

"This is ludicrous," said my lawyer. "The only thing Mickey Mouse around here is your interview, Inspector."

I made a show of looking at my watch.

Inspector Dickhead, clearly short on forensically useful questions, glared at me. "In a rush, Sergeant?"

"Not at all. Just checking the date, because I thought it may have been April Fools' day, but in here, who knows."

My lawyer puffed up again. "Inspector, have you any more questions for the Detective Sergeant about anything he's alleged to have done?"

I couldn't help myself at this point. "That's right, I am a Detective Sergeant, aren't I."

The self-important wanker ignored me and spoke to my lawyer. "We're going to charge him with being a party to the offence of assault occasioning bodily harm, with a weapon."

"Fine, Inspector, go right ahead. You can serve the summons and paperwork at my office." He threw his card across the table. "Anything else?"

"No."

"Good. We're off then. See you in court."

- 9 -

I had six months of desk duties before my trial date came up. I could have been through more quickly if I'd settled to stay in the lower court with a magistrate. But I elected trial by jury, of course. Even in this pitiful age of widespread anti-police sentiment whipped up by the social justice wankerati, any jury you could find would still rate a cop above a paedophile.

As expected, the trial was a hoot, although I kept my poker-face every single minute of it.

The star witness looked resplendent: Ronnie Redlin in his ill-fitting jail-wardrobe suit, a shocking 70s tan number, with the wide lapels. That, along with his vermiform effort at a moustache, made him look like an F-grade porn star.

For his script, he gushed forth about his appalling treatment at the brutal hands of Mickey Mouse, Donald Duck, and Goofy. All whilst I observed. He even added in the delightful detail of the Disney tune playing in accompaniment to the outrageous brutality and heinous violation of his civil rights.

I sat in the dock looking suitably dismayed at Ronnie's incredulous fantasy, making sure the jury could see my reactions.

At Ronnie's description of Goofy using the cattle prod on his testicles whilst doing the Disney dance, one of the jurors had to stifle a giggle, as the judge glared at them.

I didn't give evidence, of course. Always the accused's right not to do so. Hey, it's good enough for the scum, so why not me. Wasn't going to put myself in the prosecutor's sights for cross-examination: didn't need to face any questions I might not be able to answer honestly in court. Bullshitting a senior officer was one thing, perjury was quite another. No, best to simply stick with my lawyer telling the jury that I was pleading "not guilty" as I'd never touched Ronnie. And which sat beautifully with Ronnie reluctantly admitting to my lawyer, under superbly brutal cross-examination, that I had not, in fact, laid so much as a finger on him. No, it was all Mickey, Donald, and Goofy.

It was priceless.

Well, the jury took a mere half-hour to acquit me. Given the movement time to the jury room and back to the court, that meant they'd deliberated for an onerous twenty-two minutes.

After the foreman pronounced me "not guilty", the judge thanked and dismissed them. I made sure to bow my head respectfully and say a solemn "thank you" as they filed out.

The judge told me I was free to go. I thanked him as well.

The IA clown duo was outside, having left as soon as the verdict came in.

I grinned at them as I walked past with my lawyer. I couldn't help myself. "You fucking amateurs."

The rest of the team were standing further along the corridor waiting for me.

As we waited for the lift, Frankie turned around to the clowns. "Go get a real job, you cunts."

I've always loved Frankie's style. Or should I say Mickey's. Or Donald's. Or Goofy's. Yeah, it had never been discussed, and never would be, but he was in one of those outfits.

Even my lawyer laughed at that final insult. Well, he would. Before he was a criminal defence lawyer, he was a detective sergeant. Which is also why he was coming to the pub with us to celebrate.

Was it right? Was it wrong? Who's to say? Not me.

But I will say this: little Azalea lived.

And that's right. On any planet.

* * * * *

THE LAST COP

Frank Zafiro

"What the snap are you looking at?" the kid sneered.

He wasn't really a kid, I suppose. He could've been twenty-five or twenty-six, but he sported one of the green leather vests that were so popular these days and tied the long sleeves of his flannel shirt around his waist, knotted on the side. A bloody dagger tattoo adorned the left side of his face.

The rattling of the old subway train hurtling along the track filled the silence between us. That silence must have bothered him, because he stood, pointed at me and raised his voice. "I'm talking to you, old man! Whaddaya think you're looking at?"

"I'm not looking at anything," I answered evenly, resisting the urge to grin at the literalism of what I said.

He made a smug sniffing sound. "That's what I thought."

As if you think, shit hook, I thought but didn't say.

He balled his fist and struck himself in the chest. I didn't respond to the challenge. Gangster idiots can challenge each other any old way they want, but if they want to draw out this cop, they can damn well just speak the words. I have no patience for moronic rituals.

When I didn't move toward him, or even let go of the handrail, he sniffed again and looked me up and down. "Ain't you a little old to be a mediator?"

I didn't answer. I was seventy-three, but that was none of his business.

"Can you still pull the trigger on that Taser?" he asked with a condescending chuckle. "Is it even real?"

I didn't blink, and stood still.

His gaze swept over the rest of me, taking in the comp stick that hung from my belt and the holster strapped low on my opposite hip. I wondered if he recognized the old-style holster wasn't one of the magnetic ones the monitors carried today. That should have tipped him off, but he was a typical dumb ass, so it didn't.

"Nice badge, gramps," he pointed with a snarl. "Old style. No holograms or anything. You sure kept it shiny, didn't you? It's gonna look great on my wall."

He took a menacing step toward me. I held back a smile. This was the kind of challenge I could accept.

I pressed the mic on my shoulder. "Baker-seven-one-five, code three-seventy."

The wireless beeped and the monotone AI voice responded, *"Copy, Baker-seven-one-five. Code three-seventy. Dispatching."*

Hearing the code didn't affect him. Either he didn't know what it meant or he just didn't care. He had to know any backup, for what little it was worth, was at least two minutes away, when the near-empty train was scheduled to pull into the next station.

He took another step toward me.

I lowered my hand to the holster slung low on my hip.

His gaze followed.

I broke the snap.

His brow furrowed. "Whaddaya you got there, old duck?"

"Duck? Too afraid to speak your mind, son?" I slid the Colt .45 out of the holster and leveled it at him.

His eyes widened in surprise. "You can't carry that! Mediators can't carry firearms!"

"I'm no mediator," I told him in a growl. "I'm a cop. And I was grandfathered in."

He glanced back and forth from my face to the barrel of the gun. His mouth opened and twitched but no words came out.

"If you're still here when we roll into the station, I'm taking you in for intended theft and assault."

"I know how the system works," he stammered. "You need a warrant to even talk to me and permission from … "

I drew back the hammer on the .45, cocking it.

He turned and fled out of the subway car and into the next, the sideways flannel shirt around his waist blowing back like a cape.

I lowered the hammer and slid the pistol back into my holster.

"Baker-seven-one-five, cancel Code three-seventy," I told the tiny mic on my lapel. "Code four here now. And clear."

The AI dispatch beeped. *"Copy, Baker-seven-one-five. Code four, and clear."*

***

"Things have changed, Rammer," Harlan said. We sat in his room at the senior care center. "The whole world's gone soft."

It took a moment for me to sort out his words. The stroke made his speech difficult to understand and he refused to use a voice enhancer. "Why would I want to sound like a damn computer?" he'd said, shocking the nurse and the intern with his harsh language and archaic word choice.

"Things always change," I answered him. "That's the way of the world."

"Not like this. It's too soft now. A man can't do anything without being fined or worse."

I nodded sympathetically. If that nurse and the intern had reported him for profanity, that's exactly what would have happened. Banned words carried a heavy fine, automatically deducted from a person's financial account. A lot of good it did. The young just created new curse words, or warped old ones into profanity. The enforcement algorithm eventually caught up, banned those, and started the cycle all over again. I figured pretty soon the original slate of curse words would fall off the table and I could start using them again in public. Until then, I was limited to using them in my head. Sonsabitches couldn't do anything about that.

"No alcohol, no caffeine, no tobacco ... " Harlan shook his head in short jerks. "I'm surprised the government still allows us to eat and screw!"

I glanced at the door, which was half-closed, grateful that his speech was difficult to understand. The likelihood of a nurse or another visitor reporting him diminished that way. "I heard they require a permit for that now," I dead-panned.

"For what? Eating?"

It was a softball, and we both knew it, but I nodded, unable keep back a smile. Then I took it yard, just like he expected. "No, for screwing. They're calling it a poke permit."

He waved his hand dismissively, but I saw the delight in his eyes. "Ah, you're just being a smart ass, aren't ya?"

"Pretty much."

He heaved a sigh. "Remember the old days, Rammer?"

"I do."

He stared out the window at the faux brick wall outside. "That's all I think about anymore. The good old days."

"They weren't always so good," I reminded him.

He shrugged, a spasmodic motion. "Maybe not. But they were real."

I didn't answer. He was right. I came on the job in 2021. Just a few years later, they enacted the *Law Enforcement Protection Act*, prohibiting the use of deadly force by police. Then came the *Civil Rights Act* of 2036, which included a law making a police officer civilly liable for every action he took while releasing the agency from all culpability. The intent was to hold police officers accountable for their actions. It accomplished that, I suppose. But true to human nature, agencies took advantage and ramped up the procedural and legal requirements for patrol officers and detectives. The job went from difficult to nearly impossible. Disgusted with the perceived inability to do their job, police officers resigned in record numbers.

I stayed the course and so did Harlan. A small part of it was for the pay increase. As officers fled the profession in droves, the demand for replacements became critical. The law of scarcity kicked in and police salaries soared. Of course, a substantial portion of the gain in wages went toward purchasing personal liability insurance from companies that were more than willing to take advantage of the expanding need for this.

The biggest reason we stayed? I could only speak for myself, though I suspected Harlan's answer was the same. Simply put, what else were we going to do?

We were cops.

Staying on turned out to be a mixed bag for us. As the world changed around them, the police unions in the country slowly banded together into one monolithic fraternity, ever more entrenched and protective, trying to reverse the trend of history. In the end, they couldn't change where things were going. For better or worse, the version of individual liberty that the government was selling to the citizenry had too much momentum.

"The whole world went soft," Harlan whispered, "except for the criminals."

After the reforms, police work became a façade, a veneer of civilization that made the citizenry feel protected but didn't accomplish anything. First, officers were required to get permission to make a felony arrest from HQ. Then it was for any arrest. After a couple of court cases ruled against the police, case law forced officers to get supervisory approval to contact any citizen on a criminal matter. This evolved into requiring a warrant for that contact.

But the union's power did accomplish one thing. Veterans like Harlan and me were held to the old standards of enforcement. When the weaponry changed, and they stopped issuing guns to new officers and discouraged older officers from carrying theirs, the union got us grandfathered in and we were allowed to remain armed. Of course, they took Harlan's gun away when he retired. That was the only time I remember seeing him cry.

Tasers became the maximum allowable force, though in reality no one wanted to risk it. They issued us compliance sticks – light, plastic sticks with a mild electric current. The only times I ever removed mine from the holder was during parades for the silly salute to the Mayor, and to recharge.

We were window-dressing.

Private security slowly replaced us, for those who could afford it. Criminal court diminished and civil court became the default to resolve almost all conflict between citizenry. That, or violence. As the years passed, each incoming class of rookie police officers was less and less equipped to answer that violence. Only the contract protection hired by the rich and the often hinted at but rarely spoken threat of military intervention kept society below the chaos threshold. And eventually, the power of the police union faded until it became nothing more than a bureaucratic body siphoning off dues.

Harlan had it right.

"Monitors," he slurred, almost spitting the word. "Tattle-tells is more like it. I'm glad I left when I did."

Reduced to mostly an observe-and-report role, police officers were re-branded as monitors. Tattle-tells was an apt description for the new role.

"You're getting worked up," I said.

"I know. Feels good." He pointed down to my holstered .45. "Don't even see those beauties on TV anymore."

172

Harlan had that right, too. They whitewashed the vids to keep us safe from ourselves. "It's a new world."

"It's a wrong world."

"Said every old man ever."

"Bah!" He waved his hand at me. "It's the truth. That's the gift of being old, Rammer. It lets you tell the truth and not give a damn."

An orderly appeared in the doorway with a tray of food. She started at Harlan's profanity. Her expression fell into a mixture of surprise and worry.

"Did he just say … ?"

"'As a gift to man?'" I asked, covering for him. For all of us, really. "Yes, that's exactly what he said."

Harlan grunted.

The orderly looked relieved. She brought in Harlan's food, setting the tray in front of him. "Nurse Crider will be in with your medication in ten minutes, Mister Harlan. Make sure you eat something before then, okay?"

Harlan said something even I couldn't make out.

The orderly took that as an affirmative answer and hustled out the door. Harlan watched her go before turning to me.

"How much for one of those permits?" he asked.

I knew that eating was a messy process that embarrassed Harlan, so I left him to it. Besides, his meds would put him out within twenty minutes of taking them.

***

On the way home, I felt the jangling subway motion deep in my bones, like an ache that never ebbed. Harlan's words about how the world had gone soft haunted me as the empty stops flitted by. Hardly anyone used the subway anymore, preferring the long rolling sidewalks downtown and AI taxis for the suburbs. It wouldn't be long before the city shut the line down for good.

Harlan had been my training officer, and later my partner. His sharp mind, compassionate heart, and decisive action became the model I tried to emulate. I don't think I came close, but even falling short left me a pretty good cop.

When there used to be cops.

I hadn't told Harlan that Gene LaLiberte had retired earlier this week. Or how Joe Martinez and Hazel Vercruysse both pulled the plug only a few weeks before that. I sensed it would have depressed my old friend. Hell, it depressed me.

It also made me the last cop left working in the city.

The subway rattled to a stop. The old pneumatic door hissed open in a broken puff of air and I got off. Home was a long two blocks away, and I was deeply tired. I trudged to my tiny apartment, and opened the door. Inside, nothing but blackness.

I turned on the lights. In the kitchen, I prepared a small meal, but I could only eat part of it. I sat at the kitchen table for a while, listening to the emptiness of my home. Finally, I got up and headed toward the bedroom. I needed to rest.

They'd be coming for me soon.

***

Three shifts later, the district supervisor called me into her office before I headed out. Back in the day, she would have worn lieutenant's bars. Now, all of management had civilian titles. The uniform was a sleek top with slightly billowing leggings. I always thought that style looked like someone couldn't decide whether to make suit pants or a skirt, so they split the difference.

"Mister Ramirez," she began.

"Officer," I corrected.

She smiled indulgently, but her eyes remained cold. She didn't like me. Never had, though whether it was disdain for my kind or personal animus, I couldn't say for certain. "I wanted to renew the city's offer to you for retirement."

"No, thank you."

"Management's previous offer increased the pension by three percent ... "

"Not interested."

" ... along with a lump sum at the time of retirement."

I didn't reply.

She tried to wait me out, but that was a losing cause. I was a patient man. Finally, she asked, "Don't you think the time has come?"

"No."

"It can't be easy for you," she said. "Navigating this new world. So much has changed."

I grunted, which made me think of Harlan. Maybe I was closer to that retirement home than I thought.

"I know change is hard," she continued. "But look at all the positive results that we've seen. Individual freedom is at an all-time high ... "

And individual responsibility at all-time low.

" ... while police-related deaths have been virtually eliminated. The civil system has replaced the criminal one as the primary means of dealing with anti-social behavior. It's more effective and less expensive and the focus on treatment rather than punishment has made us a healthier nation."

Bullshit. It's made us an entitled one.

She gave me an appraising look. "Speaking of health, we both know your physical performance scores have been dropping steadily for the last fifteen years. Eyesight, cardiovascular capacity, cognitive response ... "

I raised my hand to stop her. "The job is about more than reading eye charts and walking on a treadmill," I said testily. "And there's not a thing wrong with my mind."

"That's medically debatable. There's been a deterioration, natural for someone of your age, of course, but still ... "

"I can still talk to people." I thought of the punk on the subway, and a hard smile sprang to my lips. "That's what matters."

She frowned. "So you have no intent to voluntarily retire?"

"None."

"You are aware of the pending legislation that will mandate retirement for all monitors at age seventy?"

"Pending isn't passed," I said, though I didn't have a lot of faith that the *Monitor Retirement Act* wouldn't come to fruition. It didn't matter. I'd be grandfathered in, just like all the previous instances of new laws. The precedent had been set.

She regarded me with distaste. "Tell me, then, when do you plan to retire?"

"I don't. I intend to remain a cop until I die."

There was a flicker on her face of something that seemed like cruel joy to me, but she covered it up quickly enough. "I don't think you quite understand. The *Monitor Retirement Act* has passed."

That was news to me. "When?"

"It was signed into law last night. The terms go into effect in sixty days."

I shrugged. It was a new world, once again.

Now she did smile. "There's no grandfather clause."

I stared at her in disbelief. That only made her smile more. She glanced down at her hand monitor, though I hadn't heard it vibrate or ding, and feigned sadness. "Oh, look at that. Management has withdrawn the retirement incentive. It looks like standard retirement terms apply now."

I didn't care about the money. I didn't need much. What I needed was this job. This purpose.

"End of an era, I suppose," she said, her tone a faked bittersweet one. "Have a good tour, Mister Ramirez."

***

Sixty days, I thought. And no grandfather clause.

I should have expected it. The power of the police union had eroded as the years passed, the pendulum's ultimate swing away from the overreach that the unions had overseen at their height. How long could I expect that weakened institution to protect me? All its members were monitors now, for the most part. Observe and report. Intervene only in life-or-death scenarios. And expect to be second-guessed and sued if you do.

"Now you sound like Harlan," I told the reflection in the passing store window. People strode by me as I stood on the scrolling sidewalk, watching my image crawl by in the glass and metal surfaces. At times crisp and accurate, other times warped and indistinct, there was probably some sort of metaphor in it all but I couldn't suss it out.

It's a new world, I'd told Harlan. *A wrong one*, he'd contended in return. But was it? Depending on who you listened to, the crime rate had either declined or remained constant in the last half century. Cybercrimes became the norm and physical crimes diminished but the overall numbers held steady, even in the face of the changing role of law enforcement. As cops became monitors, how much changed for the citizen?

I couldn't say. I hadn't been a citizen in more than fifty years. Any sense of context was nigh on impossible for me.

The high profile cases of alleged police brutality that brought on the reforms no longer existed, that was certain. I couldn't remember the last time I saw a monitor brought up on charges for anything other than Failure to Intervene. The days of cops being directly responsible for the deaths of citizens, or criminals, were all but finished.

So maybe all of these changes, on balance, were a good thing.

Or hell, maybe I was going soft, like the rest of the world. That's what Harlan would say.

Sixty days. Sixty days, and then it was all gone.

***

The shifts over the next several weeks were uneventful. I plodded through them. When it came time to visit Harlan again, I almost skipped it. But I knew how much it mattered to him. Besides, it was my day off, and sitting alone in my quiet apartment seemed too much like a macabre preview, so I decided to go. On the way, I realized how much the visits mattered to me, too. Harlan was one of the few connections left to that distant past, when the world was so different.

I resolved not to tell him about my forced retirement, though. That could wait until the dreaded day was closer. Hell, maybe I wouldn't tell him at all. Just show up with a suitcase and announce that we were going to be room-mates.

At the desk, Nurse Crider stopped me. "You can't go in there now," he said.

I glanced at my wristwatch, a classic Casio. "Is he eating already?"

Nurse Crider shook his head. "No, sir." He paused, then added, "I'm sorry."

That's when I knew.

***

No weather is good for a funeral. Rainy, cold, or overcast is fitting enough for the mood, but hard on the mourners. On the other hand, sunshine might be worse, with all the emotional dissonance it fosters. Today's weather, though, didn't really matter, since the entire ceremony took place indoors.

When Harlan and I were still young, before either of us got married to wives who would eventually leave us, funerals were a part of the job. Most of the time, they were for long-retired cops we never knew or perhaps only heard stories about. Occasionally, it was a younger officer. Some were line-of-duty deaths, though those diminished to almost nothing after the reforms. All were great displays of pomp and tradition, of respect and tribute, full of flags and uniforms and men and woman standing erect and still while the fallen was being eulogized.

In contrast, Harlan's was sparsely attended.

Aside from me, his ex-wife Jenny made a surprise appearance. She looked somber but not shaken. Harlan's son Cash, a food safety executive, supported her by the arm. Cash looked less somber than his mother. He and his father had long been estranged.

A few random people I didn't know attended as well. They could have known Harlan at some point in his life or maybe they were just curious observers, or looking to join the mourners for a free meal.

The officiant was appropriately subdued, but went about his duties with brisk efficiency. Harlan's achievements during his career received scant mention, breezed over in a few short sentences. In accordance with Harlan's wishes, no prayer was offered, only condolences.

No one wept.

There was no free meal.

Afterward, I joined Jenny, offering her my arm. She took it wordlessly. Her son and I escorted her back to the AI taxi that waited outside. Jenny nodded her thanks as she eased herself into the back seat. Her son said nothing. A moment later, they were gone.

***

It seemed like only a few days later before I got my thirty-day notice from the city. It included a questionnaire regarding my preferences for my retirement pension. I let it sit in my inbox, still showing the bold font of the unread message.

***

Another week passed. I walked my beat, using the scrollers when I got tired. I remained watchful, though each tour was uneventful. That's the job, I reminded myself. Ninety-eight percent vigilant boredom, two percent action-filled terror.

At least, that's what the equation used to be.

Now that equation was as indecipherable to me as Chinese algebra. The only number that I knew for sure was nineteen. That's how many shifts I had left.

***

Three days after that, I was scrolling down Fourth when I heard it. The chiming alert of the bank further down the block. Not a fire alarm, and not some advertising ploy. A robbery.

I lengthened my stride, taking advantage of the scroller to cover ground. Pedestrians scowled at me as I brushed past them, not thinking to make way for an emergency responder. Several lifted their hand monitors toward me to record my actions. The underwhelming response to the alarm irritated me.

As I drew close to the bank, the glass doors flung open and three masked figures barreled out. Two had the bulky builds of men and one the more slender frame of a woman. All three were armed, though I couldn't tell right away whether they wielded guns or Tasers. Black duffel bags were slung over the shoulders of the first two. The last one out the door, one of the men, lagged behind the other two, dragging along a middle-aged woman with him.

Hostage.

Without thinking, I drew my .45 and leveled it at them. "Police! Stop!"

The novelty of the words must have surprised them, because all three pulled up short and turned to look at me. I advanced, keeping a bead on the hostage-taker. I was now close enough to see they were all armed with firearms, too.

"What the *hell?*" the first man barked in surprise.

"Keep going!" his partner, the woman, yelled at him.

Meanwhile, the hostage-taker pressed his gun to the crying woman's temple. "Stop right there!" he ordered.

Not far away, I could hear the punctuated *yib-yab, yib-yab* of sirens. Private security was already en route to deal with the robbers.

"Come any closer, I'll shoot her!" the man bellowed at me.

I fired.

My shot flew wide, striking the window next to the bank doors, shattering it. People around me screamed and scattered. The hostage-taker flinched. So did his companions.

Undeterred, I fired again. This round skipped off of the scroller pavement.

"Crazy old bastard!" The woman robber shouted. She adjusted the heavy duffel bag on her shoulder and raised her gun.

I shot a barrage at her, squeezing the trigger rapidly. The ancient .45 bucked in my hand. Rather than the roar of each explosive blast, all I heard were mild pops. The people around me seemed to blur and move in slow motion. My bullets whizzed past the target as she ducked into a crouch.

When the last round fired, the slide of my pistol locked to the rear. My hearing suddenly became acute. The sound of the last two shell casings clattering to the sidewalk. The screech of tires coming to a stop. Doors flying open and slamming shut. Muffled screams of panic.

"Come on," the woman yelled at her companions as she stood up again. "We gotta go!"

The hostage-taker pushed the middle-aged woman to the ground in front of him. She landed hard on her hands and knees. He leveled his pistol at me. I stood perfectly still, staring down the length of my gun barrel at him. Smoke curled out through the ejection port of my own empty weapon. I waited for him to shoot, for the hail of gunfire that was meant for me, that was *always* meant for me.

"Leave it!" their leader shouted at him, already turning to flee. "There's no time! He's not worth it!"

The hostage-taker hesitated briefly. Then he lowered his gun, wheeled around, and fled after his companions.

I watched him go through the last tendrils of smoke from the spent .45. The woman who had been held hostage looked up at me. Her face was streaked with tears, her hands bloody from the shattered glass. Her shocked and angry expression spoke volumes.

Slowly, I let my hand drop. With a flick of my thumb, I released the slide and it snapped forward into place. I slid the empty .45 into my holster.

A moment later, black-clad figures in tactical gear streamed past me on both sides, their weapons trained on the retreating criminals, completely ignoring me. The tramp of their feet reverberated through me, like the bass beat of a forgotten rock and roll song that no one listened to anymore.

"Well, shit," I muttered.

* * * * *

ACKNOWLEDGEMENTS

As I said in the introduction, I've grown to love the anthology concept. Last year I published a collection of my own PI Harry Kenmare short stories, but this anthology is my first foray into publishing a collection primarily of other authors' work. I've thoroughly enjoyed the project and I'm thrilled with the end result. I'll be editing and publishing more of these, for sure.

Both writing and editing are activities defined by isolation, but getting the written word into a published form requires many other contributions, and so I've got plenty of people I wish to thank.

Most importantly for this collection, a huge thank you to all the fourteen other authors who contributed their work and entrusted me to see this project through to publication. Hope to see you all again.

And if you have enjoyed reading the authors in this line-up, then check out their other works. Details for their websites and/or social media links are included in the biographies that follow.

As always, my great thanks to my partner Ruth for her support, beta reading my draft story, and for putting up with my writing stuff spread all over our apartment.

My thanks also to my sister, Katie, and to my friend, Allan Yates, for being beta readers of the draft of my own work, an invaluable role in any writing project.

And for the professional expertise and services provided during the production stages of the project …

My thanks to J.T. Lindroos, in Finland, for the superb cover design: it is striking and captures the collection's concept perfectly. This is my second project with J.T. and I'm looking forward to many more.

My thanks to Andy McDermott and his team at Publicious Book Publishing Services here in Australia for the book production: typesetting, printing, and ebook and POD conversions.

My thanks to my friend Stephen Hill, at Dylunio here in Sydney for my shamrock logo design.

Thank you, all!

THE AUTHORS
(In order of appearance)

Christopher Allen (USA)

After a tour of duty in the United States Air Force, Christopher Allen embarked on what would become a 30-year career in law enforcement. During those years he was involved in virtually every aspect of the career field. He subsequently became a self-employed licensed private investigator where he assisted in domestic and fraud cases, as well as consulted with legal counsel regarding government corruption and capital murder cases.

In 2017 Christopher Allen began writing his first book, *Before the Thin Man: The Prequel to Dashiell Hammett's 'The Thin Man'*, for his wife Linda. They both loved the works of Dashiell Hammett and watched the entire series of movies together many times. He started his second book, *The Dead Club: A Frank DeGrae Case*, after she was diagnosed with cancer. The project was shelved during her illness. In the aftermath of her passing, he resumed writing and it was published on her birthday in 2020.

Christopher Allen credits his wife Linda with starting his writing ventures. He is currently working on a third book at a location within walking distance of the F. Scott and Zelda Fitzgerald Museum and Home in Central Alabama.

W: christopherallen.home.blog
FB: CAAllen.PI

Thonie Hevron (USA)

With 35 years of civilian California law enforcement experience, Thonie Hevron writes suspense novels based on the lives of the people behind the badge. In addition to her website, Thonie posts "Street Stories" from law enforcement veterans. Also, she hosts authors to talk about their writing craft and culture in "Writers Notes." Authors are welcome to query for posts about their newest book in "Mystery Readers Only." Her four police procedural thrillers, *By Force or Fear, Intent to Hold, With Malice Aforethought,* and *The Felony Murder Rule,* are all award winners. In 2014, she co-chaired the 2014 Pen to Published Conference for Redwood Writers. She has served as a secretary for Redwood Writers and on the board of First Alliance (Public Safety Responders Mental Health). She is retired and lives with her retired fire fighter husband in Petaluma, CA. Her hobbies are fitness, dressage and bicycling.

W: www.thoniehevron.com

Michael O'Keefe (USA)

Michael O'Keefe is a retired 1st Grade Detective from the NYPD. Working in the toughest neighborhoods in New York, specializing in homicides and other violent crime, he was born and raised on the dangerous streets he likes to write about.

His debut novel, *Shot to Pieces,* the first installment of the Detective Paddy Durr series, premiered in early July of 2016. For its realism and attention to detail, it has been included in the curriculum at John Jay College of Criminal Justice and St. John's University.

13 Stories-Fractured, Twisted & Put Away Wet is a collection of prize-winning short fiction released in March 2019.

A Reckoning in Brooklyn, a historical crime thriller released November 2019, is the prequel to *Shot to Pieces.*

Look for Book III in the series, *Burnt to a Crisp,* to debut in 2021.

He likes retirement, but he loved homicide investigation and would still be doing it if he hadn't been injured in the line of duty and disabled. He now lives on Long Island with his family.

W: www.michaelokeefeauthor.com
FB: @mikeokeefeauthor
IG: @michaelokeefewriter

Barry Lees (UK)

Barry Lees joined the UK police as a sixteen-year-old cadet in 1978. At eighteen, he began as a patrolling uniformed constable and he became a detective at the age of thirty. He worked on several murders in various roles as well as a couple of spells on a pro-active drugs unit. He was never any good at surveillance because he looked too much like a cop. In later service, he trained recruits, and since retirement from the force in 2010, he now lectures in Policing and Criminology on degree courses at the University of Cumbria, UK.

Rather than simply guess how to write, he gained an honours degree in English and Creative Writing in 2013. To date he has produced eight crime thrillers. The settings include a mental hospital, a train derailment, a fracking protest and the recent, troubled past of Belfast. Writing short crime stories is a new venture for him. It has opened up fresh possibilities for his writing. He is currently working on a collection of shorts in which he intends to explore different themes of criminal behaviour. They don't always involve a murder.

W: www.barrylees.net

P.J. Bodnar (USA)

P.J. Bodnar is a retired Half Moon Bay, CA, police officer, professional photographer, and writer. The short story in this collection, "His First", is the origin story of Officer Darren Knox, the protagonist of his forthcoming debut novel, *Half Moon*.

He lives in Pleasant Valley, NY, with his family.

TW: @PJ_Bodnar

Desmond P. Ryan (CANADA)

For almost thirty years, Desmond P. Ryan worked as a cop in the back alleys, poorly-lit laneways, and forgotten neighbourhoods of Toronto, the city where he grew up. Murder often most unkind, assaults on a level that defied humanity, and sexual violations intended to demean, shame, and haunt the victims were all in a day's work. Days, evenings, midnights – all the same. Crime knows no time.

Whether as a beat cop or a plain-clothes detective, Desmond dealt with good people who did bad things, and bad people who followed their instincts.

And now, as a retired detective, he writes crime fiction.

Real Detective. Real Crime. Fiction.

W: www.realdesmondryan.com

TW: @RealDesmondRyan

Pearson O'Meara (USA)

Pearson O'Meara is a former law enforcement professional with extensive experience in complex missing, abducted, and exploited children investigations. In 2019, after a distinguished 20-year career, she retired as a sergeant from the Louisiana State Police, where she managed the Louisiana Clearinghouse for Missing and Exploited Children and the Louisiana AMBER Alert Program. She also served as a Special Victims Unit supervisor responsible for investigating multi-jurisdictional crimes against children, including Catholic clergy abuse cases. In 2017, she was nominated by the National Center for Missing & Exploited Children for a law enforcement "Hero" award for her role in recovering four children abducted from California by their non-custodial mother and a registered sex offender.

Pearson retired to continue her education. She is currently pursuing her doctorate in law and policy and lends her expertise and technical advice to authors, novelists, and television and film producers. A lifetime avid reader, Pearson tired of academic and technical writing, so she decided to try her hand at crime fiction. "The LadySmith" is set in south Louisiana and has a swamp noir vibe. It is only the second short story she has ever written. She lives a quiet life, dividing her time between Boston and Baton Rouge.

TW: @PearsonOMeara

Ryan Sayles (USA)

Ryan Sayles is the award-winning author of the hardboiled detective Richard Dean Buckner series and numerous standalone books. His story in this collection, "Riot at the Mental Institution", features the same police department and characters that feature in his novel, *It's Ugly Because It's Personal.*

His forthcoming novel, *Like Whitewashed Tombs*, will be published by Down & Out Books in 2022.

W: www.locals.com/RyanSayles

Keith Wright (UK)

Keith Wright was a detective sergeant in Nottinghamshire Police, England, serving over 20 years in the CID, investigating serious and major crime, before retiring in 2005.

He is best known for his crime novels from the Inspector Stark series, the first of which, *One Oblique One,* was shortlisted for the best debut crime novel by the Crime Writer's Association. His fourth book, *Fair Means or Foul,* was recognised in the New York City Big Book Awards in 2020 as distinguished favourite. His books have received reviews in *The Times, Financial Times, Sunday Express* and other major newspapers.

His latest novel, *Murder Me Tomorrow,* won the Independent Press Award 2021 for best crime fiction.

Keith has written the short story anthology *Killing Dad and other crime short stories,* and had a short story published by New York's prestigious *Mystery Tribune.*

Keith lives in Nottingham, England, and is married to Jackie. He has four children.

Visit his website to read chapter samples, short stories, learn more about the author, and explore his blogs.

W: www.keithwrightauthor.co.uk
TW: @KeithWWright

T.K. Thorne (USA)

T.K. Thorne has been passionate about storytelling since she was a young girl, and that passion only deepened when she became a police officer. Graduating with a master's in social work from the University of Alabama, Thorne served for more than two decades in the Birmingham police force, retiring as a precinct captain. She then became the executive director of City Action Partnership, a downtown business improvement district focused on safety, until retiring to write full time. Her books and essays include two award-winning historical novels (*Noah's Wife* and *Angels at the Gate*); two nonfiction civil rights era works (*Last Chance for Justice* and *Behind the Magic Curtain: Secrets, Spies, and Unsung White Allies of Birmingham's Civil Rights Days*); and a dally with murder, mystery, and magic in *House of Rose*, the first novel in the Magic City Stories trilogy. She writes from her mountaintop home northeast of Birmingham, often with a dog and cat vying for her lap.

W: www.tkthorne.com

James Ellson (UK)

James Ellson was a police officer in the UK for 15 years, starting in London and finishing as a Detective Inspector at Moss Side in Manchester. When he left the police he started writing, and has been writing ever since.

His debut novel, *The Trail*, was published in 2020, and the sequel, *Cold Dawn*, will be published in 2022.

James lives in the Peak District with his wife, and manages their smallholding, which includes bees and an orchard.

TW: @jamesellson3
FB: james.ellson.98

Mark Atley (USA)

Mark Atley is the author of the novels *The Olympian* and *American Standard*, as well as a handful of short fiction. Mark promises to entertain his readers and will choose real other drama, every-damn-time.

He works as a detective for a suburb of Tulsa, OK, and has dedicated his life to crime.

TW: @mark_atley

Lisa Cutts (UK)

Lisa Cutts recently retired after twenty-five years with Kent police, having spent most of that time investigating murders for a living. For the last ten years of her service, she wrote crime fiction novels alongside her full-time job.

Murder in the Village is the first in the Belinda Penshurst Cozy Mysteries set in Kent and was published in August 2021.

She is the author of the DC Nina Foster books, *Never Forget* and *Remember, Remember*. *Never Forget* was long-listed for the Waverton Good Read Award 2013 and the winner of the Killer Nashville Silver Falchion Award 2014 for Best Thriller.

Lisa has written four books in the East Rise Incident Room series, *Mercy Killing, Buried Secrets, Lost Lives* and *Don't Trust Him.*

She writes a monthly column, *Behind the Tape*, for *Writing Magazine* answering police procedural questions from other writers.

In early 2016, she was honoured to become the Patron of Rochester Literature Festival and help establish Murderous Medway annual crime fiction festival.

As well as being on BBC Radio 4's Open Book, Lisa has twice appeared on *This Morning* to chat about TV crime dramas *Broadchurch* and *Line of Duty.*

TW: @LisaCuttsAuthor

A.B. Patterson (AUSTRALIA)

A.B. Patterson is an Australian writer who knows first-hand about corruption, power, crime and sex. He was a Detective Sergeant in the WA Police, working in paedophilia and vice, and later a Chief Investigator with the NSW Independent Commission Against Corruption.

His multiple award-winning, debut novel, *Harry's World*, introduced the jaded and flawed PI Harry Kenmare. *Harry's Quest* was the sizzling, award-winning sequel in the PI Harry Kenmare series of novels. The third novel, *Harry's Grail*, is in progress. The Harry Kenmare short stories, some previously published in the USA in *Switchblade* magazine, were collected together and published in 2020 as *Harry Kenmare, PI – At Your Service.*

He has had other short stories, all crime related, published in various anthologies.

In a non-fiction vein, he was a contributing editor to a volume dealing with the trauma for male survivors of English boarding schools published by Routledge, *Men's Accounts of Boarding Schools: Sent Away.*

For his fiction, his hard-boiled, gritty, and noir writing style has been likened to that of Raymond Chandler and Ken Bruen. He's a massive fan of both of them.

W: www.abpatterson.com.au
TW: @ABPattersonAuth

Frank Zafiro (USA)

Frank Zafiro was an officer in the Spokane Police Department from 1993 to 2013, retiring as a captain. He was fortunate enough to serve in or command almost every unit of the department during that time. Since 2004, Frank has been writing gritty crime fiction from both sides of the badge, including several police series such as River City (procedurals), Stefan Kopriva Mysteries (private eye), and Charlie-316 (procedurals). His hardboiled, darker series includes SpoCompton (criminals), Bricks & Cam Jobs (hitmen), and the Ania series (noir).

Frank lives in Redmond, Oregon, with his wife, dog Richie, and a self-assured cat named Pasta. He is an avid hockey fan and a tortured guitarist.

W: www.frankzafiro.com

* * * * *